Any Given Lifetime

By Leta Blake

An Original Publication from Leta Blake Books

Any Given Lifetime
Written and published by Leta Blake
Cover by Dar Albert
Formatted by BB eBooks

First Print Edition, 2018
ISBN: 978-1-723733-28-4

Gay Romance Newsletter

Leta's newsletter will keep you up to date on her latest releases and news from the world of M/M romance. Join the mailing list today.

Leta Blake on Patreon

Become part of Leta Blake's Patreon community in order to access exclusive content, deleted scenes, extras, bonus stories, rewards, prizes, interviews, and more.
www.patreon.com/letablake

ACKNOWLEDGEMENTS

Thank you to the following people:

Mom & Dad, without whom I couldn't be following this dream of being a writer. B & C, my lights to travel home to. All the wonderful members of my Patreon who inspire, support, and advise me, especially Sadie Sheffield. Amanda Jean for the editing work. DJ Jamison for proofing. Nick & Julie for the times I spent at their home in years past, learning about Scottsville.

And thank you to my readers who make all the blood, sweat, and tears worthwhile.

He'll love him in any lifetime.

Neil isn't a ghost, but he feels like one. Reincarnated with all his memories from his prior life, he spent twenty years trapped in a child's body, wanting nothing more than to grow up and reclaim the love of his life.

As an adult, Neil finds there's more than lost time separating them. Joshua has built a beautiful life since Neil's death, and how exactly is Neil supposed to introduce himself? As Joshua's long-dead lover in a new body? Heartbroken and hopeless, Neil takes refuge in his work, developing microscopic robots called nanites that can produce medical miracles.

When Joshua meets a young scientist working on a medical project, his soul senses something his rational mind can't believe. Has Neil truly come back to him after twenty years? And if the impossible is real, can they be together at long last?

Any Given Lifetime is a stand-alone, slow burn, second chance gay romance by Leta Blake featuring reincarnation and true love. This story includes some angst, some steam, an age gap, and, of course, a happy ending.

For Brian, for all lifetimes

Prologue

January 2012—Atlanta, Georgia

"HE DOESN'T LOOK like a Joe," Alice said, staring at her squalling son, whose face scrunched in fury and pale skin grew blotchy from crying. She pushed her still-damp dark hair behind her ear and tried to get more comfortable on the hospital bed.

"That was my brother's name," Jim said stubbornly. He reached out and touched the baby's clenched fist, which seemed to set off another round of wails. He jerked his meaty hand away, and his dark, caterpillar brows stitched together ominously. The muscles of his chest rippled as he crossed his arms.

Alice tried to place the baby to her breast, shushing and soothing him, hoping that the nurses wouldn't come into the room and try to talk her into feeding him formula again. Her milk would come in just fine. She knew it would. If he would just *latch on*, for heaven's sake.

"I promised my mom I'd name my son after my brother," her new husband pressed on. His gray eyes took on the flinty look that she'd already learned to fear.

Alice refrained from mentioning that the baby wasn't actually his son. Both of them were very bent on pretending otherwise. It was best for everyone if Marshall's memory was left with his body— blown to bits in the desert of Afghanistan. Jim had married her out of an obligation to his dead best friend, and claimed Marshall's son as his own, determined to raise him right. Alice was grateful for his help, even if she didn't have his love, or want it. Alice had tried to care for the man, but it was hard to love a man as unpredictable as Jim.

Especially after having been loved by someone as tender and thoughtful as Marshall.

"Did you hear me, Alice? I promised my mom," Jim said again. Afghanistan hadn't been kind to Jim, taking both his brother and his best friend.

"Yeah, I know you promised," Alice agreed, looking down at her son's face as he mouthed at her nipple, never quite taking it in before he started screaming again. "But…but look at him. He's just not a Joe."

"You got a better name in mind?" Jim asked, his voice implying that whatever she suggested, it better be good or else.

"Neil," she said, whispering the name that had rung through her like a bell the moment she took the baby into her arms. "Neil Joseph," she added quickly. "For your brother."

Jim chewed his bottom lip, but then he nodded once, and Alice relaxed, relieved that was the end of it for now. She smiled up at her husband, and he smiled back, tense and insincere but good enough. At least there wouldn't be a row.

For his part, Neil screamed even louder.

January 2012—Scottsville, Kentucky

JOSHUA STOOD BY the creek on his family's land in his hometown of Scottsville, Kentucky. He shoved his gloved hands into his coat pockets and studied the winter-gray sky reflecting in the ripples in the dark water. All around him the woods creaked and rustled. A squirrel chomped on a nut, eyeing Joshua suspiciously.

The creek was deep and wide, bubbling over rocks and fallen limbs carelessly. When he was a boy, he'd played in it every day, digging on its banks, jumping in up to his hips, skipping over the rocks from muddy shore to muddy shore. It had been his favorite place on earth.

He still loved it, but it had been over a month since he'd come out to the creek. Not because he'd forgotten about any of it, but because he was making an active attempt to hurt less. Somehow he'd convinced himself that if he avoided the place where he'd carefully emptied the container of ashes—all that had been left of Neil after the cremation—maybe he wouldn't feel cut to the quick.

Avoidance hadn't worked, though. So, here he was.

"Hey, Neil," he said, rocking on his heels. "I miss you."

The creek burbled and rushed. Like life itself, it was nonstop and joyful in its lack of empathy. On it went, sluicing over gravelly bottoms and slipping through woods and fields. Onward, never a glance back, just forward into forever.

"My new baby brother was born today. Remember how I told you my mom was pregnant? He arrived. They named him Sam."

He was quiet for a second, trying to feel Neil there with him, wanting some kind of connection, but he got nothing at all.

"You're really gone, huh?" he asked.

The wind blew around him, ruffling his hair, but it didn't feel anything like Neil.

"Where'd you go?" he murmured. Off with the water into the great unknown. It's part of why he'd cast his remains into the creek, wasn't it? To release him. Set him free. So why did he keep coming back to the creek looking for something he'd never find?

Joshua listened harder. "Where does the river take you? Where did you end up?" Then he smirked. "I know, I know. I can hear you telling me that you didn't *end up* anywhere, that you *died*, and any ideas I have to the contrary are just hopes and wishful thinking. You'd say I'm better off accepting reality and moving on."

Joshua ran a hand through his hair and shrugged. The squirrel decided this human wasn't quite sane, talking to himself this way, and skittered into the woods and then up a high tree. "I might be better off, Neil. But I just can't believe that." He stared up at the clouds covering the sky. The water rushed at his feet. "I don't *want* to believe that."

The grief fell on him again, heavy and useless. He made a big show of shaking it off, clapping his hands together and saying, "So, anyway, since we last talked, things have really kind of sucked. Paul is bugging me to sell my Grandpa Roger's lumber company, come back to Nashville, and live with him. He says I need to finish my degree, pick up where I left off when you…" He swallowed hard. "When you died. But I'm not ready. I'll never be ready. Nashville isn't for me. And Mom and Dad aren't capable of running Stouder Lumber. They never have been. Dad's more into the farm, and Mom's got her career as a teacher. It's on me to keep Grandpa Roger's legacy alive. Just like it's on me to keep yours alive, too."

Joshua sat down on the cold ground and wrapped his arms around his knees. "Why'd you do that, Neil? Put all of that responsibility in my hands? I'm only twenty-two years old, and it's too much." Puffing cloudy breath, he squeezed his eyes tight, thinking of all the questions Neil's lawyer still had for him. "How old were you when all of that fell into *your* hands? That's not something we ever discussed."

He was silent for a few moments and tried to think of what Neil would say to all of that. He smiled softly when he realized that in all likelihood whatever Neil said would've pissed him off.

"You'd say, 'Suck it up, buttercup.' You'd say, 'Stop taking Paul's calls if he annoys you.' You'd say exactly what I wouldn't want to hear, and…well, I don't think I like your advice any more now than I would if you were alive. But I'm glad that I know what you'd say to me. It makes you feel not so—" *Dead.* "Far away."

Joshua swallowed a lump in his throat. That was a lie. Knowing what Neil would say made him feel even more gone. He wiped at his eyes.

"I hate you for dying."

The wind blew again, chill and full of winter. Joshua bowed his head.

"I love you," he said, his breath lifting around him like smoke.

June 2012—Atlanta, Georgia

ALICE WATCHED AS the doctor examined her son. She could see the intelligence snapping behind his eyes, taking in the world around him in a wordless assessment, and it vaguely distressed her that he seemed to find it lacking.

"He's still nursing?" the doctor asked, wrapping a measuring tape around Neil's head and then making some notes.

Alice nodded. Nursing was finally going well. It had taken a while to get into the groove, but eventually Neil started eating like a champ. When he was wrapped up in her arms, gulping greedily, she felt truly connected to him in a way that she imagined other mothers felt toward their children all the time.

"He's showing excellent advances in motor coordination, and he's meeting and surpassing physical milestones," the doctor intoned, as though he was bored.

"So, he's healthy?" she asked, a little doubt in her voice. He was, after all, so *skinny* and *moody*, and somehow she felt like he was different from other babies.

"Well, he's of lower weight than average for his age, but he's not anywhere near the danger zone on the chart. Given what you've told me in the past about his eating habits, he likely has a fast metabolism. Be prepared for some marathon nursing sessions when he hits his growth spurts."

Alice picked Neil up from the table. His bobble-head jiggled on his skinny neck, and she kissed his cheek. He didn't really relax into her arms, but he didn't fight her either, and she got the sense that he enjoyed being held by her. That meant something, at least.

"Why?" the doctor asked, seeming to suddenly tune into her hesitations. "Is there something in particular that you're worried about?"

Alice let out a guilty sigh. "I just feel...I don't know, like something's missing? My friends...well, their babies are more..." She winced. "They seem happier?"

A smirk crossed the doctor's face. "Well, Mrs., uh—" He consulted the chart.

"Quinley," Alice offered, still unaccustomed to Jim's name and wishing she'd kept Marshall's. But Jim would have lost it if she'd ever suggested that. His loyalty to his dead friend didn't go so far as to allow his wife to still 'moon' over him, as he put it.

"Mrs. Quinley, your son may have a taciturn nature, true. Every child is different. But is it possible you might be suffering from postpartum depression? Are you having trouble bonding with him? Do you have an unhealthy burden of guilt, or fear that you might harm your son?"

Alice blinked at him. Guilt? A little. Bonding? She wasn't sure. She loved Neil and had since she first moment she saw his screaming little face. But he certainly wasn't what she'd been expecting. Harm him? Absolutely not. She just wanted to know that he was okay. That he would grow up to be a normal man with a normal life. She guessed the doctor probably couldn't guarantee her that.

"I don't think so," she said softly.

The doctor nodded, made a mark in Neil's chart, and said, "Okay. Well, just let me know if anything changes on that front. I know a very good doctor who specializes in postpartum emotional issues."

Alice gave him a tight-lipped smile and nodded. She cuddled

Neil close. He tensed before relaxing in her arms, and then he put his small head on her shoulder, gazing up at her with blue, trusting eyes that pulled at her heart.

The doctor left the room, and Alice got Neil's little clothes back on him. She could feel him studying her, so she whispered, "I'll always take care of you."

He waved a fist in her direction, and he almost looked like he might smile.

But then he cried instead.

PART ONE

Chapter One

May 2018—Scottsville, Kentucky

JOSHUA SAT AT a tiny table in a quiet corner of Earl G. Dumplin's diner. It was a slow day, and not many other tables were occupied. His coffee was verging on being too cold, and he considered getting up to find the waitress to ask her for a refill, but then he'd have to shift the piles of papers that he'd spread out over his lap, each precariously balanced.

There was the stack on the table in front of him that had to do with Stouder Lumber, all of which he needed to pay close attention to because he was in the middle of converting everything from paper to computer at long last, and his lumber shipping business was often full of rough roads, both literal and metaphorical. He had a lot of responsibility on his shoulders since taking over the family business—and he'd had to learn it all incredibly fast after his Grandpa Roger's death just a few months after Neil's.

Sure, Grandpa Roger had generally reliable people installed when Joshua took over, a lot of them from the local Mennonite sect, but the business itself had spent the last six years stuck in the past. Admittedly, that'd been appealing to his horse-and-buggy-driving employees, but things had to change if they were going to stay profitable. It was time Joshua got a grip on all the paper his Grandpa had used to track everything and converted it to digital programs and processes. That included dealing with tons of old contracts covered in legalese about trucking and transportation all of which made his brain want to run out of his ears in an effort to escape the boredom.

Then there was the stack on his left knee. That had to do with the Neil Russell Foundation for Advanced Nanite Research, including the latest applications for grants and funding. The massive amount of money that had been left behind for Joshua to handle after Neil's death wasn't something he'd ever expected for several reasons.

First and foremost, he hadn't known Neil had changed his will to make Joshua the beneficiary of his estate. They'd only been together as a couple for nine months when Neil died. They hadn't even made their relationship physical yet—what with Joshua being a skittish country boy stewing in internalized homophobia, and Neil being a very busy research scientist with a healthy commitment to waiting until Joshua was 'ready.'

Joshua had known they were in love, believed it with his whole heart and felt it in his bones, but he'd committed the folly of youth: he'd also believed they had time. It wasn't until after Neil's death that he'd fully understood, though, just how devoted Neil had been to him. The inheritance had come as quite a shock.

Second, Neil had always lived frugally. His apartment in Nashville had been unremarkable—obviously, since he'd been Joshua's next-door neighbor—and his clothes had been a uniform of black jeans and black button-up shirts that looked like they could have been purchased at JCPenney or even Walmart. Neil had once told Joshua that his parents, before their deaths, had been upper-crust society types, and that he'd attended prestigious private schools growing up. But he'd never really spelled out what that meant in numbers. So Joshua had always assumed the money was long gone, used up to pay for Neil's college and PhD, most likely.

It wasn't until Neil's estate went through probate that it became clear just how truly wealthy Neil had been. Nearly a hundred million dollars in old family money inherited from his parents, plus

Neil's own investments in experimental medical technology that had paid off over the years, had all been left in a trust for medical nanite research after his tragic death, along with strict instructions that Joshua should be in charge of running it and be given quite a hefty salary for doing so.

That had been almost as shocking as Neil's death itself.

But Joshua took his position as head of the board seriously and personally. In fact, he'd been accused of being *too* involved recently, which made him laugh because of course he was 'too involved.' The foundation and its funds were all he had left of Neil, weren't they? He'd do whatever it took to make sure Neil's contribution to medical science would never be forgotten.

Immediately after Neil and his grandpa's deaths, Joshua had discovered the only way to survive his grief was to work his butt off, and then he'd just never stopped. In the stack on his right knee, there were applications for grant money from medical nanite research organizations as far away as Hong Kong and India, and he intended to examine them all thoroughly before meeting with the rest of the board to discuss them the next week.

Yet he was being encouraged by *certain people* to loosen his grip, to hand everything over to someone 'more qualified' and start moving on. But Joshua had no intention of doing that. Even if Paul, his former roommate and best friend, thought he was losing himself in it all.

Paul had thought Joshua was losing himself in Neil when he was alive, too. But if he'd truly lost himself in Neil back then, things would have been different between them.

Very different. Regret tasted bitter as hell.

Taking a sip of his cold coffee and blocking out the *ka-ching* of the old-fashioned cash register by the door, Joshua shuffled through some of the Stouder Lumber paperwork on his lap. He barely noticed a stranger who walked into the diner and spoke to Earl behind the counter. It was only when the man came to stand directly by Joshua's table that Joshua looked up.

"Mr. Stouder? I'm sorry to interrupt. A man at your lumber company said you'd be here. Uh…do you have a minute?"

Joshua looked up into dark brown, soulful eyes beneath a shaggy mane of brown, wavy hair and couldn't bring himself to say he was busy. After a formal introduction, Joshua insisted on moving to the clean table beside them, one not stacked with papers, so that they could talk on more equal terms.

Lee Fargo moved with grace despite the scarified evidence of former burns. They climbed over his exposed forearms and under his shirt, then up the right side of his neck, stopping just beneath his chin, as though some kind of mercy had spared his face.

Joshua swallowed hard as Lee told his story. It wasn't the first time a donor recipient had sought him out. A woman who'd received one of Neil's kidneys had contacted him by email, and they'd had a long correspondence about the hope afforded to her, especially given anticipated upcoming medical breakthroughs in nanite nephrology. He'd received letters of thanks from a number of people: parents of a few children who had received some of Neil's skin, a woman who'd had her sight restored with one of Neil's retinas, and a young man who'd received Neil's surviving lung. It was always overwhelming. But this was the first recipient who had sought him out in person, and Joshua didn't know what to say.

So he simply listened.

Lee had been in a fire while he was in his sister's house. He'd been burned on over sixty percent of his body after going back inside to save his nephew, who was trapped in the upstairs bedroom. His nephew hadn't lived, and Lee had barely made it himself.

"Thank you," Lee said, reaching out and putting his hand over Joshua's fingers clutching the handle of his coffee cup. "I can only imagine how difficult it was for you to lose your partner. Someone like Dr. Russell must have been really special."

"He was unique, all right," Joshua said, swallowing the sadness and going with a smile.

"Oh yeah? Tell me about him," Lee said, leaning back again. "I'd love to know more about the man I have to thank for my skin."

Neil's skin. Joshua wanted to reach out and touch, even though he knew that given the rate of cellular overturn, the amount of skin on Lee's body that would have still been Neil's was negligible.

"Well, he was sometimes a jerk," Joshua said honestly. "He was intense, arrogant, and too Northern for most of us Southern good ol' boys to handle." He wrinkled his nose, trying to seem playful, but he knew his grief was showing through.

"Yeah? But you loved him, right?" Lee's brown eyes were dark and earnest. Joshua couldn't help but think he was handsome, even with the scars marring his neck. "So, he must have had some winning qualities."

"Winning," Joshua said softly. "Yeah, he liked winning."

"Competitive, then?"

"Competitive doesn't cover it. He usually won." Joshua went silent and felt a darkness swell.

"At?"

"At everything."

And then there was that last time. When he tried to beat the odds for the sake of love. And lost.

"I'm sorry," Lee said, moving back in his chair. "I didn't want to cause you pain. It was selfish to ask too much. I should have thought." He jerked his thumb over his shoulder. "I'll just...."

Joshua reached out and touched Lee's forearm to stop him from getting up. The skin was slick and gnarled under his fingertips. "No, please. Stay. I'd like to tell you about him, if you still want to hear."

"Of course I do," Lee replied, and he settled back in his seat.

"That's why I'm here."

Joshua nodded and then waved at a waitress. "First, let's get you some coffee."

"That'd be nice. Thank you."

October 2010—Nashville, Tennessee

THE POUNDING ON the door didn't stop.

Joshua wrapped the towel around his hips and dashed into the living room of the apartment he shared with Paul. He grabbed Magic by the scruff of her neck and jerked the door open, out of breath and still wet all over.

Joshua had noticed before that their neighbor was handsome, in an uptight, professorial sort of way. That is, if a skinny, uptight professor with short, dark curls could also be a hot, sexy all-black-wearing dominant type with a perma-scowl. And given the sharp glare and set jaw Joshua was greeted with when he jerked the door open, this guy was proof positive that a professor could embody both those vibes.

His entire body rang with an electric buzz as he stammered a greeting. But the man's grimace and grunt of anger as Magic broke free of Joshua's grip and leapt up against his firm chest quickly wiped away any imagined charm.

"Your dog is a nuisance!" the man exclaimed, under assault from Magic's eager tongue and paws. On her hind legs, Magic was nearly as tall as he was, which put the man at somewhere close to five-nine, and probably a hundred and sixty pounds soaking wet. Just a few more pounds than Magic herself.

Joshua tried to grab at her, but failed to get more than a handful of shedding fur. "I'm sorry. Let me just…. Magic! Down! Come on, girl! Inside!" He lunged, catching hold of his dumb dog, and tried to wrestle her off the man. But, in the process, he lost his towel.

With cold air on his dangly bits, and a writhing, happy dog rubbing all over him, trying to get back to her new friend, he managed to get his apartment door open again, and shoved Magic back inside, slamming the door on her.

"Nice ass," the guy said, dusting dog hair off his black shirt and jeans.

Joshua scrambled to grab the towel from the floor. His wet skin tingling with hot embarrassment, he wrapped the towel around his body, and opened his mouth to stammer another apology. Magic barked sharply. Once. Twice. Three times.

"And that's what I'm talking about," the man snarled. "That bark."

Joshua tied his towel around his waist again, panting and sweating from the effort he'd expended trying to get his idiot dog off the neighbor and back through the door. Worse, his damp skin was now covered in short, dark, dog hair, so his efforts in the shower were completely undone. He'd probably be late to work now, too. He groaned, humiliation stinging his cheeks, and he raked a hand through his hair. "Sorry. So sorry. About my dog and…and about my ass."

"The ass was no hardship," the man said. "The dog, though…"

Joshua ignored that, wiped a hand over his sweaty upper lip, and went on, "She's just a big puppy. Not even a year old yet. I adopted her last month and—"

"I know damn well when you adopted her because that's when my quiet evenings at home turned into a nightmare symphony of dog whines, barks, and outright howls." The man glared at him so hard, Joshua was afraid his already tight-feeling skin might peel off.

"Oh. I, uh, well." Joshua held his towel tighter. "My roommate and I work most nights and—"

"And from what Mrs. Saunders across the way told me at the mailboxes this morning, your dog barks all damn day, too." The man raised a harsh brow.

"She does?"

The man crossed his arms over his chest. "Where are you all day that you don't know?"

"School?"

"You're in college?"

"Yes."

"And your muscle-bound roommate I see going in and out? Where's he during the day?"

"Also school."

"And you both thought it was a great idea to get a puppy, huh?"

"Well—" Paul hadn't actually endorsed the adoption of Magic, and he wasn't much help with her even when he was home. But Joshua wasn't about to admit that right now. He held onto his towel a little bit tighter.

The man raised a brow and went on. "A big, hulking puppy with an appetite for attention and exercise. The education system is abysmal, I know, but you're a country boy, aren't you?" He looked Joshua up and down like he could see every single farm-spent hour written into the muscles of his body. He licked his lips, shifted to his other foot, and cleared his throat. "You should have known better."

Joshua stared at the man. Speechless, and conscious of the way his dick had reacted to the incredibly obvious once-over he'd just received, he shivered. He'd been trying hard not to have those kinds of thoughts about men anymore. He really had. But just one look from this imperious, slightly older man had Joshua's balls tingling. He bit into his lower lip, trying to tamp down on his reaction before it became horribly obvious.

The man sighed, pinched between his eyebrows, and waved at the door to Joshua's apartment. "Invite me in?"

"Uh, why?" Images of the man stripping off Joshua's suddenly much too-small towel and dropping to his knees flashed wildly through his mind. He held back a whimper.

The man's brows jumped to his hairline, as though Joshua were a total fool. But then he sighed heavily and rolled his eyes. "I guess I should introduce myself first. I'm Neil Russell, your next-door neighbor. I'm also the guy currently standing between you staying in this apartment building or getting kicked out for pet violations." He grimaced. "So, if you'll let me in, I have some thoughts on your dog situation."

Joshua's cock thickened as he gazed at Neil's mouth—soft, but hard, too, like it bit out every word thoughtfully, precisely, without any mercy or forgiveness. He wondered what a man like that might do in bed. Not that he'd ever had a man in bed before. Not a soft one, or a hard one, or a man his own age. No men ever. Not in his bed, not anywhere. But he wanted to know what this man would be like, tugged close against him, taking him apart precisely as he—

God help him! He needed to get his mind out of the gutter.

Neil sighed again. "Hello? May I come in? Or would you rather I invited you to my place? Or should I just call the apartment manager and have you evicted?"

Joshua gasped.

Neil blinked irritably, which Joshua hadn't even known was a thing someone could do. He put a thumb to one eye and pressed softly, and then said in a kinder tone, "I thought it might be better to share my ideas with you inside your apartment, where you can put on some clothes. But if you insist on chatting here in the hallway while standing there in nothing but a towel, fine by me."

"No, no, you're right. Um, come in." Joshua turned back to the door, his stomach flipping wildly. "But I can't promise Magic won't jump on you again."

The man rolled his eyes, which Joshua suddenly realized were a bright, piercing blue. "Lead the way."

May 2018—Scottsville, Kentucky

"SO WHAT HAPPENED after that?" Lee asked, his dark brown eyes dancing with amusement. Joshua hadn't shared how he'd reacted physically to Neil that first morning in the hallway, but his predicament of being caught in only a towel was still a funny one. Especially the part where he lost it.

"He came in, I got dressed, and then he proceeded to bless me out for a good ten minutes about the idiocy of two students with night jobs adopting a dog like Magic. I had to agree with him."

"Did he want you to get rid of her?" Lee had long, tapered fingers, some of them also scarred, and he drummed them on the side of his coffee cup as they talked.

"No. Not really." Joshua laughed under his breath. "As it turned out, he was a massive softy when it came to dogs and, well, animals of all kinds. People irritated him but animals held his heart. He was a vegetarian, even, and refused to perform any of his nanite research on animals—which I've continued to insist on to this day."

"He was a nanite researcher?" Lee's voice inched up an octave with interest. Joshua knew the news had recently been covering some advances in nanite cellular repair. He'd done some of the interviews about it, even, since Neil's foundation was funding so much of it. In the upcoming years, nanites might be able to change the surfacing of Lee's scars.

"He was. One of the best." Joshua swallowed a lump in his throat and went on. "Anyway, no, he didn't want to get rid of Magic. Instead, he cozied up to her while I was getting dressed, and by the time I came back into the room, he'd basically taught her to sit. Something I'd failed at for weeks. He was amazing with that kind of thing."

"Dogs know if someone's a good person," Lee said, with a tender smile that grabbed at Joshua like a hook.

"Yeah. And Magic adored him from the start." He returned Lee's smile tightly. "In the end, he offered a proposition that I almost refused because I didn't understand the way his mind worked yet. He was gruff, impatient with me—with all humans, really—and I wondered if he had some nefarious plan for Magic because it was too good to be true." Joshua let his mind go back to that moment in his old, shared apartment: Neil on the sofa with Magic, surrounded by Paul's beer bottles and the detritus of two young men living together away from home for the first time. Magic had nuzzled Neil's hand, and he'd given his first smile to her—bright, sweet, and surprising. Joshua sighed. "But she was snuggled up at his side, and he stroked her with this gentleness that got to me…" He swallowed again, worried that he would cry for sure this time.

"He offered to help with her?"

"Yes. He offered to train her, to take her with him running in the mornings before he left for work, and to keep her at night in his apartment if Paul and I were out. In exchange, Paul and I had to pay for her food and vet bills, and in the end? Magic was Neil's dog. She basically lived there, and we just took care of her when Neil couldn't." He laughed. Then wiped his eyes. "Of course, it was Magic who…" He shook his head violently. "I'm sorry. I can't talk about that."

Lee's eyes softened. "How he died?"

Joshua shook his head again. "I can't." His voice was gruff.

"No, of course not. I never wanted you to. Thank you for everything you told me today. Do you mind if we just have a coffee together now? Talk about other things?"

Joshua gave a watery, grateful smile, and he noticed again how warm and caring Lee's eyes were, and he let himself reach out to take hold of Lee's hand.

Chapter Two

August 2018—Atlanta, Georgia

"I T'S JOSHUA." NEIL stopped playing with the old cell phone Alice had given him to take apart and pointed toward the TV screen. "He's on the news again."

She studied Neil's face as he stared with a slightly open mouth at the flat-screen mounted on the wall. "He looks sad," Neil said, and there was worry making his already gruff little voice sound even gruffer. "I don't want him to be sad."

Alice knew who was on the screen without looking. Joshua Stouder, a man close to her age, from Scottsville, Kentucky. Neil had only been five or so the first time they saw Joshua Stouder on the national news, discussing some kind of medical research his foundation was funding. He claimed it had the potential to change traumatic-injury treatments forever. It involved the use of tiny robots called nanites. Alice didn't really understand the details, or care to for that matter, but little Neil had stood up, abandoning his blocks. He'd pointed at the screen on the wall and said, "*That's Joshua*," in a voice containing more awe than she'd ever heard him display. He'd always been a child who seemed to find everyday miracles not only to be old hat, but really kind of annoying.

At the time, she'd been startled and even found it amusing. Neil had talked of someone named Joshua for a long time. In fact, one of the first things he'd ever informed her of, when he was only about thirteen months old, was, "I want Joshua." She'd asked him who Joshua was, and he'd stared at her like she was stupid and shrugged his tiny shoulders in a gesture that was spookily old on a baby.

As he'd continued to tell her about Joshua, usually in off-hand comments, and sometimes with a mournful sigh and an announcement that he *missed* Joshua, she'd become worried that this imaginary friend of his might not be so imaginary. But she hadn't been able to fathom where Neil might be seeing a man of that description. She was home with him during the day and kept a close eye on him when they went out. Still, she'd had a neighbor come over and add locks to Neil's bedroom windows, just in case. Her paranoia had grown that out of control. What if someone was messing with her son? She'd worried about that endlessly, even though Neil had just glared at her in annoyance when she asked him if Joshua ever visited him when she wasn't in the room, or came in through his windows at night.

But when she'd looked toward the screen that day when Neil was five, she'd been shocked to see a man named Joshua Stouder who did look remarkably like the person Neil had told her about. A quick internet search brought up even more evidence that was too accurate to be a simple coincidence. Not to mention, the scariest thing of all: Joshua Stouder had been involved with a nanite researcher at Vanderbilt University, a man named Neil Russell. A man who, photographs revealed, more than a little resembled her own little Neil. It was spooky, and she'd barely slept that night, she was so freaked out.

The next day, she'd asked her friend Marie, a fellow military wife, "Do you believe in reincarnation?"

Marie had laughed and said, "Yeah, and tarot cards, and astrology. Oh, and also I can tell the future by the marks on my toilet paper after I wipe my butt."

Alice had never mentioned reincarnation to anyone after that. Still, the thought lingered. Especially because it unnerved Alice how Neil talked about Joshua as though he knew him. And some of the other things he said—things about medicine, Boston, and nanites—couldn't be explained, but it was all information that research told her Dr. Neil Russell would have known a lot about.

Now, Alice watched Joshua on the screen again. This was the fourth time in as many days he'd been shown on the news. He wasn't talking, though, just sitting in a courtroom looking alternately sad and angry. His arms were crossed over his chest, and his gaze rarely left the back of the defendant's head. One Beau Allen of Bowling Green, Kentucky, who was on trial for sabotaging a Stouder Lumber truck, causing a highway accident that had killed one woman and left her husband paralyzed.

The reporters stated that Mr. Joshua Stouder was in attendance in hopes of convincing the judge to refuse to accept the defendant's plea bargain. A dark-eyed reporter with glasses said, "Mr. Joshua Stouder is on record saying that Mr. Allen is a dangerous, unstable man who was let go from Stouder Lumber a month before the truck was sabotaged, allowing the logs to roll free onto the road. He does not believe that Mr. Allen is reformed and, should he be released, would continue to be a risk to society."

Alice hoped that Joshua's testimony would take place in the judge's quarters, or else Neil would insist that they save it to the computer so that he could watch it over and over. She had practically memorized the interview Joshua had given to a show called *Louisville Now* about the Neil Russell Foundation and its research into nanites. It was a simple little piece, but Neil had watched it at least a hundred times, and Alice had nearly lost her mind.

Neil had discovered the interview through some search protocols he'd installed on the computer to notify him when Joshua Stouder appeared in print, on film, or anywhere online. Jim would have killed her for letting Neil use the computer at all, but she couldn't stop Neil from being who he was, and so she just tried to minimize the damage. Neil was so dang smart, though, that 'the damage' was surprisingly nonexistent.

Alice tried to comply with most of Jim's wishes with regard to Neil. She felt like she owed him that much for stepping in after Marshall's death, providing a home and income for her, and being a father for Marshall's son. And Jim clearly felt that she *did* owe him given how often he'd brought all that up in their arguments over the last six years.

He'd accused her of pretty awful things and a lot of ulterior motives whenever he'd been drinking. But the truth was she'd married him in desperation, and he'd married her out of some misplaced desire to be the hero. He hadn't been able to save Marshall from the IED, but he'd saved Marshall's girlfriend and baby from poverty. His motivations had been good. His execution less so. And the reality was they weren't a good fit as a family.

She'd told Jim that once when Neil had been three years old, and it hadn't been a pretty scene. She was still humiliated to think that the neighbors had probably overheard the way he yelled at her, the things he'd said.

Especially about Neil.

Neil had been a strange child from the beginning. He was never chubby or darling, but always kind of scrawny and somehow indignant about *everything*, as though he was furious that he'd even been born into the world. Sometimes Alice felt guilty about that, even though she didn't know why. It wasn't like she'd give him up for anything, but it'd always seemed so clear to her that he had somewhere else he'd rather be. Though, given that he was a kid, Alice had no idea where that was.

Then he'd been…well, precocious wasn't even the word for it. He'd spoken his first sentence at barely one year, and he never went back after that, sounding like a strange, abrasive little professor trapped inside the body of a tiny child. It unnerved most people and infuriated Jim. "Tell that kid to shut the hell up!" he'd told her one night. "I don't need a fucking brat lecturing me."

She hadn't known what to do. There was no way she could ever ask Neil to be anything other than what he was, but Jim had hated being humiliated by a child. And of course, that was the way he saw it, which was just ridiculous, but there it was. She was relieved when Jim was deployed again and dreaded each of his returns.

She still felt the cold hand of panic grip her whenever she remembered Jim's last two-week visit home. He'd punched a hole in the wall and grabbed her arm a lot harder than she wanted to admit, all because six-year-old Neil had taken apart the new touchscreen mobile device that Jim's mother had bought them for Christmas. Neil had managed to pry it open and was investigating the circuits when Jim walked in and found him.

"Do you have any idea how much this cost?" he'd yelled.

Neil had stared up at him, his tiny face unwavering. "I can fix it." He'd sounded so certain, calm, yet totally irritated with Jim.

"Alice!" Jim had screamed. "Look at what your son's done!"

Alice had tried to placate him, saying, "Just give it to him, Jim. He can put it back together."

"Put it back together? He's ruined it."

Then Jim had grabbed Alice's arm and jerked her. She'd seen Neil stand up out of the corner of her eye, and she'd shaken her head at him. He'd stared at her with unblinking, intense eyes and looked like he might step forward at any moment. That was the last thing she wanted.

"Fuck!" Jim had yelled, and punched the wall, leaving a hole behind. He'd stomped out of the house, taking the touchscreen mobile with him.

"Idiot," Neil had assessed in his little gruff voice. "I was going to fix it."

Alice had burst into tears, which seemed to freak Neil out. He'd walked over to her, his bony little legs sticking out of his shorts and his hand outstretched. She'd wiped at her face and said, "Don't, Neil. Just don't."

He'd seemed to understand and dropped his hand, looking down at his socked feet and shaking his head, like he was still sure that Jim was an idiot, and Alice had to agree.

That was six months ago, and unless something changed, Alice was worried how they would manage when Jim returned for good. She'd spent more than one long night wondering if she might be able to find a way to make it on her own. Single motherhood would be hard, no doubt about that, especially with a child like Neil—he didn't look like a six-year-old, or talk like a six-year-old, or act like a six-year-old—but it had to be better than fearing for their safety.

After Marshall died...well, Jim had said everything she wanted to hear. He'd been full of promises of happiness and a home for her and the baby. Alice still thought Jim had meant every word of it, too. But then Neil had been born, and he wasn't what Jim had expected in a son. Unfortunately, Jim wasn't the kind of man who could deal with that.

Alice knew that someday soon, they'd have to go.

The news show left the Stouder Lumber case behind and moved on to discuss some brands of infant formula that had been recalled due to bacteria.

Neil turned to her, his blue eyes focused on her face. His expression was intense, focused, the way it always was whenever he started thinking about Joshua. Suddenly, he smiled. "Joshua's mother had brown hair, too," Neil said, leaning against Alice's shoulder to touch her hair with his small fingers. "I never met her. But I know she was different from you. She preached to him about gay being a sin. I'm glad you're not like that."

Alice smiled sadly and kissed his forehead. "Being gay is beautiful. All love is beautiful," she assured him.

Neil nodded, his lips in a thin line. "Love sucks, actually." Then he kissed her cheek and said, "But you're okay. I like you."

Well, if that wasn't high praise from her son, then she didn't know what was. And even though she knew it wasn't the kisses and endless 'I love yous' she'd imagined throughout her pregnancy, Neil's approval was good enough for her.

A WEEK LATER Marie showed up at their house with the twins in tow, crying her eyes out. Neil didn't like Marcus or Meredith, even though they were the same age, because they wanted to throw balls or pretend to be things and people they were not, which as Neil had declared to Alice, were stupid games and, more importantly, a waste of time. The only reason he ever agreed to go to their house at all was to play with their dog, Rocco, a stinky old hound whom Neil adored. It was unfortunate that Alice was allergic to dogs and cats because she thought Neil could have benefited from having one around, since he found human friends so hard to come by.

Alice tried to shoo Neil away from the kitchen table where he was working on a small robot made from a few old scavenged cell phones and a remote control or two, as well as some Legos she'd scored from Goodwill for only a dollar. She told him to go play with Marie's kids, but he peered grimly at Marcus and Meredith, and shot Alice a look, before turning resolutely back to his work.

Alice sighed, brushed her hair out of her eyes, and sent Marcus and Meredith in to watch cartoons in the other room while she made a pot of coffee for Marie, who was crying too hard to speak.

"Is it Danny?" Alice asked softly. She knew all too well how it felt to get bad news.

Marie shook her head, blew her nose loudly into a paper towel, and said, "No. My mom."

Neil sighed heavily, as though Marie was annoying him by

sitting at his table, and Alice lightly slapped the back of his head in warning as she passed by to deliver Marie her coffee.

"It's that mass in her chest," Marie warbled.

"Cancer?" Alice asked.

Marie snuffled. "No, it's a tumor, really big, they say. But probably not cancer. Thank God. But still—"

Neil looked up then, interest in his eyes. "Where's it located?"

Marie glanced his way, surprised to be addressed by Neil. Alice couldn't blame her. Neil usually ignored Marie at all costs.

"I—I—don't know," she said and started to cry again.

Neil clucked his tongue. "Location, location, location. Important in real estate and tumors." Then he turned back to his robot while Marie stared at him aghast and confused. After a moment, Neil added, "Not cancer, huh? If you're gonna have a big mass in your chest, it's always best if it's not cancer. One day, nanites will go in and destroy cancers before they can grow." He paused, frowned, and then said as if it somehow cost him, "I'm sorry that day didn't come sooner."

That was the closest to empathy Alice had ever heard Neil give to anyone other than her or Joshua. The fact that her son had an opinion about the location of tumors qualified as creepier-than-average behavior, and she found that, as usual, she had no idea what to say. Marie wiped her nose and stared at him. Neither of them asked what they were really thinking: "Where did you even come from?"

She wasn't sure either of them truly wanted to know.

September 2018—Scottsville, Kentucky

JOSHUA PULLED OFF the road on his way out of Scottsville Square to investigate a new bike shop that had opened alongside the highway. Joshua wouldn't call himself much of a cyclist, but he'd been considering purchasing a new one to get to and from the lumber offices on days when it wasn't too muggy or too cold. It seemed like the progressive, green thing to do, and it wasn't like he couldn't use the exercise. Besides, he hadn't known that a new shop was opening, and he was curious about who was behind it.

The store was small, but the front room was very neat, with rows of shiny bicycles of all sizes and colors lined up, ready to be tried out. Joshua stuffed his hands in his pockets and walked around, looking at the merchandise, trying to decide if he preferred the racing models to the touring bikes with little baskets on the front. Gay, maybe. But so was he.

"Can I help you?"

Joshua blinked. "Lee? What are you doing here?"

Lee wiped his hands on a dirty cloth and grinned. "I own the place." He motioned around. "Like what you see?"

Joshua looked him up and down. Lee wore a pair of jeans and a tight, long-sleeved cotton shirt, straining over his biceps. Even with the scars twisting up the side of his neck, Joshua had to admit to himself, yet again, Lee was handsome.

Joshua swallowed. "Yeah, I...uh...." He scratched behind his left ear a little nervously and looked away, turning his focus on the yellow bike with the white basket. He pretended to examine it. "I didn't expect to see you here."

Joshua hadn't counted on ever seeing Lee again after that day in Earl G. Dumplin's diner. He'd thought about him a few times, though. He'd considered emailing even but had never been able to come up with a pretense on which to 'check in.' It didn't seem like it was appropriate to contact the skin recipient of his dead lover to say, "Hey, you're really good looking and seem nice, smart, and like a genuinely decent person. Want to hang out?"

After six years, Joshua wasn't in mourning anymore, and he was not dead—definitely not dead—*and* he did have a libido. A thriving one that he was tired of trying to ignore. Scottsville wasn't a great location for picking up other gay men, and he'd never been the type of guy to find the idea of Grindr appealing. That still hadn't changed. Nor was he going to drive down to Nashville or over to Bowling Green for some random hookup. So the fact that Lee played a role in the fantasies that filled his mind in the showers some mornings ever since they'd met said a lot about how much he'd liked the man. But who knew if Lee was even gay?

Lee put his hands on the handlebars of a small kiddie bike, leaning forward in a way that showed off how nicely his shoulders connected to his chest and neck. Joshua didn't know what it was about the posture, but it made his stomach curl with lust, and he felt his cheeks heating up.

"When I was here last summer to meet you, I kinda liked the place. Small town. Simple living." He looked directly at Joshua with a bit of meaning in his eyes and a smile that was decidedly suggestive somehow. Joshua's stomach fluttered. "Nice people," Lee went on. "I've been looking to start my life over somewhere, and this seemed like the perfect spot."

Perfect. Scottsville was far from perfect, but warmth bloomed in him over Lee's appreciation of the town's potential.

A few minutes later, Joshua looked at a green-and-blue touring bike with a brown basket—still gay like him, but less aggressively so—and listened to Lee talk about the care and upkeep of such a bike. Eventually, heart in his throat, he interrupted the shop-talk to ask, "You said you wanted to start your life over... Why's that?"

Lee went quiet, and then he slipped his hand into his dark hair and shook it out, like he was freeing some part of himself.

"That was invasive," Joshua said. "I'm sorry."

Lee shrugged, swung a leg over the bike Joshua was considering, and sat down. "I don't mind. You shared a lot with me when I met you last time. I consider us friends, and friends are free to ask questions." He smiled, and the tilt of his lips made Joshua's heart ache. "Too many memories."

Joshua swallowed hard. "I know what that's like." It was why he'd never gone back to Nashville, wasn't it?

Lee smiled again, his full lips stretching to reveal his white, straight teeth. "You know how it is. I knew you'd get it."

"Yeah."

"Back home, everyone knew me the way I was before. Even after six years they can't get over what happened to me. I get sick of the pity on their faces. I'd rather see people look aghast at first and then just get over it than deal with another old friend always looking at me like that."

Joshua put his hand on Lee's shoulder. "I don't know why they'd pity you." He swallowed and then just said it, "You're so handsome."

Lee's face went soft. "Thank you for not saying 'still.'"

Joshua shoved his hands in his pockets to keep from touching Lee's cheek. "You are."

Lee shrugged. "Maybe it's my problem, then. Maybe I'm the one who's changed." He stood up and stretched his arms over his head, which caused his shirt to lift a little, revealing more scars on his stomach. "Want a cup of coffee?" he asked, gesturing to the back room of the shop. "We can talk about other things. Warm up to each other some more, maybe."

Joshua pressed his lips together in a smile and nodded. He had some time. "Why not?"

There was a small kitchen in the back, along with a window looking out on rolling green fields and telephone wires. Lee gestured at a small table, and Joshua took a seat. As Lee set about boiling the water and producing a French press from a cupboard, he smiled at Joshua. "Tell me more about Neil."

"Why do you want to know?

"You don't have to say anything you don't want. I just feel like he's what we have in common. And I like the way you look when you're talking about him."

Joshua watched as Lee carefully poured the grounds into the press. Not many people wanted to hear about Neil anymore. Most of his family and friends were of the opinion that it was well past time he healed up and moved on. "All right. What do you want to know about him?"

"You said you met when he blessed you out over your dog and then basically stole her from you." They both laughed. "But how did you fall in love after that?"

Joshua's stomach flipped. He didn't know if it was anxiety at being offered a chance to talk about Neil, or a reaction to the bubbling attraction he felt for Lee. He delayed until Lee had joined him at the table, waiting for the familiar sound of boiling water to begin. "Well, it was a slow start between us, but I fell fast."

Oh, how Joshua rued that he had refused to ever do more than kiss Neil for fear of what that would mean. He'd come out in the end, hadn't he? Alone and grieving, he'd shouted his queerness to his family, and no one had turned their backs on him. If only he'd been brave enough before Neil was gone.

But he'd been young, and he was learning to forgive himself for that.

He wondered what Lee needed to forgive himself for. He supposed there was only one way to find out, and maybe that involved being the first to open up. He could be brave enough to do that. Besides, it really was good to have an opportunity to talk about Neil.

"It started with Magic, like you said, but I was slow on the uptake," Joshua began. "Mainly, because I didn't realize he'd stolen my dog, as you put it, until he'd stolen my heart, too."

April 2011—Nashville, Tennessee

JOSHUA CROSSED HIS arms over his chest, sulking as Magic raced after yet another tennis ball he'd thrown, only to bring it right to Neil's feet instead of his. The dog park was crowded for a Tuesday afternoon, probably because the weather was finally decent after a wickedly cold winter and a wet spring. Green flowed from grass to tree, and the sky shimmered a hot, thick blue.

Magic's black fur rippled over her quivering body as she waited eagerly for Neil to pick the ball up and throw it for her. He bent gracefully and did just that, demonstrating a form in his pitch that Joshua hadn't anticipated given his normally uptight, tense way of holding himself.

"So are you done being mad now?" Joshua asked.

The entire walk from the apartment, Neil had been on his phone yelling at one of his lab assistants, and Joshua had wondered if he should really be crushing on a guy who had such a cutting tongue. Would he talk to Joshua that way if he got angry? What would happen if Joshua got vulnerable with him and opened himself up?

Not that he ever would. Or could. It didn't matter if Neil was hot and sexy. It didn't matter if he was so good with Magic that it melted Joshua's heart and half his brain, too. It didn't matter that when Neil yelled at his assistant, Joshua just wanted to sling an arm around him, hug him close, and kiss him until he shut up. Because Joshua wasn't acting on those thoughts. Ever. He knew better than that. He just needed to shove them down deep into a box and keep on going.

"I'm done being mad," Neil said, but he didn't sound like it. His voice still held an edge of irritation. "Where's Paul lately? Haven't seen him coming or going."

Joshua stiffened. Neil asked about Paul a lot when he was picking Magic up or dropping her off, or just telling Joshua that he was *keeping* her like he was prone to do of late. "His grandpa's sick back home in Scottsville. He had to take a leave from school to help out."

"Ah." Neil glanced at him out of the side of his eye, and then bent to retrieve the ball Magic had brought back to him. She gave a little jump and bark of delight. He threw the ball even farther. "How do you feel about that?"

Joshua wrinkled his nose. Was Neil Russell, nanite researcher at Vanderbilt and grumpy-ass, dog-stealing neighbor really asking him about his feelings? And why? "I hope his grandpa is okay, I guess. It'll be hard on everyone if he dies."

"Will it be hard on you?" Neil narrowed his blazing blue eyes on Joshua. Then he made the hand motion he'd taught Magic early on. It meant 'down and stay,' and Magic did just that. She dropped to the dust at Neil's feet, panting, and contented herself with watching the other dogs play.

"Not really? I mean, if Paul moves out, paying the bills will be tough, but..." He shrugged. "I mean, I don't really know his grandpa."

Neil's brow quirked. "And my grad students say I'm cold. Wow. Blizzard levels here."

"Why?"

"Your boyfriend's grandpa is on the brink and you're just worried about the bills? I'd say your relationship is headed over the falls, too, in that case."

"Paul isn't my boyfriend," Joshua whispered, looking around to see who might've overheard. "I'm not..." Joshua swallowed down the word gay and the lie along with it. "I mean, he's my friend."

"You're not what?" Neil glared at Joshua, obviously daring him to deny himself.

"Paul's my friend."

"Got it. And you're not *what?*"

Joshua swallowed hard and stared at Neil's lips. They were held tightly, ready to bite out more sharp words if necessary. Joshua told the truth. "I'm not into him."

Neil's mouth twitched, and then he nodded sharply. "Good."

"Good?"

"Yeah. Good."

"Good because…?" Joshua swallowed hard, adrenaline making him lightheaded. "What? You don't like gay guys?"

Neil laughed then, hard and long, bending over to put his hands on his knees, his straight shoulders shaking with the force of his laughter. Joshua had never seen him lose it like that.

"What?"

"Oh, I like gay guys," he said, between getting his wind again and wiping at his eyes. He stood up straight and graced Joshua with one of his rare smiles. It was so sweet and bright that it almost hurt to see. Then he gripped Joshua's bicep hard. "I like them a lot."

Joshua swallowed hard, gathered his courage, and confessed, "I'm gay."

Neil's expression softened. "Me, too."

"You're the first person I've told."

Neil stared up at him for a long moment before jerking his head back the way they'd come. "Let's head back. I've got beer in the fridge and a Takeout Taxi menu in my junk drawer."

"I don't know. I haven't ever…"

Neil rolled his eyes. "We're just going to talk."

Joshua looked around to see who might be watching as Neil put his hand out as though to take hold of his. And then, with a rush of feeling like none he'd ever known, electric and hot, Joshua took the offered fingers.

Then he let Neil guide him and Magic home.

September 2018—Scottsville, Kentucky

"SO YOU TALKED?" Lee asked.

"We talked." Joshua sipped his coffee. "This is good, by the way. What brand do you use?"

"But you didn't *just* talk," Lee said with a wink as he reached behind him and grabbed the tin of coffee off the counter to show him the label.

"We did actually. That first day, anyway. I was way too skittish about who I was and how I felt to do anything more. Just holding his hand felt like a life-or-death event."

"I get it. When I came out to my family, I was terrified, but it was hardest to come out to myself. Admitting the truth of my feelings was scary as hell."

Joshua bit into his lower lip, considering Lee for a moment. "I had wondered…"

"If I was gay?"

"Yes."

"I hope that's because you'd be willing to go on a date with me."

Joshua closed his eyes, heat in his cheeks.

"Is that a yes?" Lee asked.

"Why would you want to?"

Lee laughed. "You're handsome, kind, and obviously a loving guy. Why wouldn't I want to go out with you?"

"I feel like maybe I've misled you."

Lee's eyebrows drew down, and he seemed to brace himself. "How's that?"

"I'm not the blushing virgin I was when Neil took me back to his apartment."

Lee chuckled. "I'd hope not."

"But not because of Neil…"

Lee's dark eyes grew quizzical. "I'm not sure I understand."

"I never slept with Neil. Before...yeah." He swallowed thickly. "Before he died."

Lee's eyes softened. "I'm sorry." Then he put his hand out and touched Joshua's wrist. "I'm not sure what that has to do with me asking you out? Or how you've misled me?"

"You have this idea of me as this loyal grieving widow, but the truth is different from that."

"I don't follow."

"I loved Neil. I loved him a lot, but I never gave him—" Joshua broke off. "I never gave him all of me. I saved sex because I was afraid that being with a man wasn't meaningful the way it was supposed to be. That it was a sin like I'd been taught. In the end, the guy I was with? It was meaningless because I didn't love him, not because of his gender. Afterward, all I could think was that I'd betrayed Neil. So that's the kind of man I really am. A coward."

"Do you really think so?" Lee took Joshua's hand, squeezing gently. "In your heart of hearts, is that what you think?"

Joshua felt hot tears behind his lids. What was wrong with him? Why was he confessing this to Lee, a virtual stranger, and then crying about it like some hurt little kid? Like he was back to being the old Joshua in Neil's apartment, too young and dumb to love himself?

Lee squeezed Joshua's hand again. "You haven't misled me at all. You're the man Neil fell in love with, and I see exactly why."

Joshua wiped at his eyes with the back of his free hand and whispered, "Do you?"

"Yeah."

Joshua cleared his throat, but he still couldn't look at Lee when he said, "I'd like to go out on a date, if you still want to."

Lee chucked his chin up, gazing into his eyes. "I can't think of anything better."

Chapter Three

January 2019—Atlanta, Georgia

NEIL HATED TRUCKS. Alice didn't understand why, but the sight of a semi-truck had been enough to set him off from the day he was born. It all came together one night when he was seven, and he presented her proudly with a comic book he'd made in his art class.

The comic was a gruesome thing, and it was accompanied by a note from his teacher requesting a conference to discuss it.

The opening scene of the book showed a man in a hospital bed with his chest open, his purple lungs and heart exposed for all the world to see. Next to him stood a man with a sharp knife, possibly a scalpel, and brown eyes. The dead man on the hospital bed was labeled with a very precise arrow and the word "ME."

The next panel showed a man with light-brown hair, dark brown eyes, and a wide smile; he was labeled, unsurprisingly, "JOSHUA." Then there was a drawing of a black dog labeled "MAGIC." Alice touched the drawing carefully. She'd heard less about Magic than about Joshua over the years, but the dog wasn't a surprise, either.

The next page declared it ten hours earlier. This was followed by a sequence of comic panels showing Magic and a man running on a sidewalk in a city, Magic breaking free of her leash, and the man dashing after her.

And then a truck. A semi-truck.

The next page showed Joshua crying, and the final page was

back to the man on the hospital bed. This time he was missing some limbs. A green-scrub-covered surgeon off to the side clutched a heart. It was not a Valentine's Day heart. No, of course not. This was her Neil, so it was a very detailed drawing of an anatomical heart, complete with aortic and thoracic valves and lots of blood dripping off the surgeon's elbow. No wonder the art teacher wanted to meet with her.

It was times like this she was grateful that Jim was deployed again.

"You were hit by a truck?" she asked Neil, carefully setting the comic book on the coffee table, amidst his clutter of tech journals and gadgets.

"Yep," he answered, looking up at the ceiling with pursed lips. "It sucked."

"Yeah, I can see that it would."

"Magic..." He frowned. "I think she died, too. I tried to save her. But I think I was too slow. I think if she'd lived, I'd know." His lips twisted. "Poor Joshua."

"Yes."

"I guess you can't expect to go up against a semi-truck and win. But I didn't even think. I loved her and..." He sighed. "I wish I'd saved her."

And again, Alice felt guilty. She knew now where he'd come from, and where he longed to be. Somehow, she almost felt like it was her fault that he was only a small child and not already grown man who could go find his Joshua and start his life with him over again.

"I think 'sucked' might be an understatement," she said.

Neil chuckled, a rarity that warmed her soul.

"I don't think Shakespeare had enough curses to cover it," Neil commented and then went to his room to poke at his latest project again: an experiment that involved dealing with nanites and rapid cellular repair.

Sometimes she was afraid to ask.

July 2020—Atlanta, Georgia

ALICE LEFT NEIL with Marie when she went to meet Jim at the old house. She'd moved out and into a new apartment a few days before he returned from his latest deployment abroad, and she had no intention of telling him where they were living now. She didn't trust him not to stalk them or worse.

"What the hell, bitch?" Jim asked, waving his arm around the empty living room. "You took my shit?"

"It wasn't *your* shit," Alice said softly. "It was our shit. And I'm leaving you with the house and the money in our joint account. I'm not asking you for anything more, Jim. Not another cent. So, please…just let us go."

"'Please let us go,'" Jim mocked. "Like I want you or your little bastard around anyway. Freakish little brat."

Alice didn't defend Neil. It was pointless, and it would only piss Jim off more. She had to concentrate on one thing, and one thing only: getting out of there unharmed and securing his agreement to sign the divorce papers.

She noticed the empty beer bottles by the clump of blankets on the floor. Most of the blankets still had their price tags from where he'd purchased them at Walmart. When her eyes flicked back up to his face, she swallowed and wished that she hadn't come alone. She should've taken Marie up on having her brother, Shane, come with her.

"He wasn't even Marshall's," Jim said, spitting out the word. "My best friend *died* thinking that kid was his. Lying cunt."

Alice quivered and started to back up toward the front door of the house. She'd told Jim before, a hundred times, she'd never been with anyone else. There had only been Marshall, and then him. But she knew where this conversation ended up, and she was just glad that Neil wasn't here to see it because he'd blame himself, like he always did. And it wasn't his fault. He couldn't help who he was, or who he'd been born to be.

The first punch was always the hardest to take, and Alice only had to suffer through three before she managed to wrench the front door open and stumble outside, clutching at her ribs and trying not to cry. The neighbor, Mrs. Chandler, was smoking on her front stoop, and she waved at Alice cheerily, her smile fading as she took in Alice's face.

"Need help, darlin'?" she called out.

Alice shook her head, fumbled with her car keys, and got the car door open. She glanced over her shoulder to see Jim standing in the doorway, one hand on the jamb, the other on the door itself, shaking his head at her and glaring menacingly, almost daring her to come back.

Mrs. Chandler looked between them and then stubbed out her cigarette and went inside.

Alice took a deep breath and drove away.

She didn't go straight to Marie's house, though. She wanted to get herself together before she picked up Neil. She hated to see the guilt on his face when he knew that Jim had hurt her. He wasn't a very open child, but when he did feel something, he felt it deeply, and she'd seen the way he looked after her fights with Jim in the past. Dark circles would appear around his eyes, and he'd spark inside with a rare warmth, a sad, guilty devotion and affection that made up for everything awkward and trying about him, and he'd stroke her hair while she cried.

There were times when she felt like the world's worst mother for allowing him to do that, to comfort her that way, but most of the time it just felt like the two of them against the world, and she was growing accustomed to that.

Grateful Jim hadn't punched her face, she was able to wipe the tears from her face and stop crying after only an hour or so. She cleaned up in the McDonald's bathroom, splashing water on her red, tear-stained cheeks.

When she finally showed up at Marie's house, Neil was sitting on the front step. His skinny legs were tucked up almost to his chin, and his piercing, intense gaze followed her car into the drive. When she got out, he stood up and ran to her. His arms felt too small and slight around her body. She held him and rubbed his back, and when he peered up at her, he searched her face.

"So...." she said.

He stared up at her, and she could feel him assessing her, taking in every detail of her face, body, and hair.

"It's over," she said. "Hopefully he'll send in the paperwork. And if he doesn't, then he doesn't. I don't care. We'll never see him again."

Neil nodded shortly. "Good. I...I'm sorry."

She patted his soft, spongy chestnut brown hair. "Shit happens, Neil. Every Southern girl knows that. But you're not the shit. He is." Neil seemed unconvinced, so she grabbed his chin and made him look at her. "You're special. You're not like everyone else. And maybe some people will hate you for that. But I love you. God help me, I do. And I'll do anything for you. You're my son."

Neil looked like he might say something cutting; sometimes he did when she was too sentimental. But he just said, "I love you, too."

She cleared her throat and tried not to cry. He almost never said it, but she always knew it was true. Still, it only hurt in the good way to hear.

"I love you, too," he said again. "And I promise to make it all up to you. I'll make you proud."

April 2021—Atlanta, Georgia

NEIL SAT IN the dark in his room, curled up in the bed, an underlying hint of pain softening his usually sharp expression. Alice sat on the floor by his bed, reached out a hand to him, and wasn't surprised when he didn't take it. She sat there for over an hour, and it was only when she stood up to leave that Neil spoke. His voice was rough and tired. "He got married. Joshua. Got married."

Alice sighed and turned back to the bed, sank down to the floor, and said, "Neil, you have to let this go."

"I'm glad," Neil said, straightening his shoulders. "I'm glad for him. I want him to be happy. At least, I did. I *do*. I don't know. He can't wait around for me to grow up." He tensed his body as though annoyed with it and said with quiet rage, "Look at me. I'm just a little boy."

Alice didn't know what to say to that. She never did when Neil confided these thoughts to her. If she had more money, she'd seek counseling for them both. Though she couldn't imagine Neil ever actually talking to a counselor. And there was no way she was going to pay exorbitant fees for sessions she had no doubt would devolve into staring contests and possibly insults. From Neil, not the counselor.

"Who did he marry?" she asked, not certain if it was the right thing at all.

"The man he's been seeing. Lee Fargo. He's a nice guy."

"How do you know?"

"Facebook."

Alice knew Neil followed Joshua on social media outlets, but she hadn't realized he was also tracking Joshua's friends. Though, of course she should have known that. She still looked at Jim's account sometimes, following links to his new girlfriend's page, and she didn't even love him. Not the way Neil still loved Joshua.

Neil went on, "He posts pictures of them together and stories about their life. I hadn't looked at his page in a few months. Because it hurts."

"I know, baby."

"But when I look, I get to see Joshua's face at least."

"Yes."

Neil tensed all over. "So I missed the engagement announcement. But I should have known. They've been together a long time." Neil rolled over so that his small back was to her. "Joshua looks happy in the pictures."

"You deserve to be happy, too."

Neil shrugged and covered his head with a pillow.

The next evening, Alice stirred the canned soup she was heating for dinner and watched as Neil signed onto Facebook to look at Joshua's wedding pictures again. Seeing the pictures of Joshua obviously soothed as much as it hurt. The pot began to rattle on the stove, and she turned the heat down.

Day by day, moment by moment, she'd watched Neil realize that any hope he'd had of hurrying up into adulthood so that he could be with Joshua again was vanishing. Today that hope was entirely snuffed out. Joshua had a husband now, and a new life. Even if he still remembered and loved his old Neil, the one called Dr. Russell, Joshua had moved on.

And that was only right. Alice couldn't begrudge Joshua that, even if it killed her to see her little boy grieve.

"Neil," she said gently, snapping him from his obsessive clicking through the photos. "Soup's ready."

Neil rubbed at his eyes, turned his computer off, and stood up. "Not hungry. Going to bed." He left the kitchen and headed down the hall to his bedroom.

Alice bit her lip as his bedroom door shut. With a sigh, she sat down at the table to eat. But the soup didn't seem very appealing to her anymore, either.

August 2011—Nashville, Tennessee

LOVING JOSHUA WAS frustrating as hell.

But Neil was accustomed to frustration. He was a scientist, after all. Patience, calculations, and re-tries were what his life was made of. It didn't mean being stuck with blue balls for the fourth day in a row was any fun. But he could wait. For Joshua.

"Can I see you tomorrow?" Joshua asked, his ripe, soft lips swollen from the teenage-like make-out session they'd just engaged in for the past hour and a half. His eyes were dark and hooded, his expression soft and sweet.

If only he'd agree to go to the bedroom and let Neil into his hands, and mouth, and ass. Neil would make everything so good for him.

"Don't you have to work?" Neil asked, brushing his thumb over Joshua's mouth, letting it sink into the wet heat. "Bring home the bacon?"

Joshua groaned and sucked on Neil's thumb, closing his eyes. He panted softly when Neil pulled it free. "I hate my job."

"Most people do."

"I want to stay here with you."

Neil smiled. "You can come back over after work. I'll be here with Magic. You could spend the night."

Shit. He'd pushed.

Conflict warred in Joshua's eyes, and Neil knew the moment he'd shut down against the growing lust between them. Sadness combined with shame as the young man he loved whispered, "I can't do that. Not yet. Maybe not ever." Joshua squirmed. "My family won't understand. I *can't* be gay. It's not—"

Neil stopped his words with his thumb again, letting Joshua

suck on it a moment. He wanted to tell him that nothing was going to change about his feelings. That ignoring them, repressing them, would backfire eventually. But he didn't want to end the night on a sour note. He loved Joshua too much to send him off angry. It used to be that he valued the truth; now he just valued Joshua. He kissed his mouth. "Go home. You're tired."

"And I need to jerk off."

Neil groaned. "Asshole." He bit back the suggestion that they take care of it together.

"Will you jerk off, too?"

Neil swallowed and nodded.

"I'd like to see that." Joshua's voice was soft, full of yearning.

"You could."

Joshua's eyes lit up and then the fire guttered out again. "I have to go. C'mon, Magic. Paul's home."

The giant roll of fur, more like a log than a dog, really, huffed from the bed in the corner and didn't move.

"I guess she's staying here."

Neil stroked his fingers along Joshua's jawline. "Come back after your shift. Stay with me tonight."

Joshua backed into the hallway, his mouth still red but his eyes flashing danger. "I can't. I've told you. And I probably won't come over tomorrow, either. I have the late shift. So I guess I'll see you and Magic... I don't know." He winced. "Later."

"Later," Neil murmured, watching Joshua unlock the door to his apartment and rush inside.

Joshua's loud, angry cry of frustration that came as soon as the door was shut was expected, but it still made Neil tense up. He hated how Joshua hated himself. But what could he do about it except wait...and love him? He hated to admit it, but he'd fallen for the kid from the start, when Joshua had bitten into his lip and stared innocently down at him while wrapped in nothing but a towel.

And that was why he wasn't going to pressure Joshua anymore. Not for another kiss. Not to spend the night. Not for anything physical at all. Neil could wait.

When the time came, he'd show Joshua how good it could be between men. How wrong his parents were to call it sin. He'd have Joshua begging for him to go beyond their current lust-soaked, fully clothed gropes. Yes, when Joshua finally asked to have sex with Neil, he would make him sing out in gratitude and praise.

For that, Neil could wait. Because he was in love. And when love came for a man, there was no denying it. Love was big, powerful, and strong as fuck. And he—serious, focused, never-loved-anyone-before Neil Russell—was flattened by it. He'd wait as long as it took for Joshua to love him back.

He'd wait forever.

Chapter Four

April 2022—Scottsville, Kentucky

JOSHUA WAS SURPRISED by the message he got from Paul. He and his boyfriend Fisher were going to be coming up from Nashville to visit with Paul's grandma and wanted to get together. Joshua was excited to meet Fisher. After all, he'd been with Paul for quite some time now.

Paul had invited Joshua to meet Fisher once before—in Nashville—and asked him to bring Lee.

It they'd gone, it would have been the first trip that Joshua and Lee had taken together.

Well, except for the visit to Lee's sister in Louisville. That had been a tough trip. She was still grieving for her lost child, and just the sight of Lee, with all of his scars, seemed to undo the year of therapy that she'd gotten under her belt. When she'd lost her crap, yelled at Lee, and then slammed upstairs to a bedroom, her boyfriend had asked them to leave, and they had.

Joshua had held Lee while he cried, rocking him back and forth on the hotel bed and rubbing his scarred back. Their mom had died when Lee was twelve, and their dad had abandoned them when Lee was sixteen. His sister was the only family Lee had left. And now she couldn't bear to be near him.

"You've got me," Joshua had whispered. "You've got me."

It was as he'd held Lee on the hotel room bed, the vacancy light shining red outside their window, Joshua had finally understood why Lee couldn't forgive himself, and it broke his heart. Because he understood all too well. He hadn't even been there the morning of Neil's death, hadn't had a single chance to save his life, but he still blamed himself for living.

He and Lee were both survivors, and they both struggled with guilt.

The Nashville trip to meet Fisher and see Paul had never happened though. Joshua couldn't lie to Lee about the reasons why, not like he could lie to Paul. The truth was he'd let perfectly normal issues at Stouder Lumber become emergency-sized in his mind, until he'd been able to convince himself that it was right to put the trip off indefinitely in order to resolve them. When, in fact, the problem—a few of the Mennonites struggling with the newest computer program he'd installed—wasn't a big deal in the scheme of things, and could have easily waited a few days. He simply couldn't make himself go back.

Maybe if Paul wasn't still living in the same apartment, the one they'd shared beside Neil. Maybe if Joshua hadn't held Lee on that hotel bed as he sobbed, and understood in his own heart how impossible it would be to ever go back to the places or the people death stole from them.

Still, Joshua had always wanted to meet his old friend's new lover, and so he was excited by the fact Paul and Fisher would be coming up to Scottsville this time. He didn't even know what Fisher looked like since Paul wasn't on social media, and neither was Joshua, really. Lee was on Facebook, though, and posted tons of pictures and videos of them online, but Joshua only updated the Stouder Lumber account when there was news to impart, and clicked 'like' on things Lee told him he should. So he was curious about the man who'd stolen his old friend's heart.

Over the phone, Paul told him, "I've been wanting to show Fisher around Scottsville and Bowling Green anyway. I'm grateful Grandma's still alive. I've told Fisher about how she and Gramps took me in when I really needed a home after Dad kicked me out. Fisher wants to thank her."

Joshua had always admired the blasé attitude Paul's grandparents had taken when he'd jumped out of the closet by making out with the town's hotshot quarterback when he was fifteen. Eric, the quarterback, hadn't fared as well, being cast out of his parents' house, too, and then bullied by his own team until he finally left for college the next year. Eric had stayed with his former girlfriend's family in the time between. It'd been a cold, awkward, scary time for every young queer in town. But Paul's grandparents had been steadfast. Evidence that there could be warmth even in a blizzard of fear.

In the end, Joshua's own folks had been surprisingly chill about his coming out, too. Maybe because he'd been so devastated by grief at the time that his homosexuality was the least of their concerns. Besides, they said, they'd suspected when he'd moved in with Paul after leaving for school, since Paul was out already. Though they'd hoped since he was attending a religious school, he'd keep it to himself.

And he had kept it to himself. Until he hadn't.

Seeing Paul again, after all that Joshua had been through, after all the changes in his life—well, he was kind of nervous. What if Paul didn't like Lee? What if Joshua didn't like Fisher? What if Paul wanted to talk about Neil and Magic? And what if that was more than Joshua could handle in front of a stranger?

Lee, though, was relaxed, saying, "He knew Neil, and you knew Neil. That's a blessing, isn't it, babe? Were there any other people who really knew him?"

"Not really. Just Chris, but he's..." Joshua raised a shoulder and let it fall. "He's Chris."

Most people in Scottsville knew Chris from his job at the nearby resort, and also as the swishiest queer in town, but only a few really knew about Chris's background in Nashville.

"Chris at Barren River?" Lee asked, surprised.

"Yeah."

"Knew Neil?"

"They were friends."

Lee blinked. "There's a story there. I can't believe we've been together almost four years now and I haven't heard it."

Joshua laughed. "I don't know why I never told you about it. I guess there isn't much to say. If you know Chris, then you know he's friends with everyone who doesn't treat him badly because of his, you know, everything."

Chris was...Chris. He'd been a drag performer in Nashville, and a pal of Neil's from the years when Neil had hung out at gay bars—a pastime he'd given up as 'boring and stupid' by the time he'd met Joshua. But Chris he'd never given up. They'd been friends until the end.

"I still remember the first time I met Chris," Joshua said, a smile on his lips. "He was hanging out at Neil's place, Magic on his lap, and a big old plastic cup in his hand. It was full of rum with a dash of some kind of juice so he could call it a cocktail."

"Sounds right."

"He didn't stand up when I came in. He just put out his hand, and said, 'I'm Chris. And who are you, sugar-tits?'"

"Sugar-tits!" Lee laughed. "I can see him saying that."

"Yeah. I think when he did drag shows, he used female pronouns, but otherwise..." Joshua trailed off, remembering the ease between Neil's snark and Chris's sparkle. He'd been jealous at the time. Which seemed silly now that Chris had married a big, beefy Kentucky farmer and taken on a passel of stepsons. Talk about complicated.

"How did Chris end up in Scottsville?" Lee asked. "I always assumed he'd been born here and never got out."

"No, he's a transplant. Like you. He came up to check on me after Neil died. Stayed a few days and somehow met Dale Richards while pumping gas—I know, right? They exchanged numbers, started texting, and the rest is history."

"Wow."

"Yeah."

"Well, then, if it's just you, Paul, and Chris in the world who really knew Neil, then we should be grateful for this visit," Lee said again. "I'd like to hear Paul's take on the guy who loved you so well."

Joshua kissed Lee then, grateful and sad all at once. He loved that Lee didn't want him to forget Neil, and that he never suggested Joshua should 'move on' or 'get over it.' His patience was beautiful. But sometimes he felt like Neil's humanity, the reality of him, got lost in Lee's near-hero worship of the man who'd donated his skin, and the ideal that Joshua had loved. The reality was that Neil could be a pill, and sometimes it weighed on Joshua that he let Lee believe in Neil's purity.

A week later, when Paul stepped out of the giant, white SUV and onto the fresh green, rolling field that extended out from Joshua and Lee's small, white farmhouse, Joshua couldn't stop smiling. Paul looked the same as he ever did: big, tall, and like he lived on a bench press. His tanned skin and blond hair glimmered in the Kentucky sunshine.

"This your new place?" Paul asked, nodding toward the house Lee and Joshua had moved into not long before, taking over the only empty place already built on the Stouder family property—the others were already spoken for by aunts, uncles, cousins, and Joshua's parents. "No wonder I could never lure you back to Nashville if you had this waiting for you." He grinned and gave Joshua a big hug.

Fisher followed right behind him, and his steely, firm gaze met

Joshua's. "Glad to meet you," he said, putting out his hand.

"You, too." Joshua smiled a little at his firm grip.

Salt-and-pepper hair and a weathered face made it clear that Fisher was a good ten years older than Paul. He was a chiseled guy, wearing an old Army T-shirt and jeans, and bearing himself with the ramrod straight self-assurance of an ex-military officer. His bear-paw hand was rough and calloused. It turned out he was a mechanic and they'd met when Paul brought his car in for some work.

Lee stepped out of the front door, and a whole new round of introductions took place. As they walked inside, Fisher's big hand stayed on Paul's lower back. Lee directed them into the living room where drinks were served and a discussion of how best to barbecue the steaks began. Lee and Fisher went out back to start the grill, and Paul chattered on about their life in Nashville, and how eager he was to see his grandma.

Slowly, Joshua relaxed. It was good to see Paul again. It didn't hurt nearly as much as he'd thought it would, even when Paul brought up Neil and Magic.

"He loved that dog. Wasn't that into me, though, was he?" Paul said, leaning against the counter separating the kitchen from the living room. "He used to stare at me back before you got together, and if laser beams could have shot from his eyes, I'd be dead." He chuckled and tossed back the last of his bourbon. "Got any beer?"

"Sure," Joshua said, turning toward the refrigerator and pulling out four, then popping the lids on two. "I thought he stared at you because he was into you," Joshua admitted with a chuckle. "I was jealous as hell."

Paul laughed. "You always were an idiot when it came to knowing a guy was interested."

"Neil was hard to read."

"True. Lee isn't. He's wild about you."

Joshua grinned. "He is, isn't he?" He gazed out the window to the back patio where Fisher and Lee were laughing and gesturing at the grill. "He's brought me back to life."

Paul came around the counter and pulled Joshua into a big hug. He pounded Joshua's back and said, "After Neil and Magic, I was scared we'd lose you, too. But you pulled through it. I'm proud of you. Neil would be proud of you, too."

Joshua's throat closed up, and tears stung his eyes. He pulled away and punched Paul on the shoulder. "Asshole. Don't make me—" He waved at his face.

Paul grinned. "Let's take these beers out to our men."

That night in bed, Joshua cuddled up with Lee and wondered what Neil would've said about Fisher being so much older. Joshua chuckled.

"What?" Lee had asked.

"Just thinking about Neil."

"And you're smiling. That makes me happy, babe."

Joshua shrugged. "He made me happy. And seeing Paul today, hearing him talk about Neil, it reminded me that I shouldn't let his death change that."

"Nope."

Lee kissed his head and after a respectful moment said, "So, this Fisher guy. Paul's a bottom."

"Seems like," Joshua said.

Lee cackled softly and grabbed Joshua's ass, squeezing. "Can't believe Neil ever thought you and Paul were together."

Joshua laughed. "I know. Neil was rarely wrong, but when he was, he was extra wrong." He grew thoughtful. "Paul and Fisher are probably happy staying at Barren River, and they said Chris gave them one of the best rooms with a good view, but maybe we should have asked them to stay with us?"

"Where?" Lee asked. "Our place is kind of small. Oh, wait, were you thinking they could stay in our bed? Naughty, naughty

Joshua."

Joshua rolled his eyes and threw a pillow at Lee's head. "We could turn the office into a guest room like we keep talking about."

"In a few hours' time? I don't think so." He laughed again. "I think a foursome is clearly the only solution to this problem."

"Don't be a smart-ass."

"Also I like the office." Lee reached into the bedside table for a bottle of lube. "Let guests stay at Barren River or another hotel. That's what hotels are for!"

"True."

"Now, get on your hands and knees. No more talk of foursomes."

Joshua laughed. "I kind of think Paul would flip out if that happened."

Lee snorted, guiding Joshua up to his hands and knees and running a finger over Joshua's sensitive anus. "Just Paul, huh? You know I'm kidding, babe."

Joshua didn't manage to ask if the lack of additional bed partners was something Lee regretted because he tended to lose track of his thoughts when he was being fingered open with such focus and determination.

Then Lee was over him and in him, taking his time and letting Joshua fall apart on his cock, before he pulled out to shoot onto Joshua's back. Lee kissed Joshua's sweaty neck and gave him three of his fingers to ride. Joshua moaned and writhed on them while he worked to bring himself off, until finally a string of curses fell from his lips and come splattered the sheets below.

"All mine," Lee whispered as he rubbed his come into Joshua's skin and then pushed his cock back in for a second round. "Not sharing."

Joshua squirmed as Lee pounded his prostate. He didn't want to share either.

Chapter Five

August 2022—Scottsville, Kentucky

THERE WAS SOMETHING going on. In the past several months, Joshua had started to become somewhat paranoid that Lee was having an affair. There were whispered phone calls in the kitchen late at night that ended abruptly when Joshua walked in. Plus, Lee had been getting home late from the shop so often that Joshua decided to drive down there himself one evening to hang out since Lee couldn't break away. But the shop had been closed up and the lights were out. Lee was nowhere to be found, and calls to their mutual friends didn't turn him up.

When Lee had shown up at their house later, he'd been super apologetic for worrying Joshua, and made some weird excuse about having gone on a night bike ride through the woods to clear his mind.

"Of what?" Joshua had asked.

"Just work stress, babe," Lee had replied.

Joshua didn't think there was anyone Lee was interested in, though. He wracked his brain trying to think of a single, solitary man that he'd seen Lee check out since coming to Scottsville. The only one he could think of was a young Mennonite man who worked in the lumber yard, Zeb Reimer. But, well, that would be a lost cause for Lee even if there *was* anything to be jealous about. Zeb was very devout, straight, and married with two children. And even if he wasn't straight after all, he'd have a lot of cultural programming to get past before he'd commit the double sin of homosexuality and adultery. More even than Joshua had had to overcome in his own quest to be true to himself despite his upbringing in a conservative church.

So, no. Not Zeb.

But maybe there was someone else? Someone that Joshua had overlooked? Or possibly someone he'd never met before? There were always people coming through the store, some from as far away as Louisville or Nashville, looking to have their bicycle repaired on their long-distance bike tours. For all Joshua knew, one of them could have caught Lee's eye and, possibly, his heart. Joshua hoped that he was being an idiot, hoped this wasn't a case where love destroyed him again.

"Hey," Joshua said, answering Lee's call.

He was at his desk at the lumberyard, ostensibly working on some Stouder Lumber schedules but actually worrying about Lee and wondering if his marriage was on the rocks or not. He supposed the thing to do was to just ask, get it all out in the open, but he didn't want to come across as unreasonably jealous if he didn't have to be. What he needed was some proof.

"I need you to come down to the Medical Center," Lee said.

Joshua sat up straight. "Why? Are you okay? Are you hurt?"

"Everyone's fine. I just… You're just needed here. Can you get here as soon as possible?"

"Sure, yeah. Yeah." Joshua stood up and started gathering up his things. "Are you sure you're all right? Is it my mom? Dad? Sam?"

"Shh, Joshua. Relax. It's all fine. Just come."

Joshua was frustrated when the call went dead before he could get any more out of Lee, and he considered ringing back, if only to ask *where* in the hospital he should meet him. But he didn't want to waste any time, just in case there was something Lee wasn't telling him. He shot off a few texts demanding answers as he raced to his car, but only got one word in reply.

Cafeteria.

THE CAFETERIA AT the hospital was completely decked out. There were streamers, and balloons everywhere, and tons of people who yelled, "Happy Birthday, Joshua!" when Joshua raced through the door.

He stopped dead, shock rolling over him. Happy birthday? It wasn't until next month. He stared agog for a few minutes at the crowd around him, and then grinned, shaking his head, amused and annoyed with himself for having doubted Lee. Lee, who was there clapping, his face all lit up with happiness and pride at succeeding in his surprise.

Joshua took Lee into his arms and kissed him on the lips.

"I can't believe you!"

"I can't either!"

Joshua laughed and looked around. Paul was sitting on the other side of the room with Fisher, near a table boasting a giant cake and a podium with a microphone. Joshua started to head that way, a wide grin on his face, when suddenly, he stopped. Aside from Paul, Chris and Dale, Chris's oldest stepson Declyn, Joshua's parents and little brother, Sam, he didn't know anyone in the massive crowd.

"Uh…what's going on?" he asked, chuckling in confusion. "Did you have to hire attendees for my party or something?"

"No, Joshua." Lee's dark eyes softened with love. "This is your present." He gestured to everyone in the room. "Every person in here, including me, benefited from Neil's life. I tracked down every former graduate student of his that I could find—privacy issues made that hard, but I managed to find some. And, wow, Joshua, a lot of his lab assistants didn't like him very much, even all these years later. Said he was impatient and yelled at them a lot. Talk about holding grudges!"

Joshua didn't know if he was going to laugh or cry. He bit on his lip, his smile hurting, and a lump forming in his throat.

"I also found every person I could who'd received any organ donation from him after his death. Again, privacy issues prevented me from getting a full list, but I had the names of the people who'd emailed you in the past, plus others who'd given permission for you to contact them. I invited them all and their families." He motioned around again. "This isn't even everyone. But every person here? They're here because they knew and admired Neil, or they benefited from his life through organ donation. So, happy birthday, Joshua." Lee put his hands on Joshua's shoulders and looked into his eyes seriously. "So long as all of these people exist, so long as *you* exist? Well, to quote Celine Dion, babe—his heart will go on."

Joshua burst into laughter at the same time he burst into tears, pressing his hand to his mouth he tried to hold them back, but it was impossible. Lee hugged him tight.

A chant of "speech, speech, speech" began, and Joshua shook his head, not sure if he could get it together enough to even begin.

Still, Lee steered him to the front of the room and positioned him in front of the podium. Joshua cleared his throat, looked out at the room full of people, caught his mother's eye, and cleared his throat again. She smiled encouragingly at him, her gray eyes glinting with pride. He remembered when he'd been with Neil, in the closet and afraid, he'd thought if he ever came out, he'd never see that pride in his mother's eyes again.

Now look.

Pride for him. And pride for Lee.

Even pride for Neil, though she'd never known him.

He'd underestimated them all.

"So...." he started. "Wow. I don't know what to say."

There was applause at that.

"Well, first, I do. Thank you. Thank you for coming here and for remembering Neil. He was...well...he was sometimes an asshole."

Laughter spattered through the room.

"But he was never anything but gentle with me, even when he shouldn't have been, maybe. Even when, looking back, I wished he'd pushed me harder than he did. I know he was tough on his students, but he was only ever tender to me. And I loved him."

Silence fell, but it lasted only a beat, and then there was more applause.

"Neil loved when his work got attention," Joshua said. "He was always puffed up like a peacock every time his work was published or cited by a fellow researcher. He liked everyone to know that what he did was important. He wanted to change the world with nanites. And I suppose, given the work his foundation does, he has. But somehow I think he'd be appalled by this...this big show of sentimentality. He'd probably say, 'What are you doing? This is ridiculous! Don't waste your life on boring birthday parties for my idiot boyfriend. Go do something real with your time!'"

The crowd shuffled nervously.

"And you know what I'd say to that? 'Stuff it, Neil. This one's for me.' And to all of you—thank you. So much. I...I truly appreciate it." Joshua turned to Lee who was standing behind him, and he took his hand. "Thank you. I love you. Thank you for doing this for me. You're amazing, and I'm so happy that I met you, and that I can have you in my life."

"Ditto, babe," Lee said. He jerked his chin toward the room full of people, directing Joshua's attention back to everyone that Neil's life had touched. "Happy birthday."

PART TWO

Chapter Six

September 2027—Scottsville, Kentucky

JOSHUA WOKE UP sweaty and sick to his stomach, on the verge of tears. It had been 'the dream' again. Well, one of them. He had two dreams that came frequently enough to earn that term of familiarity. At least it wasn't the one that woke Lee up, too, though that one left Joshua less conflicted, if only because Lee knew about it. There really was no way to hide the jerking sobs that usually woke them both.

After that dream, Lee would rub his back and tell him, "It's okay. It was a long time ago. You're here with me right now."

It was what he needed to hear because in the dream the present didn't exist. He was back there, in the hospital, and Neil was dying, hooked up to machines and covered in blood, brain already dead and gone forever. And people were telling Joshua, not asking but telling him, that it was time to say goodbye, to do what Neil would have wanted, to give his organs away. So much responsibility, so much grief and pain, and he hadn't even been prepared for it. He hadn't known that Neil had changed his will. The terror and the gut-wrenching pain filled him up like an ocean, and he'd wake up from the dream sobbing, "Neil, Neil, Neil," with the drumming of his heart. It was kind of stupid that it hurt that much. It had been fifteen years. He should be past all of this by now.

He'd tell Lee as much afterward, wiping the snot and tears off of his face, half-laughing, but his mouth still twisted up with old pain.

"Shut up," Lee would whisper good-naturedly. "I hate that you hurt so much, but I love that you're the kind of person who loves that hard. It's selfish, but I'm glad to know that if I die, you'll still miss me this much years later, too."

Joshua laughed a little between leftover sobs. "You better not die on me."

"If I could make that promise, I would."

Joshua would let Lee hold him then, resting his cheek against Lee's now scar-free shoulder. They had faded away two years ago when Lee had signed up for a trial of one of the highly experimental cellular-nanite treatments that Neil had been working toward before his death.

Joshua was glad for Lee's sake that the scars had gone, but, strangely, he missed them, personally. They were part of the man he'd fallen for, the man who'd made him laugh, and love, and be happy again after he'd lost Neil. And even if they were considered by most to be unfortunate and unsightly, Joshua had loved every inch of every scar with all of his heart.

Joshua often wondered what Neil would have thought of how far nanites had come. How excited he would have been to see the outcome of their use to repair cellular damage. Joshua could only imagine the look of excitement and power that would have come over Neil's face when he realized what his work had accomplished.

Neil never got that chance. Instead, Neil had ended on a hospital bed with his hand in Joshua's. And when Joshua had nightmares of that day, the pain was still intense and vital. It swelled viciously inside of him.

But that wasn't the dream he'd woken up from all sick and sweaty. This time it was the dream Lee didn't know about. The one Joshua dreaded the most. In it, Joshua sat at Earl G. Dumplin's diner, sipping at his coffee and messing with the new tablet he'd just picked up, trying to program it to alert him to issues with his lumber trucks via satellite tracking, when Neil sat down across from him.

Joshua cried, "Oh my God! It's you!"

The amount of joy that filled him was immeasurable. It was relief, happiness, and utter bliss all at once. Tears came to his eyes, and he took Neil's hand, and he didn't even ask; he didn't even need to know. Where Neil had been? Why he was back? None of that was important. The only thing that mattered was he was there now. And he was perfect, and handsome, and looking at Joshua with all of the love in the world.

"I've missed you so much," Joshua would always say, and he grabbed Neil close. Neil smelled the same—like soap and shampoo and his skin. "I'm so glad you're here. We can do everything we were meant to do. We can be together."

Neil looked happy in that way that only Joshua understood, his eyes warm and narrowed, and Joshua felt as though he was going to burst into a million joyful pieces, because he was with Neil, and he wouldn't have to miss out on any of it now.

Then, every time, Neil would open his mouth and say, "And how will Lee feel about that?"

All of the joy, all of the bliss, would crumble into a pile of sick dread around his feet. He'd take Neil's hand and stare at him, devastated as he tried to process the joy, the hope for what he wanted with Neil, and line it up against what he had with Lee: the peace and happiness they had together, the love they shared, the *life* they'd built. He'd feel a cold, sweaty panic well inside of him because he couldn't give it up. He couldn't give either of them up.

And then Neil would put his hand on Joshua's cheek and say very seriously, "It's just a dream, Joshua. Wake up."

Wake up.

Joshua hated those dreams. He'd spend the next day feeling grief-stricken like he'd lost Neil all over again, and feeling guilty, too, like he'd betrayed Lee's trust. He'd been unable to choose.

He'd wanted it all. And he'd betrayed Neil for wanting Lee, and he'd betrayed Lee for wanting Neil, and most of all, he was angry that his subconscious would do that to him. Torturing himself was something he didn't do anymore. It was a bad habit that he'd made himself outgrow. Because it hadn't made him not gay. Because Neil wouldn't have wanted it. Because Lee was a good man, and they had a happy life together. The list could go on.

It was morning, though, and the dream had come and gone.

Joshua took deep breaths, trying to cast aside the feelings left behind like debris in its wake. The sun streamed through their bedroom window, and it was a beautiful fall morning. The wind chime on the front porch rang like aural glitter, and he swallowed hard, determined to focus on all that was beautiful and alive.

He listened to Lee's gentle breathing beside him, and when he turned onto his side, he found his younger brother Sam asleep on a bed they'd thrown together on the floor for him. Sam had wanted to spend the night in order to get away from their parents' fighting, so Joshua and Lee had let him.

Thinking of his parents, Joshua groaned and rolled onto his back, throwing his arm over his eyes like he could block it out of his mind. But he found the drama rolling there like a movie. His dad had slept with another woman, a new teacher in town named Marissa Laurie. Joshua had only met her once at the restaurant at Barren River Lake resort when he'd been having dinner there with his attorney discussing some Stouder Lumber issues. Ms. Laurie was there having an after-school-hours drink with his dad, and Joshua had known, immediately known, what was really going on.

He'd pulled his father aside and said, "Listen, Dad, if you don't care what this would do to Mom, at least think of Sam."

His dad had denied that anything inappropriate was happening, and Joshua had gone home with his stomach in knots, helpless and afraid. Because, really, what was he going to do? Demand that his father own up to something that might not have happened?

But it had happened, of course. And now his mom and little brother were hurting.

Joshua sat up, and Lee shifted. His arm flopped over to Joshua's pillow, the scars almost entirely erased now; just a slight discoloration remained. Joshua put his feet on the floor and carefully stepped over Sam. He smiled down at his brother's sprawled form—fifteen years old and gangly.

Joshua headed to the bathroom to take a piss. He could still feel the heat of Neil's hand on his cheek from the dream, and he fought the urge to bring his own hand up to wipe the sensation away. As much as he always hated the dream and the loss he felt every time, he longed for it, too. To feel that touch again, to see Neil's face. It was worth the pain.

Lee was still asleep when Joshua was ready to leave for work, but Joshua returned to the bedroom to kiss his temple and push his wavy dark hair away from his forehead. He stood by the bed and watched him sleep for a long moment. Joshua smiled and whispered, "I love you."

Then he stepped over his younger brother again and got on with his day.

JOSHUA HAD AN early meeting with another member of the Neil Russell Foundation board to review some standouts in a recent spate of nanite-technology-related grant requests from some rather young scientists. Each of them would need in-depth investigation to prove that they had something to offer the world at large and weren't just another group of college kids with big egos.

Morning had never been Joshua's time, and he stopped off by Earl G. Dumplin's to pick up coffee. There was quite a breakfast rush, so while Joshua waited, he let himself remember the dream. He took a deep breath and let the rush of joy when he saw Neil sweep over him again, and he tried not to feel guilty about it.

Eventually, though, the guilt crept in and ruined it again. So, he turned his attention to the ways Earl G. Dumplin's had changed in recent years. They now took touch-free payments direct from phones, and servers could take a payment at the table with just a tap of an app. It was silly to resent change, but he missed the old *ka-ching* register and the feel of dollar bills in his fingers. Just like everywhere, as time marched on, the place just didn't feel the same.

Joshua remembered when the local hospital had approved refitting their entire system a few years back. He'd always hated the hospital bracelet that had marked Lee as a patient when he'd been checked in for various nanite skin treatments over the years. Now bedside fingerprints and retinal scans had taken their place.

The last time Joshua himself had been in the hospital, he'd been in for tests determining whether or not he'd be a good candidate for a new, experimental nanite technology. The doctors had promised that the advanced cellular-repair capabilities could extend his life exponentially, and as it turned out, he'd been accepted into the trial. A few weeks later, nanites had been fed into his bloodstream during another overnight stay, and the microscopic robots had set to work on repairing wear and tear, bolstering his immune system, and even eking some additional functionality out of his already healthy pair of lungs. For several months afterward, he'd felt superhuman.

Joshua thought Neil would be pleased at the advancements his work had made. After recovering from the worst of his grief, Joshua had always taken good care of himself—for Lee's sake, and his own, but also because he knew that Neil would have wanted him to live a long life. The nanite technology basically ensured that when death finally came his way, hopefully many years from now, it wouldn't, at least, be due to his failure to take every opportunity to stay healthy.

Though Joshua was grateful to live a longer, healthier life than he'd ever imagined, he didn't feel entirely comfortable with some of the new changes at the hospital itself.

"Why?" Lee had asked when Joshua mentioned it, looking up from the novel he was reading on his tablet.

Joshua had shrugged, rubbing a hand over his wrist loosely, remembering the plastic bracelet he'd worn in the hospital before. "I don't know. It's just when I was a kid and was in the hospital for my appendix, wearing a bracelet made me feel safe, I guess. Like they were going to take care of me."

"You're such a sub, babe. It kills me." Lee's lips had twisted in amusement, and he'd winked at him. "Don't worry. When we get upstairs tonight, I'll make you feel safe. That should make up for it."

Joshua had rolled his eyes. Trusting Lee *did* make him feel safe, but that wasn't the point. He'd sighed, amused but also feeling like Lee hadn't taken him seriously.

"What? You don't think I can make you feel safe? You don't know that I'll always take care of you?" Lee had put aside the tablet and flashed a heated glance Joshua's way.

Joshua had grinned. "Oh, you always do," he'd whispered. "It's one reason why I love you."

"I'm glad there's more than one," Lee had said, laughing softly.

In general, Joshua didn't have a problem with technological advances that led to medical miracles, and nanites were definitely among those. He did have his doubts, though, about the wisdom of some of what the scientists were doing. It seemed to be verging on a world too removed from the 'home' of his youth for his liking. And, if there was anything Joshua needed to stay the same, it was Scottsville. People came and went. Romances started and died.

Children were born and grew up. Everything was always in flux, true. But the thing that kept Joshua sane was knowing every nook and cranny of his little corner of the earth.

Scottsville.

The town he'd run to when he'd lost it all. The town that brought him Lee, and love, and a way to live again.

But Scottsville was changing. And it was disconcerting, to say the least.

Still, today he soldiered on cheerfully, getting his coffee at Earl G. Dumplin's, nodding at fellow locals and grinning when he ran into Chris in the parking lot outside. He hadn't seen his old friend in awhile, but he was happy to see him now. Chris held his and Dale's youngest, a baby they were fostering from a neighboring county.

"Hey, Chris. Hey, Beth," Joshua said, kissing the baby's cheek. He ran his hand over her downy head.

"I'm going to be late," Chris said, shoving his long hair behind his ear, distracted. "Gotta get her to day care and then dash to Barren River to work."

"Sure," Joshua said. "I'll just let you go."

"Okay, but…" Chris grabbed his arm and smiled softly. His teeth glinted in the morning sun. "You okay? You've got that vibe like the world's gonna tumble down if you don't hold it up with your own two shoulders."

Joshua smiled. "I'm fine. Had a weird dream."

"Oh." Chris tilted his head, an uncanny perception in his dark brown eyes. He pushed another tendril of hair behind his ear. Beth chewed on her fist. "Well, if you need to talk, you know where to find me."

"I do."

It still amazed Joshua that Chris had made his home in Scottsville of all places. He'd never quite understood how it was possible that the man he'd met in Neil's apartment, the former drag queen, had come to be the stepfather to farm boys and foster kids. But he had, and he loved it. Not to mention, he'd found a good job at the state park's hotel and settled into being the town's most obvious queer with a kind of grace Joshua envied.

"How's Dale?" he asked before Chris could get away from him. "I know you've both been dealing with a lot since his accident." Dale's leg had gotten crushed by his tractor the summer before, and the damage done had been extensive. While he'd healed, he still had nerve pain that caused him a lot of trouble.

Joshua had been instrumental in making sure that Dale got signed up for an upcoming medical trial of newly developed, experimental nerve-repairing nanites. It still amazed Joshua how nanite technology had progressed from skin repair, like Lee had received, to the mending of internal organs and vascular trauma.

He sometimes thought about Neil's extensive injuries after the accident, and it blew his mind to think that had nanite technology been developed to the extent it was now, maybe Neil's own work could have saved him. At least nanites had saved thousands of other people lucky enough to reap the benefits of the technology Neil had devoted his life to. Well, if they had enough money to access the treatment anyway. The inequity in the availability of the nanite medical treatments was something Joshua was working to correct with quite a few grants. Including the one funding the trial Dale would be taking part in.

The trial was to be held out of Emory in Atlanta, Georgia. Apparently, developing nanites for nerve trauma had an exceptionally high degree of difficulty. Joshua remembered Neil going on about the whys of it back in the day, but he'd tuned out the particulars, mainly taken with the shapes Neil's mouth made when he talked. But an idea dreamed up by some young kid—a genius, apparently, who'd submitted plans to the researchers at Emory—had made neurological nanite medicine more feasible. Despite the age of the kid—only fifteen—the theory was sound, and Emory was working out the kinks to get a trial up and running. After some string-pulling and a nice donation, Dale was number one on the list of candidates.

"Dale's looking forward to the treatments," Chris said. "We both are."

Joshua knew Dale was a trooper and rarely complained, but he also knew from the look on Chris's face that he was still in too much pain.

They talked about that for a moment, and Joshua reassured Chris that the trial would start soon.

"The older boys are big enough to take care of themselves, but sometimes…" Chris trailed off and looked meaningfully at Beth.

"Why don't we babysit tonight? Give you and Dale a chance to get some rest?"

Chris smiled. "Would you mind?"

"We'd love it."

Chris kissed his cheek. "Thank you. I'll drop her by at six. Love you, Josh. You're still a good egg." Then Chris was gone, his long hair blowing out behind him and his skinny ass swishing back and forth like a broom. Beth waved goodbye over Chris's shoulder, and Joshua blew her a kiss.

Sometimes he was sad that he and Lee had never made a family together. They'd talked about adopting early on, but Lee had been resistant to the idea. After a small argument, the truth had come out. Lee admitted that he felt too guilty to have a child of his own when he still blamed himself for his sister losing hers. No matter how irrational the guilt was, it lingered, and Lee couldn't escape it.

Joshua understood that. He still felt guilty that he hadn't been there that morning when Magic jerked free of her leash and darted into the road. Hadn't been there to stop Neil from following her…

As he headed toward his car, he called Lee to let him know about the change in their plans and his agreement to look after Beth that night. Even though Lee didn't want kids of his own, he loved babies, and Joshua knew they'd enjoy Beth for the night.

"Morning, sleepyhead," Joshua said when Lee picked up the phone still sounding groggy. "Time to wake up!"

Lee groaned gently.

"I ran into Chris. He asked us to look after Beth tonight."

"Mmm, 'kay."

"Make sure Sam gets to school on time."

Lee grumbled under his breath, but Joshua could tell he was getting up. "Weren't you helping your grandpa run Stouder Lumber by his age? Can't he get himself up?"

Joshua laughed. "Not quite. I was a little bit older. Besides, you know he's a night owl."

"Yeah, well, whatever. I'm exhausted this morning."

Joshua frowned. They hadn't done anything strenuous the night before, not with Sam by the bed. It seemed like Lee was complaining lately more and more often of exhaustion.

Joshua chewed on his bottom lip.

Lee had been one of the first to receive the original prototype nanite treatments, and there had been quite a few unknowns associated with those early trials. On the surface, everything appeared to be fine—the nanites had repaired his scars. But some patients who'd undergone the same nanite therapy with the same early prototypes were beginning to show indications of problems. The nanites hadn't behaved as they were supposed to. The tiny robots, instead of doing their work and then dissolving, had become 'overzealous,' as some reports described it, sticking around to 'repair'—aka destroy—perfectly healthy tissue elsewhere in the body. This often led to sudden collapse and, in several cases, death.

Joshua hesitated. They'd argued about whether or not Lee needed to see a doctor just a few days before when he'd been too tired to go to work. Lee had insisted he was fine, and it wasn't big deal. He claimed he was just rundown from work, and that Joshua was worrying too much. While Joshua was starting to have his doubts, he also hated to start their day with another argument.

Deciding to talk about it over dinner, he said instead, "Well, should I cancel on watching Beth tonight?"

On the other end of the connection, Lee moaned, gasped, and made a strange sound.

"What's wrong?" Joshua abandoned his resolve to wait until dinner and turned on the car, pointing it toward home. "Are you okay?"

"It's fine," Lee said, still gasping a little. "It's nothing. No worries, oh-husband-of-mine."

Joshua felt a nagging doubt. Suddenly, the dream of Neil seemed like an omen. "Was it that pain again? In your chest? Did you ask the doctors about that, Lee? You said you would."

"It was nothing. I pulled a muscle working out. That's all."

Joshua swallowed and kept driving toward home. "Last time you were in for a checkup, didn't you ask them to do a blood test? Did they make sure the nanites had dissolved the way they're supposed to? Those early prototypes—"

Lee cut him off. "I'll drop by the doctor's office and ask them when I go into Bowling Green on Monday. All right?"

Joshua wanted to push for him to call about it now, but he knew Lee was stubborn and an agreement to go in on Monday was better than expected.

"Babe, I'm not blowing it off," Lee said gently. "But I know my body, and I'm fine."

"It's just—" Joshua stopped. He'd lost so much in his life, and he was happy now. He sometimes felt like he was waiting for the other shoe to drop, waiting to lose everything again.

"I know," Lee said. "That's why I'm going in. I don't want you to worry. It's a big day today with that sales rep from Nashville coming in to show me the new bikes, and tonight we'll look after Beth, and Sam again, probably. Then it's the weekend, babe, and I want to relax with you. Monday's the soonest I can fit it in. But I promise to go. Okay?"

Joshua shoved aside his fear and said, "I love you."

Lee laughed. "Tell me something I don't know."

"Okay, I'm wearing red underwear," Joshua said, waggling his eyebrows, hoping to break the tension he still felt. He found a place to turn around on the road and start back toward the lumberyard.

Lee laughed again. "No, you're not."

Joshua chuckled. "What if I am?"

"You're not," Lee said. "You act like I don't know you."

Joshua grinned.

"I'm shaking your kid brother awake right now. You should see the scowl on his face. Wakey-wakey, baby-cakey."

"Go 'way," Sam's angry mumble came from the background. "You suck."

"Hey, Joshua, I think he needs to be tickled awake, what do you think?"

Joshua heard Sam screech, and then Lee said, "I love you. Bye, babe," and the connection went dead.

Joshua grinned, heading back toward Stouder Lumber.

As he finally settled at his desk, he brought his hand up to his cheek and touched where he could still feel the barest phantom touch from Neil in his dream. He wiped it away and cleared his throat, determined to focus on the present.

Chapter Seven

August 2027—Atlanta, Georgia

NEIL DIDN'T LIKE it when his mother cried. She was a special woman, and he'd always owe her for having raised someone as difficult as him and not just giving up, tossing him to the foster-care system or putting him in an oven and roasting him alive. He knew how rough it had been for her.

More than that, though, he loved her. She was funny, smart, and tender.

He patted her back awkwardly and said, "Mom, it's just across town."

He stopped short of saying that she could visit whenever she liked. If he had anything to do with it, he'd be far too busy designing and helping to run a massive experimental nanite study while simultaneously earning his medical and engineering degree at Emory University. Maybe she could stop by and bring him something to eat? Even that seemed like an interruption.

"And you're sure that you can't live at home?" she asked. "You're only fifteen, Neil. You're still so young."

Neil frowned. Only fifteen. If only he *felt* fifteen, then everything would be different. Instead, he'd felt thirty from the time he was born and had the memories to go along with it. He didn't have linear access, though. His experience of his prior life was a mix of instinctual knowledge and sudden, sometimes overwhelmingly specific, memories. He knew enough of his prior incarnation to know that he would have disdained the very idea of an individual soul that passes from life to life. And yet, here he was, a prisoner in a fifteen-year-old body. He sometimes told the Neil-From-Before, the one who still wanted to dispute that this was even possible, to suck it.

"Yeah, well, deny it all you want, but I've never been young, Mom."

He'd tried calling her Alice once because he'd never had the awe of her that most kids seemed to carry for their mothers. He'd read in some schmaltzy book in his pediatrician's office when he was six years old that to every child the word for God is 'mother,' but for him the word for God had always been 'fuck you, why did you do this to me, you son of a bitch.' Assuming God existed at all, and he still had serious doubts on that score. The word for the woman who loved him despite the fact that he was probably the furthest thing from the child she'd dreamed about was just Alice, as far as he was concerned, and that sufficed.

Alice seemed comfortable, the most respectful choice, really, because it set them on par as equals. And while Neil didn't really see her as being on his intellectual level, it was a good thank you for loving him, protecting him from Jim during those scary young years, and for dealing with his crap.

Alice, though, had been furious. He'd winced when she slammed her hand on the kitchen table and said, "What did you just call me?"

"Uh, your name?"

"Uh-uh, buster," she'd said to him, pointing a finger at him in a way that was nearly threatening. It was something Neil was not accustomed to from her, and he shrank back.

"I gave birth to you, do you hear me? I don't care how smart you are, how much you remember about a previous lifetime, or if you freak out your peers and teachers by correcting everybody about everything. Nor do I care that you don't look a damn thing like me, or like Marshall for that matter. I don't care if you'll always be more advanced than I am in every way, but I spent thirty-six hours enduring labor to *push you out of my vagina*, and you will call me *Mom*. Do you understand me?"

Neil had nodded slowly and said nothing for a few minutes. He'd waited until she started eating her dinner again before he said, around a mouthful of warm mashed potatoes, "Well, I'm not more advanced in *every* way. You've got the cooking thing down."

It had been a huge concession for him, and he'd known that she knew it. It had been an apology of sorts, and she'd clearly known that, too. Her lips had quirked up and she said, "And you can't heat a pot of beans to save your life."

Neil had smirked.

She had shaken her head. "If you paid attention to cooking the way you pay attention to your experiments, you'd be just fine."

"Thanks…Mom," Neil had said and cleared his throat.

He'd never called her Alice again outside the confines of his own head. He figured Joshua would be proud of him—not only for making a choice to do something that was no sweat off his back and which clearly meant a lot to her, but also for actually loving the woman. Alice was, all in all, a good mother, and Neil enjoyed being around her, which was saying a lot.

Now, though, at the not-so-tender age of not-so-fifteen, Neil was leaving home, and Alice seemed to be having a hard time handling it. In some ways, he didn't understand why. It wasn't like he made life easy for her. From the time he was quite small, he'd been instrumental in ostracizing her from any kind of community. It hadn't been on purpose. Being him just seemed to do it.

He was different this time around. Even in his prior life, he'd been difficult to know and like, but now it was like all of his impatience, irritability, focus, and social awkwardness had been distilled by lost time and rage. He was no one's idea of a fun person to be around.

But Alice was still young and beautiful, in Neil's admittedly biased opinion, and he saw his moving out to be a good thing for her. Maybe she could date again. Find someone to build a life with. Hell, it wasn't even too late to have another child—maybe the next one would be normal, and be the kind of kid that Alice deserved. He wanted that for her.

At the same time, Neil knew he'd been Alice's whole life from the moment he was born. She'd worked to give him the best education she could until he'd gotten his first scholarship to university classes at the age of twelve. And she'd done it all alone.

Her parents weren't dead, but they might as well have been as far as Alice was concerned. She'd told him the year before, on a rainy, drab Christmas Eve when she'd had a little celebratory wine as they opened presents—renewed subscriptions to medical and engineering journals for him, and a microscope for her (okay, it was for him; he was a terrible son)—about how her folks had been addicts. Her earliest memories were drenched in the scent of marijuana, but it had progressed from there to much harder drugs over time.

"And then, when I was nineteen, I met Marshall Green," Alice had said, toying with a ribbon from the wrapping. "He was handsome, and he promised to take care of me. I moved in with him as fast as I could. And I was pregnant with you before he left for his first tour in Afghanistan." Alice had sipped her drink and sighed. "He was a good man, your father."

Neil had rolled his lips in and bitten back the reply that Gerald Russell, the man who'd died in a car wreck in Boston nearly forty-five years ago, was his father. Neil had only seen photos of Marshall and a few video clips, but he fully remembered Gerald's sharp nose, quick wit, and long fingers that shuffled cards and drilled him with questions about the rules of gin rummy. But he was glad to carry

Marshall's last name now, instead of that asshole Jim's. That was another thing Alice had done for them both after they'd left—erased Jim's name from their legal documents.

After a few quiet moments, Alice had sighed and said, "Parents. Can't live with 'em, can't be born without 'em."

Neil had nodded. "Some aren't too bad, though." He'd wanted her to know how he felt. It could've been worse: At least she loved him and let him do what he wanted with his life. And he loved her, too.

Alice had shrugged. "You probably had it better last time around."

It was the first time she'd ever mentioned Neil's family from his prior life. He'd thought about telling her before—about the wealth, the house, the travel, and the boats. The loneliness, the pressure, and the loss. The fear he'd felt when his parents had died, and he'd been left alone with all that money and all that responsibility. But he hadn't. It'd seemed like something she didn't need to hear. But there were so many things that he remembered that he'd never shared with anyone. Part of him longed for her to know.

Watching Alice twist the ribbon around her finger again, he'd decided it was time. If she thought they were better than her, then that, at least, was something he could set straight. She was the parent who'd loved him unconditionally.

"Why don't you ever ask about them?" he'd asked.

"About your parents from your life before?"

"Yeah." He had licked his lips quickly, surprised by the zip of nerves.

"It makes me feel guilty," she had said, swallowing another mouthful of wine. "I mean—if she was great, better than me, why would I want to hear that? And if she wasn't...then why would you want to tell me? It's better left in the past, isn't it?"

"She wasn't better than you," Neil had said. "And she wasn't worse, either. She was just different."

Alice had shrugged.

"And she had to put up with a lot less, too. I didn't have all of these pesky memories last time around. I was an actual child then, not a freak."

"Neil," she had started, but he put his hand up.

"Don't, Mom. It's fine." He'd stood, went to her chair, and knelt in front of her. "I just want you to know. She wasn't better than you. If she'd had to deal with me, the way I am now, she'd have probably murdered me in my sleep."

"You don't know a mother's love," Alice had said softly.

"I know your love," Neil had said. "And even though everything about being stuck here in this body wanting something I don't think I'll ever have sucks. You don't. You don't suck, Mom, and I love you."

"Ah, Neil." She'd laughed, tears shining in her eyes. "Ever honest. And I love you, too."

Now, nine months later, standing beside Alice in the parking lot in front of his dorm, Neil brushed a tear from Alice's cheek and said, "Mom, you know I hate it when you cry."

"They're happy tears," she lied, and Neil groaned.

"Right."

"Let me have my feelings, Neil."

"All right." She'd always let him have his feelings. All of his anger and rage, all of his love for Joshua. He'd itched with helplessness his whole life, and she never told him he was wrong for it. "But don't feel them too long."

Alice laughed through her tears. "You don't get to tell me how long I get to wallow in my empty nest."

Neil loved Alice's laugh and big smile, and despite his best comedic efforts, they were far too infrequent in his opinion. He tucked her long brown hair behind her ear, kissed her wet cheek, and said, "Okay, Mom. I've got a meeting in fifteen minutes. You have to go. I'll talk to you later."

Alice nodded, threw her arms around Neil, and squeezed him so tightly that it hurt to breathe.

"It's okay, Mom," he said awkwardly, patting her back. "This will be good for you."

She huffed a laugh, pulled back, and looked up at him before forcing a bright smile. "Okay, kiddo. Just remember, you can always come home. No matter what."

Neil felt a strange tug in his chest, and a small lump came to his throat. He coughed and kissed her forehead and backed away as she got into her car. He didn't watch her drive off, hustling back to his new dorm room to get his papers ready for the meeting. But when he walked back through the parking lot on his way to the professor's office, he suddenly wished he'd hugged her one more time before she'd gone. And then he shrugged it away.

He'd see her again soon enough.

Chapter Eight

October 2030—Atlanta, Georgia

THE FIRST TIME Neil had sex after having been forced to endure childhood and adolescence all over again, he was eighteen years old, and it was with his roommate.

It came as a pretty big surprise to Neil, too. He was under no illusions about his physical attractiveness. He was bony and looked young for his age. It'd been the same in his first life, too, when he'd been nearly twenty-five before he'd grown into himself. Neil remembered that when he was Neil Russell, sometime after his twenty-fifth birthday, he'd had no trouble getting laid, but before that it'd been a parade of disturbing blowjobs with closeted jocks and bullies. At least he'd skipped that particular brand of misery this time around, even if he'd been so horny that if it *was* possible to go blind from masturbating, as his first mother had informed him decades ago, he absolutely would have.

His third year at Emory had started out well enough. Neil was rarely around, and his newly assigned roommate, Derek, was a huge improvement over the prior year's asshole. At least Derek was gay, which took away the burden of having to worry about whether his sexuality would be a problem that might result in injuries.

Neil had never told his first two roommates because he'd never felt entirely safe to disclose that information. They were both raging heterosexuals, and jocks to boot, so he'd always been a little concerned that they'd find his homosexuality threatening and kill him in his sleep during some steroid-fueled panic attack.

It wasn't like being up front with anyone about his sexual preferences mattered much those first years. He was an underage, scrawny genius; no one wanted to fuck him anyway, and he'd been far too absorbed in his actual work to risk his life to get laid. His hand had never failed him yet.

Then Derek came along. He wasn't just 'out'; he was ridiculously gay. He moisturized and had gobs of hair gunk sitting all over their communal sink. He didn't flap around much, but he said things like, "That's my bitch," and he spoke openly to anyone who would listen to him about his endless hunt for sex on the various apps available. And since Derek often mistook Neil's silence for 'listening,' Neil heard about Derek's craving for cock a lot.

Neil thought Derek was a good-looking guy. A little skinny, maybe, but he had cheekbone-length dyed black hair that fell down over his dark eyes, and that contrasted nicely with his pale skin. Neil only admitted to himself after the first time they fucked that he'd ever noticed any of these things about Derek's physical attractiveness. At first, they'd just lived together, and that was that, and that was fine with Neil.

But one night, after hours and hours in the lab, working out some kinks for the next stage of the upcoming nanite trial, Neil came home to find Derek sitting on the sofa in nothing but a pair of loose yoga pants, his cock out, jerking off to some porn on the wall-sized screen that Derek's parents had provided.

Neil shut the door behind him, surprised that Derek didn't stop what he was doing or act at all ashamed. Instead, Derek motioned at him.

"C'mere. You top, right?"

Neil nodded. Yeah, he preferred to top. He remembered that from his prior life—the clench of a guy's ass around his cock, the grunts a guy made as he'd thrust inside. Neil was hard before he could even turn the lock on the door and drop his bag to the floor.

There was no preamble. Derek had condoms, and he wanted to be fucked. Neil wasn't about to argue with that. As Neil's cock sank into Derek's tight, gripping ass for the first time, his eyes rolled back, and he groaned in pleasure; his nipples ached, his balls drew up, and he got four thrusts in before he was filling the condom with his jizz. It didn't matter, though. It had been so long for him, and it was so good. For once his youth was on his side. He quickly got another condom in place, while Derek wriggled his ass in open invitation, and then Neil fucked him hard enough that Derek scrambled at the carpet, cried out, and threw himself back onto Neil's slamming cock in happy abandon.

They went at it over and over for four delirious hours. Neil's balls ached, and his legs shook when he tried to stand up afterward. Derek smiled, limp and drooling, as he lay facedown on the carpet beside the sofa, his ass still up and his hole clenching at air.

Neil was covered in sex and wanted to wash it off, get some water and food, and then rest—alone, in his own bed. He hoped Derek wasn't the cuddling type. Neil tried to convince his legs to do their job long enough to make it to the shower, but he collapsed against the sofa before making it three steps. His dick was still twitching and his balls twanged hard as he panted there, gaining strength for another push toward the bathroom.

Oh God, he suddenly realized—he hoped Derek didn't expect anything *real* from this. He groaned as the thought dawned on him and reality finally overrode his lust-addled mind. He'd fucked his roommate; things could get awkward now.

"Jesus, you're hung," Derek murmured. It was the first thing he'd said aside from 'more,' 'harder,' 'please,' and 'fuck' since he'd asked if Neil topped. "I feel like you turned me inside out, man."

Neil swallowed and rubbed a hand over his eyes. He'd already done his duty and looked at Derek's ass to make sure it was okay. It'd been a little red, but otherwise anything Derek was feeling was just a stretch, and he'd be fine.

"Listen," Neil said. "We're…roommates. This was—"

Derek rolled over to his back, grinning blissfully. "Don't tell me we're not doing this again, because we so are. But if you don't wanna be my boyfriend, that's fine. Just fuck me through the floor like this and we'll call it win/win, okay?"

Neil was uncertain. He'd experienced this kind of thing before. Back in his first life, there'd been a fellow graduate student, and he'd fallen for Neil after promising that he just wanted sex. But that was a different time. Another life. *Derek* was different, from a new generation, and he seemed completely fine with casual sex. Neil had heard it going on through the thin wall separating their bedrooms often enough to know just how fine Derek was with that.

Besides, Derek was a decent guy. Neil didn't want anything bad to happen to him. If fucking Derek kept him from picking up so many random strangers, then maybe it would keep him safe, too. Homosexuality wasn't the big deal it used to be, but there were still plenty of homophobes in the world, and rapists didn't disappear just because it was okay for gays to get married just like the straights these days.

"Don't worry." Derek pulled himself up to sit on his ass, wincing a little as he did. "I know where I stand. And this way you won't be upset when I throw you over for a real boyfriend." He eyed Neil's limp cock and grinned. "Though with that thing hammering my ass whenever I want, I'm not sure how eager I'll be to find one."

Neil stared at Derek and decided he was sincere.

After a shower, a sandwich, and a nap, Neil knocked on Derek's bedroom door, and sixty seconds later he had a cock in his mouth and a mouth on his cock. It was just as good, if not better, than Neil remembered, and when Neil blew his load, grunting in pleasure and clutching at Derek's slim hips, he decided it was a fantastic arrangement.

Chapter Nine

I T WAS AFTER about three weeks of fucking that he and Derek actually became what Neil would consider to be friends. He hadn't had many friends in his life, not in this one and not in the one before, but Derek was easy going, helpful, and pretty smart for an English major, in his science-biased opinion.

Neil knew it was dangerous to let things overlap, but Derek seemed sincere in keeping the sex separate from the rest. They never cuddled after, or talked to each other while still sweaty and covered in come. It was all sex until they were satisfied, and then they went their separate ways.

The friendship came in and around that. Neil would work in the lab until he couldn't see straight, and then come back to the apartment, fuck Derek if he had the energy, go to sleep, and wake up to do it all over again. Somehow, though, he found himself lingering over breakfast with Derek and chuckling at Derek's conversation, but the true tipping point came when Derek asked him about his books, the stacks and stacks of them lining his bedroom.

"So, what's up with the fascination on reincarnation?"

"It's a hobby." Neil tried to herd Derek back out of his room, but Derek wasn't having it.

He plopped down on the bed and waved a beat-up copy of *Old Souls* at Neil. "Obviously, but why?"

Neil shrugged.

Derek opened the book, flipping through some pages. He tilted his head to read some of the notes Neil had made in the margins. "Do you believe in reincarnation?"

Neil took a slow breath and then said, "Does it matter?"

"I believe in it," Derek offered. "My grandmother said she was a weaver at the court of Queen Victoria in her past life."

"A weaver, huh? Not Queen Victoria herself?"

"Nah. Never even met the queen, she said." Derek shoved hair off his face and shoved the pillow under his head to get comfortable. "I think it makes sense, you know? Energy to energy. Soul to soul."

"I don't," Neil said. "I don't think it makes sense at all."

"Well, you're a scientist, so..." Derek shrugged. "If you don't think it makes sense, why do you read about it then?" He pulled the book from Neil's bedside table. "*Where Did You Go: The Surprising Journey of Life Beyond Life*. I mean, you're really into this!"

"I do believe in it," Neil confessed, his palms going sweaty. "I just don't think it holds up scientifically."

"More mysteries on earth than...wait, how does that go?"

"It's Shakespeare. I thought you were an English major?"

"I study poetry." Derek put the books aside. "So why do you believe in reincarnation?"

Neil licked his lips, his stomach flip-flopping. What did he have to lose by telling Derek? He already said he believed in past lives, too, and he didn't seem like the kind of guy to decide Neil couldn't fuck him anymore because he thought he was born again. "I remember who I was before I died."

"Cool!" Derek enthused, smiling. "Were you like, I dunno, someone cool? James Dean or one of the Romanov children? Anastasia maybe?"

Neil snorted. "I was a nanite researcher."

Derek rolled his eyes. "Way to miss an opportunity, dude. You're saying you were just...you?"

"Yeah. I was just me. But I had another name and lived in Nashville." He couldn't believe he was admitting all of this aloud to someone who wasn't Alice.

"How boring."

"I guess so."

Derek tilted his head. "Do you know how you died?"

"I was hit by a truck."

"Fuck," Derek winced. "Sorry, man. That's crappy."

"It is."

Derek patted the place next to him. "Sit. Tell me more."

It wasn't as though Neil let it all come tumbling out, but still, gradually, Derek came to be the only person aside from Neil's mother who knew all about his past life and Joshua. Neil even showed him the videos of Joshua that Lee had posted to Facebook over the years, and they discussed at length Neil's memories from his first life.

Derek was pretty fascinated by it all, but he never made fun of Neil or suggested that he was crazy. It was a relief to have someone else who accepted his reality as truth. Though Neil himself still sometimes wondered in the wee, sleepless hours of morning if it was true at all, or if he was simply delusional, if not schizophrenic.

But, as far as Neil was concerned, a fuck buddy and a friend wasn't a bad trade-off at this point in his life. If he couldn't have Joshua, he didn't see why he needed to be a friendless monk. He supposed he deserved a little pleasure outside of his work.

Neil also knew that if it wasn't for the sex, the friendship would never have happened. If they hadn't been fucking, then Derek would never have been in Neil's bedroom, or, if he had, Neil would've accused him of snooping or looking for cash or something worse. But sometimes they screwed on Neil's bed instead of Derek's, and Neil would get up, shower, and go back to the labs, leaving Derek blissed out on the mattress.

Some part of him had to have known it was only a matter of time before Derek would notice the collection of books, all of them on reincarnation, and ask about them. It wasn't common for young people to have paper-and-ink books anymore, and he had a lot of them. Neil could admit to himself that maybe he'd wanted Derek to ask. Maybe Neil was lonely, and Derek was as good a potential friend for him as any. It wasn't as though he could share the truth about himself with any of his professors or his fellow scientists without doing harm to his career. As far as Neil was concerned, between the orgasms and the expectation-free company, Derek's friendship served him well.

It turned out that Alice liked Derek, too. Neil wasn't the best son ever, but he submitted to her request for monthly meals together, so long as they were held at his apartment with Derek. That way he could zip out of the lab, eat takeout with her, do his sonly duty, and go right back to the lab afterward. That plan backfired the night he got wrapped up in his work, forgot about their dinner plans, missed her text messages, and returned to the apartment to find her and Derek sacked out on the sofa watching old romantic comedies and drinking hard cider like old pals.

After that he was always on time to meet his mother for their dinner dates. He hoped that would put an end to the inappropriate fraternizing between his mother and his fuck buddy, but it didn't. He returned from his lab one evening seeking sex and dinner to find Derek talking over video call with Alice. He stood, dumbfounded, outside Derek's door listening to them discuss the 'reincarnation thing.' Like it was no big deal, and when Derek looked up and saw Neil standing there, he went on talking to Alice like it was normal and like Neil wasn't there listening.

"Yeah, I agree. The problem isn't that Neil's hot for someone older. Lots of guys have hopeless crushes. It's more than that, and he's gonna have to let this one go," Derek said, sticking his tongue out at Neil and motioning toward the kitchen where Neil could smell some Chinese takeout waiting. "I mean, as far as this Joshua guy's concerned, Neil's dead. And he *is* dead. Well, not our Neil, but the other Neil. You know what I mean." He muted the microphone so that Alice couldn't hear. "It's your mom. I got the Lo Mein like you like, okay? I'll be off in a minute. Unless you want to talk to her?"

Neil just stood and stared at him. Derek rolled his eyes, blew his hair away from his face, and unmuted his mic. "Alice, listen, I've gotta go. We can talk about this more later, okay? But don't worry so much. Neil's okay. He works a lot, but he's eating plenty. And he actually smiled twice yesterday, so either it's a sign of the apocalypse or he's doing pretty all right."

Neil wasn't smiling now. Hell no, he wasn't. "Have you told her that we're fucking, too?" he asked as soon as Derek disconnected.

"No. Do you want me to?" Derek stomped into the kitchen, got some plates out, and put them on the table. "I could tell her all about how you make me come so hard with that big dick of yours that I see stars. Think she'd like that?"

Neil knew Derek was messing with him, but it pissed him off all the more.

Derek sighed. "Listen. She's lonely, okay? She's got this big, weird thing in her life—"

"You mean me."

"Yeah, you. And she needs to talk to someone who gets it. When she found out I knew everything and that I believed your story, she was so relieved. Don't deny her that. Besides, I like her, okay? She's kind of awesome. And one day, when you're off...being you...she might need a shoulder, and I might need a mother figure who isn't actually my mom. So, just chill. And eat your Chinese food."

Derek took his plate to his bedroom and shut the door. Neil

stood and stared at the boxes of food for a minute and then filled a plate, before knocking on Derek's door. "So are we going to screw or what?"

Derek threw something soft against the door. Neil heard whatever it was bounce against the opposite side. "Call your mother and maybe we'll fuck after."

Neil sighed. He didn't really have time to talk to Alice. But he supposed it *had* been almost a week. He sat down with his meal and phoned his mom.

"Hey, Mom," he said around a mouthful of food. "I can't talk long, but how are you?"

OF COURSE, THE next time Alice came to dinner, she spent the entire time asking him why Derek couldn't be his boyfriend.

"Because it doesn't work like that," Neil said, calling on all the patience he could muster, thankful that Derek was out with some of his other friends for a change. He wanted to be a good son to Alice. He did. It was just that sometimes she made it really hard.

"You can't tell me he's not good looking enough. He's adorable, Neil, and he's smart. He makes me laugh all the time, and I've even seen you chuckle around him. So...why not?"

Neil stared at her. "Mom," and he had to refrain from calling her Alice in pure frustration. "Find a boyfriend. Get your own life and stay out of mine. I've told you this before. *Listen* this time, for the love of—"

"Neil," she said seriously, "is this because of Joshua?"

Neil ignored that. "What makes you think Derek would even be interested in dating me? We're roommates. We're friends. That's it."

Alice narrowed her eyes and took a bite of her pizza, chewed a moment while glaring daggers at Neil. "You're having sex with him."

Neil practically choked on this soda, and coughed before drinking some more, just to have something to do with his mouth so that he wouldn't curse at her for being so damn nosy. "Did he tell you that?" he finally asked.

"He didn't have to."

Neil didn't believe her, and she clearly knew that, because she went on to say, "I made an educated guess based on how you look at him, and how he behaves around you, and how that's changed over the last few months. He cares about you, Neil."

"We're friends. Who have sex. We both want it that way."

Alice sighed. "You could be happy, if you'd just let yourself."

Neil swallowed his soda and stuffed more pizza into his mouth. He couldn't talk to her about it. She was right, after all. He could pretend that he was like everyone else, pretend that Joshua wasn't alive out there being Joshua, being the best thing that Neil had ever known, and he could *try* to fall in love with Derek. But that was the thing. He shouldn't have to try.

"What I remember of love—romantic love," he clarified, "is that it isn't something you try to make happen, or that you have any control over at all. If I was going to fall in love with Derek, I would have fallen for him by now. I like him. He's a good guy. We enjoy what we have going. But I'm not going to marry him and make a family with him. I'm not going to become a different son. I'm sorry that I'm always a disappointment to you."

Alice's expression went very serious. "You're not a disappointment," she said. "I love you, Neil. I just want you to be loved and to experience happiness. It's all I've ever wanted for you."

"I don't think that's in the cards this time around, Mom," he said. "But right now, I'm not miserable. I've got my research and a decent roommate. Right now…well, it ain't bad."

Alice kissed his forehead and left the discussion behind. For that, Neil was grateful. And later that night, rocking his aching cock into Derek's tight body, Neil kissed the sweaty skin of Derek's neck and thought, "Nope. This ain't bad at all."

Chapter Ten

November 2030—Atlanta, Georgia

NEIL STARED AT his phone's touchscreen in shock. The social media announcement was plain and left no room for questions:

> *Lee Edward Fargo left this earth suddenly Friday afternoon. Friends and family will be received at the Harwood and Strode Funeral Home on Lois Moore Drive. In lieu of flowers, please donate to World Bicycle Relief, which mobilizes children worldwide in order to help them complete their education.*
>
> *Please refrain from texting or calling. Joshua is with his family and needs some space to grieve. He knows that you love and care for him.*

The university cafeteria bustled mindlessly around him, no one knowing or caring that the entire world had just turned upside down. Neil shoved his tray back and scrolled through the comments looking for details. Sure enough, Chris—ah, Chris, how he'd missed him over the years—posted in reply to someone named Kath Henderson's questions about how and what had happened:

> *Yes, an aneurysm due to the early nanite treatment, Kath. Joshua was with him. It happened at breakfast. They were alone together. Poor Joshua.*

Then further down in response to a Gary Lowe:

The nanites didn't dissolve properly. A genetic predisposition causes that problem sometimes, especially with the old nanites. I don't know a lot about it other than Dale doesn't have the genetic issue Lee did. Is it wrong of me to thank God for that? Most of what I know about the older nanites and those issues comes from the news.

Gary Lowe then asked if it was a total shock or if they'd known it was a possibility.

Joshua told me Lee already knew about the lack of dissolution of the prototype nanites, but they'd hoped to find a way to resolve it before something like this happened. Joshua is devastated. He's with his mom and brother. You know his father passed suddenly just last year? It's been a rough time. The Mennonites who work for him at the lumberyard have the whole family covered for food, though. Thanks for asking.

Neil's blood ran cold. He read over the comments again. Clicked through to Joshua's page to scroll through post after post of condolences, and stories about Lee, and photos of Lee with whoever was commenting with their sorrow. He clicked open a picture of Lee standing alone beside Cummins Falls in Tennessee. His shaggy, dark brown hair was wet and hung around his still-scarred neck, and his eyes sparkled happily. The caption said, "Fun trip to the Falls with Lee Fargo. Nanite treatment for his scars begins next week."

As he stared at the pictures, a new post came up on Joshua's page. It was from Joshua himself, and Neil swallowed hard. He could count on two hands the number of posts that Joshua had made himself over the years.

Losing Lee is like having my heart torn out and my arm cut off. I can't breathe. I can't stop crying. I know you all loved him and that does more good for me than anything else. When I lost Neil, my first love, I thought I'd never feel pain that bad again. I was wrong. Thank you for all your words of love and shared grief. We'll have to make it through this together. Lee would want that for me...for us.

Neil blinked at his phone, mind whirring. He had no idea what to do, how to proceed. He hadn't realized how comfortable he'd become over the years with the knowledge that Lee Fargo was taking care of his Joshua. And now...

Due to his invention and the lack of rigorous testing before implementation in humans, Lee was gone, and Joshua was in pain. He pinched the bridge of his nose, breathing in and out slowly, trying to calm his racing mind. He had to fix it.

But he didn't know how.

He walked dully back to his rooms, his thoughts darting every which way into the past, present, and future, tearing apart his old nanite schematics and cursing the greed that had led to his work being pushed out into the world before it should have been.

Pushing into the apartment, he grunted at Derek who greeted him with an enthusiastic grin. "Hey, you're home early. Are you horny or something?"

Neil said nothing, slamming into his bedroom and tossing book after book onto his bed. *Journey of Souls, Many Lives, Many Masters, Soul Survivor,* and more were flung heedlessly onto the mattress until the pile teetered and books slid off onto the floor.

"What are you doing?" Derek asked, leaning in the doorway, watching wide-eyed. "Are you okay?"

"Fuck all this," Neil said, tossing *20 Cases Suggestive of Reincarnation* over his shoulder. "Fuck this shit, fuck my life, fuck my research. Fuck it all."

"Whoa, whoa," Derek said softly, putting out his hands. "What's going on?"

Neil didn't reply, shoving an entire shelf of books out onto the floor and shouting at the top of his lungs.

Derek grabbed him from behind. "Shh. Come on. Shh."

Neil struggled against him, but even stringy Derek was stronger than he was. He collapsed against Derek's chest, breath coming in heaves.

"Talk to me," Derek murmured, running his fingers into Neil's hair. "Tell me what's going on."

"Lee died."

"Lee who?"

"Lee Fargo. Joshua's Lee."

"Oh." Derek sat them both down on the edge of the bed, the change in angle of the mattress causing more of the books to slide with a crash down to the floor. "And?"

"And he'll never forgive me," Neil murmured. "I'm the reason his husband's dead."

"You had him murdered?" Derek asked, mouth falling open, though he wrapped his arms around Neil even tighter.

"What? No, you idiot. He died from nanite dissolution failure."

"In English?"

"Rogue nanites killed him."

"Damn." Derek loosened his grip and Neil could breathe a bit more, but the despairing pain came rushing back.

"I don't want to do this anymore," Neil said quietly.

"Do what?"

"Be me. Be this." He waved at the cascade of books and pushed away from Derek's embrace. "It's time for me to move on. Forget Joshua. Forget the past."

Derek frowned and shoved his dyed black hair out of his face. "Because Lee died? I don't get it. Isn't this what you've been waiting for?" He paled a little and went on like he didn't even want to say the next words but forced them out anyway. "Now you can find Joshua, tell him the truth. Be with him."

"Are you insane?" Neil scoffed. He stood up to pace but was blocked by the mess of books. He kicked one. "That's the stupidest thing I've ever heard."

Derek's eyes flickered with hurt. "Hey, now."

Neil wiped a hand over his face. "No, I'm the stupid one. Thinking that one day he could ever meet me and I could...that we could... That was a dream, Derek. A stupid kid's dream."

"I don't think you were ever a stupid kid."

"I was a broken one. A freak. You and Mom are right. I should have let this go before now."

"Why, though? Before now Lee was alive and you had no chance."

"That's not the only reason."

"Right. Because Joshua was happy, and you didn't want to hurt him. But now Lee's gone, and, yeah, that's sad, but if you just give Joshua some time to grieve..." Derek waved his hand around.

"Then what? After letting Joshua hurt for a year I just show up and say, 'Hi, I'm your dead boyfriend from twenty years ago. How's it hanging?' He'd never believe me."

"I believed you."

"Because you're..." Neil waved at him. "You."

"What's that mean?"

"You're gullible."

"Thanks, asshole. Also, no one says, 'How's it hanging?' anymore." Derek chewed on the inside of his cheek, thinking. "You'd know things only he'd know, wouldn't you? Things you said to each other. Things you did together. How could he argue with that?"

Neil stared at him, his gut churning. Hope and despair and a weird grief he didn't understand because he'd never known Lee, not really, mixed inside him like a highly reactive combination of corrosive chemicals. "True. But how can I do that to him? It would be selfish."

"So?"

"He's just lost his husband."

"I'm not saying drive up there right now and tell him everything. I'm just saying that this is your chance. Eventually."

Neil shook his head. "It's been twenty years. He's forgotten about me." The words of Joshua's post floated in his mind. *When I lost Neil, my first love, I thought I'd never feel pain that bad again.* Maybe he wasn't forgotten, but he was in the past: dead, buried, and grieved.

What kind of asshole would he be to rip that scar open?

Derek tugged him close again. "You just need a good fuck to clear your head," he whispered, unbuttoning Neil's dark shirt. "It will all look better after an orgasm."

Neil gave in, pleasurable oblivion preferable to the unbearable tumult of feelings inside.

Several hours later, Derek was asleep beside him in bed, the books were still all over the fucking place, and Neil's balls ached from coming. He stared up at the ceiling, considering the speckled plaster.

He wouldn't purposely reach out to Joshua. But if the time came where they met face-to-face due to nanite research or some odd accident, then he would take it as a sign from whatever source had brought him back. As for what he'd do or say at that time, he'd have to hope he could wing it. There was no amount of practice that would ever make it easier to say he had once been Neil Russell. Maybe the most he could ever hope for would be to simply be in the same room with Joshua again, as Neil Green, nanite researcher and grant applicant, and be content with that.

Until that time arrived—if it ever did—Neil would dedicate himself to making sure all of his future nanite trials and treatments went through the most rigorous trials and tests before moving on to human subjects, the way he'd wanted to do from the beginning. If only he'd been old enough to have any say in the matter. But, at the time of the proto-nanites' introduction to human testing, he hadn't even been in college yet.

Careful not to wake Derek, Neil climbed out of bed, bypassed the books, and found his computer. Then he made an anonymous donation of money he didn't really have in honor of Lee Fargo to World Bicycle Relief.

It was the best he could do.

PART THREE

Chapter Eleven

October 2032—Bowling Green, Kentucky

THE BARREN RIVER Resort conference room was the same as it had been for as long as Joshua could remember: wood paneling on the walls and a long, beautifully polished table that took up the length of the room. The windows looked out on the shining lake, and the sky reflected in it. Geese flew in from the northern climes and dropped into the lake with a splash.

Joshua stuffed his hands into his pockets, wondering if perhaps he'd been wrong to insist that they have the meeting here instead of the lumber offices. After all, it was just going to be him and two people from Emory University. The pomp and circumstance of the resort conference room was unnecessary. He wondered if it was too late to ask for a smaller room, just to reduce the formality.

"Mr. Stouder," Brian Peters, his contact from Emory with whom Joshua had worked in the past, called to him jovially. His silver-blond hair was cut shorter than usual, and his glasses glinted with the sun through the window. He was slightly taller than Joshua, but trimmer, with a narrow wrist and slim fingers.

Joshua greeted Brian with a smile and an open palm, shaking effusively.

Joshua hadn't seen Brian since before Lee's death. After nanites rewrote both his and Lee's bodies—erasing Lee's scars and improving Joshua's health and extending his youth—Joshua had thought nanites were the answer to every doctor's and patient's prayers. Not to mention the anti-aging effect of nanite creams, which repaired cellular damage to surface skin! Joshua was vain enough to enjoy the fact that, for anyone who could afford it, it was possible to look years younger than one's actual age. And then, of course, there was Dale's success story. The nanites had repaired his leg and all the nerve damage, and that had been the cherry on top of the proof pudding, as far as Joshua and Lee had been concerned.

But in the end, the prototype nanites that had removed Lee's scars had also caused Lee's death. And in the darkness of grief, Joshua had found himself asking a lot of difficult questions about whether or not he could stomach funding further nanite research. The increase in nanite-related deaths in recent years indicated to Joshua that an overzealous application of a too-new technology had been allowed without appropriately rigorous testing and trials.

It'd been almost two years since Lee had collapsed and died. Joshua was gradually coming out of the worst of it, but despite many persuasive grant requests, he still hadn't authorized any more nanite funding to be sent out. And he wouldn't. Not until he was guaranteed he'd be working with someone responsible and fastidious enough to go through the rigorous testing that Joshua would require now before any nanite experiments went to human trials. That's part of what Brian was promising him.

"Where's your protégé?" Joshua asked just as the young man entered the conference room. He was the entire reason Brian had wanted to meet in person.

"Dr. Green is a genius," Brian had said during their conference call. "If you don't at least meet him, you're not being fair to yourself or to the world at large. Admittedly, he's egotistical and demanding as hell, but that's why he's so impressive. Brilliant. Knows more about nanite development than I do and has a mind that can solve problems before they even start. So while he might not be the sweetest pill to swallow, I hope you can look past his poor social skills, Mr. Stouder."

But Joshua didn't know if he could look past what he saw now.

His chest went tight, and he couldn't breathe. He stared at the kid in front of him, dressed casually for such an important business meeting in a black button-up shirt and dark jeans, both of which made him look even skinnier than he already was. He couldn't have been more than twenty, with blue eyes and curly, chestnut-brown hair, a long neck, and a jawline that was remarkably similar to…was very much like….

The realization struck him like a blow, and he felt the world tip as though going off its axis.

The boy was identical to Neil at that age.

Joshua knew it. He knew it without any pictorial evidence, or reason to believe, but it remained true all the same.

"Mr. Stouder," Brian said proudly, "may I introduce Dr. Green? He's the young man I've been telling you about."

Joshua licked his lips and put out his hand, taking Dr. Green's long, cool fingers into his own to shake. The grip was firm and too familiar. Joshua let go and, still feeling the tingling imprint of Dr. Green's hand on his, tucked his hands under his arms to stamp out the sensation. He tried to say something, but nothing came. Dr. Green's lips twitched into a small, familiar smile, and Joshua blinked. Memories flooded through him, hard and fast. He pressed a hand over his eyes, trying to get a grip.

"Mr. Stouder?" Brian asked, sounding worried. "Are you okay?"

Joshua took a deep breath through his nose and forced himself to be present. He tore his gaze away from Dr. Green's blue eyes and looked at Brian. Dots swirled in his vision. "I'm sorry. I need a moment. I'll be right back," Joshua said, and he stepped out into the hallway, booking it toward the balcony facing the lake.

He pulled open the exit door, and when it was safely closed behind him, he took a few long, deep breaths of the cooler air. A few memories of Neil raced through his mind as he pressed the heels of his hands to his eyes again. What would Neil say? He muttered to himself, "Get a grip, Joshua. You can do this. Go in there, hear them out, and tell them whether or not they can have your money. He's just a kid, not a ghost."

Not a ghost. Joshua took another long breath, studied the shimmering lake for a moment, and on the exhale shook his head. He laughed softly at himself. He'd been silly to freak out like that. He didn't know why he'd even let the resemblance get to him. It probably wasn't even as strong a resemblance as he'd imagined.

Joshua stepped back into the conference room and swallowed. The kid, Dr. Green, looked so much like a young Neil that Joshua was immediately awash in sweaty panic.

"I apologize," Joshua said, breathless again. "I didn't get a lot of sleep last night." It was true enough. He'd had nightmares most of the night about Lee's death.

Dr. Green looked at him with an expression that could only be described as *perceptive*, and Joshua felt exposed, like Dr. Green knew exactly why he had taken off out of the room.

They all sat down at the conference table as Joshua went on, "I'm ready to hear your proposition, though I have to warn you in advance, because of my past, your chances aren't great."

"I guess some things don't change," Dr. Green murmured, and Joshua blinked at him.

"Excuse me?" Joshua asked.

"Ignore him," Brian said. "Social niceties escape him at times, despite being the most amazing student I've ever met."

"Scientist," Dr. Green corrected. Even his voice sounded like Neil's had.

Joshua shivered hard, like he was cold, and his teeth chattered a bit.

"And he's great with dogs," Brian said, obviously trying to take the edge off the strange moment. "He trained my Muppet to behave in just a few hours' time. My wife was thrilled."

Dr. Green shrugged, not meeting Joshua's eye any longer. "I like dogs."

"I don't know why you don't have one," Brian said with a smile. "Might get you out of the lab more if you did."

Dr. Green shrugged, a gesture so intimately familiar that Joshua couldn't breathe.

Joshua put his hand over his mouth to hold back a sound. He wasn't even sure what it would be, exactly—a sob? A moan? Something that hurt deep down, something that shouldn't hurt as much as it did. That much he knew for sure.

He's a *kid*, not a *ghost*, Joshua told himself again.

"Did you grow up with dogs?" Joshua asked, choking on the words.

"No," Dr. Green said. His gruff voice rubbed Joshua in all kinds of ways. "I always wanted one, but my mother was allergic. And there wasn't enough money to go around as it was, so no allergy shots. Besides, it wouldn't have been fair to add another mouth to feed." He held Joshua's gaze. "It's important to make good choices about when to bring an animal into your life."

Joshua stared at him, cold trickling through his veins. "When did you learn to train dogs?"

Brian darted glances between them, a frown gathering between his brows, obviously trying to make sense of the weight in Joshua's tone.

Dr. Green didn't answer the question. Instead, he asked his own. "Are you in need of a dog trainer?"

Joshua shook his head hard. "No."

"Are you okay, Mr. Stouder?" Brian asked, tilting his head.

"I'm fine. I think I ate something that disagreed with me. Let's get started," Joshua said, gesturing toward the files Brian had brought along. He blinked at his own lie. He never lied. So why had he now?

They settled down to business with Joshua at the head of the table, and Brian passed him a thick folder of documents. Joshua opened it and began to flip through them to avoid looking at Dr. Green more than he had to. He wasn't going to lose his mind. Not right now. Not in a business meeting.

Joshua blinked at the pages in front of him, trying to make sense of the words, wondering if he just needed to call off the meeting entirely, or reschedule it for a day when he wasn't so tired and emotional. He hated to waste Brian's time, though. He needed to get himself together.

"As I was saying," Brian said, giving Dr. Green a warning look that Joshua interpreted as a scolding in advance for whatever Dr. Green might be about to say. "I'm sure you're familiar with Dr. Green's work from the information I provided."

Joshua couldn't say that he was familiar with Dr. Green's work at all, actually. He supposed he really should have spent some hours getting familiar with the information. There was a time when he would have stayed up all night to do just that. But, since Lee's death, he didn't see the point in a lot of things anymore. And working his ass off was one of them.

It was strange how grief was so different each time he lost someone. When Neil and his grandfather had died, work was the thing that saved him. When his dad had passed away, he'd been strangely balanced about it all, but then Lee had been there to soothe his pain. Since Lee had died, though, things seemed to matter a lot less to him. Stouder Lumber was still an occasional hassle, but Joshua had learned to compartmentalize it. All in all, he just didn't have the desire to invest so much in the world now.

Lee had been gone almost two years, and Joshua was doing just fine. But 'just fine' was different from what it had been before. It was a lot quieter and more sedate; there was time for sitting and staring out a window, or reading a book, or planting a garden in the back yard the way they'd talked about for years but had never done.

Life was bittersweet now. Joshua missed the man he'd planned to grow old with, but he also felt like he'd been really lucky. Damn lucky. He'd had Lee for *years*. He'd known the details of him, and the stories of his childhood, and the feel of him in his arms. While he could honestly say that losing Lee hurt like hell, like a part of him had been amputated without warning, somehow all that they'd shared between them tempered it.

It was easier than when he'd lost Neil. Because even twenty years after Neil's death, Joshua was still haunted by the things—big and small—he didn't know. Things that no one would *ever* know about Neil. And he was regretful of all they hadn't had a chance to share.

Losing Lee was hard, but Joshua knew which kind of grief was worse.

Joshua realized that Dr. Green was talking, and had been for some time. His voice was low in pitch and yet expressive, rolling up and down in ways that were achingly familiar as well. Joshua shook his head, trying to stop thinking of Neil's chuckle, or the way he'd cup Joshua's cheek after kissing him, or rub a thumb over his lower lip.

Joshua didn't think he could do this.

"...nanites shouldn't be misused for vanity," Dr. Green was saying. "They are quite possibly the greatest healing tool of all time. And yet how are they typically applied? For our petty desires to be the hottest, most attractive people possible. Tossing them into moisturizers so that we can look fifteen forever—look at *you*, for example, Mr. Stouder—"

Joshua's eyebrows went up, and he blinked at Dr. Green.

"You look thirty instead of forty-two. Despite your recent turn against nanites, it's clear to me that you've benefited from them.

Free-radical-destroying mini-machines, great in moisturizers and fantastic for repairing damage to skin, but given too quick of an exposure and the wrong genetic make-up, the vascular system can't handle them, and next thing you know? Aneurysm. Also known as artery-go-pop. I believe you're familiar with that."

Joshua clenched his jaw and remained silent. Dr. Green was clearly referencing Lee's death.

Brian's eyes widened, and he stared at Dr. Green like he was an alien. His mouth opened as though to comment, but Dr. Green plowed ahead, his words tumbling out like even he couldn't stop them.

"But nanites could be used for so much more than that. I've been working on models that could repair human tissue previously considered too damaged to salvage. I've even been working on a way to get nanites past the blood-brain barrier. Deaths from catastrophic injuries could drop drastically if my research is successful." Dr. Green pressed the palms of his hands together and tipped them toward Joshua in a gesture so intimately Neil-like that Joshua had to take another deep breath.

"Mr. Stouder," Dr. Green said, his eyes piercing. "Are you still with us?"

Joshua swallowed. He sounded so much like Neil. *Just a kid. Not a ghost.* It was time to get a grip.

"I'm with you." Joshua crossed his arms over his chest. "Don't forget *I'm* the guy you're wanting to sweet talk into giving you a bundle of money for a project I'm not exactly sold on."

Dr. Green narrowed his eyes even more and said, "As I was explaining, *Mr. Stouder*, in the most recent project I've been working on, the nanites can reverse severe brain trauma. They engage with glucose, merging and becoming part of the cell, in order to cross the blood-brain barrier effectively. At that point, they begin to repair pathways to allow for neural communication, or what we scientists refer to as the schnizzle in your nizzle, in order to—"

"The schnizzle in your nizzle?" Joshua scoffed. He turned to Dr. Peters. "Brian? Are you seriously asking me to give funding to a project on *nanites*, and let's just leave aside my current issues on that particular subject, where the lead scientist—who, by the way, looks barely out of high school—refers to brain activity as 'the schnizzle in your nizzle?'"

"It's very old slang, Mr. Stouder," Dr. Green said oddly. "I can speak in scientific terms only, if you prefer, but I doubt you'll be able to follow me."

Joshua didn't think he could take another minute of this disconcerting likeness to Neil. The voice, the expressions, even the brutal straightforwardness. It was ridiculous, and Joshua couldn't be expected to cope. He rubbed his face and said, "Sorry, Brian. That's it. I'm out of here."

Brian opened his mouth to speak, but Dr. Green interrupted, "Really, Mr. Stouder? You're going to walk away just like that?" His body trembled, and his eyes blazed. There was something in his tone, something that made Joshua remember all too clearly that first day by his apartment door and the resulting ten-minute scolding he'd received from Neil. "I know you're a country boy, but haven't you learned over the years?"

Joshua paused. The arrogant little jerk was definitely taking it too far. "Excuse me?" Joshua asked again. "And just what do you think you know about me?"

"More than you know about me," he replied.

"Neil," Brian said in a strong tone.

Joshua narrowed his eyes, heart skipping. "What does Neil have to do with this?"

"Not that Neil," Dr. Green said, obviously annoyed. "Clearly you didn't do your homework, Mr. Stouder. He's talking to me."

"You?"

"Yes, me. My name's Neil Green." He crossed his arms over his chest.

Joshua gasped. The words punched him in the gut, and he blinked at the kid in shock. "I'm sorry, what did you say your name was?"

"You heard me," Neil Green said, but his voice was soft now, tender, like he cared. "I doubt it's a name you'd forget. Or maybe I'm wrong about that?" He tilted his head, his tone going so very gentle so that it tingled up Joshua's spine. "Twenty years is a long time, after all."

Joshua stared at him. "So you've done *your* homework on *me*. Good to know. Having a similar name to my dead lover means absolutely—"

Dr. Green laughed, a familiar sound that shook Joshua to the core. He blinked at Joshua almost coyly. "Lover? Isn't that stretching the truth a little bit?"

His blood simultaneously drained from him and rushed so hard through his veins that he couldn't hear or see straight. How the hell could Dr. Green know that he and Neil had never consummated their relationship physically?

Dr. Green's bravado wavered, and he reached out to Joshua with regret washing over his face. Joshua recoiled. It was one thing to sit there *looking like* Neil, and *being like* Neil, it was another thing to throw Neil in his face.

Joshua pointed his finger at Dr. Green. "Maybe you can talk to other people like that, Dr. Green, but it isn't going to work with me. I'm not impressed by your so-called 'genius' or your rude, inappropriate comments about my past or me. As for giving you money? I think you can pretty much assume you lost all chance of that when you brought up my dead *lover*, yes. So, Brian, if you want to call me when you find a head scientist who can summon a little respect—"

"Respect?" Dr. Green said. "I do respect you. I've always respected you."

Joshua blinked at him, shook his head, and said, "You don't know how to show it, Dr. Green." Joshua stood up, leaning over to put his hands flat on the table. He peered into Dr. Green's blue, and upsettingly familiar, eyes. "You're just a kid, so let me spell this out for you. In the future, you'll want to remember that the guy with the money has your balls in a vice. And they? Just got crushed. Have fun doing your research without funding."

Joshua dusted his hands off and turned around.

As he left the room, he heard Brian bark something at Dr. Green, and Joshua was momentarily tempted to stay and see how well the kid took a verbal beatdown from his advisor.

Somehow, he thought Dr. Green would hold his own, but he headed toward the stairwell, got out of the building, and into fresh air as quickly as he could.

Chapter Twelve

NEIL HAD NEVER loathed himself so much as he did when he closed the Barren River hotel-room door on Brian Peters' still talking face. He hadn't heard a single thing Dr. Peters had said to him after Joshua walked out of the room, and he didn't think he needed to hear whatever Dr. Peters was saying now. It couldn't be harsher than what he was telling himself.

You blew it, idiot. You had this one chance, this one opportunity, and you blew it.

One chance for what? He'd never had a chance with Joshua. Not in this lifetime. He'd been an idiot to come up to meet with Joshua himself. He should've insisted they apply for grant money elsewhere, and if there wasn't another foundation that would even consider something as experimental as what Neil was suggesting, then he should have insisted that Dr. Peters come alone.

But he hadn't been able to resist the idea of being in Joshua's presence again.

Neil ran a hand over his mouth. God, his stupid *mouth*. It was like he'd been possessed, and sentences had come burbling out before he could stop them. He'd never had something like that happen before in this life or the last. It was like all of his nerves had sharpened him into the worst version of himself, the one he only let slip to lab assistants who fucked up, and sometimes to especially shitty baristas.

Fuck.

He didn't want to hurt Joshua. He'd never wanted to hurt

Joshua. But the expression on Joshua's face when Neil had made the anxiety-driven jab about Dr. Russell having never been Joshua's lover had clearly struck at pain deep inside. Neil had wanted to swallow his own tongue, choke to death on it, and *not* come back in another life remembering everything again.

Hell, if he could only be sure of that, he'd have offed himself a long time ago.

It was exactly like he'd known it would be. Painful, awkward, and, yeah, seeing Joshua, sitting beside him, watching his face move through various emotions as he'd regarded Neil had been terrifying, so he'd lost his mind and been an ass. At the time, it'd seemed better than grabbing Joshua, kissing him, and declaring himself the reincarnation of Joshua's long-lost lover.

Lover.

God, Neil wished he'd been Joshua's lover. If he had those memories, too, maybe he'd have been able to cope a little better. Maybe he really could have left it all behind when that truck barreled down on him and Magic. But instead he was stuck with all of this longing. The longing that had foolishly led him to apply for the grant and then come here with Brian.

He'd been an idiot. A foolish, selfish, heartless idiot.

Neil sat on the bed, head in his hands, and stared at his shiny shoes purchased just for this trip. He remembered getting ready for the meeting, the anticipation and fear that had rushed through him in an endless loop. He'd stared at himself in the mirror, looking at the line of his nose, the angle of his jaw, and he'd wished he were somehow ten years older. He'd wondered if Joshua would recognize him, if he'd see the similarities, or if he'd just be some dorky kid.

He could admit it now. He'd wanted Joshua to know. And yet the recognition in Joshua's eyes had been horrible to see. Joshua had looked ill, like he could barely stand to look at Neil, and that had cut. Was Joshua so desperate to forget him after all? Had he moved on since Lee's death to mourning for his husband more than he'd ever mourned for Neil? For a split second, Neil wished Joshua had never met Lee. The thought lacked generosity and love, but it was there all the same.

Neil fell back on the bed, stared at the ceiling, and thousands of memories poured through him. Scottsville had seemed freakishly familiar when he'd driven into the town after the hour-drive from the Nashville airport with Dr. Peters. It was exactly as Joshua had described it to him all those years ago. A town frozen in time. After they'd arrived at the Barren River Resort, he'd stayed hidden in his room freaking out, waiting for the meeting to start.

The meeting that had just gone oh-so-very badly.

When he'd seen Joshua standing in the conference room, eyeing the table, with his hands stuffed into his pockets and his light-brown hair curling at the temples like it always had, Neil had thought his heart would hammer out of his chest. He'd heard people say things like that before, describing an intensity of hollow, ringing fear that he remembered from the truck accident, but now that he'd experienced it again, he couldn't shake the reverberation of it from his body.

And then Joshua had seen him, too.

And his face...his face had said so much. Neil shivered remembering the way Joshua had paled, going green at the gills. Joshua had been horrified by the resemblance he saw, and Neil couldn't blame him. There'd been times in the past, when he'd been hanging out drinking a coffee in the campus cafeteria, or looking up old, dusty books on reincarnation in the library when he'd seen someone who resembled Joshua. Someone with light-brown hair that hung down in their face—the way Joshua had worn his hair when Neil first met him—or someone with the same slope to their shoulders and bounce in their walk. And he'd hated that person. He'd never talked to any of them, and he never would, but he hated them for looking like Joshua, for making Neil remember in a visceral, aching way exactly the thing he could never have. The thing he needed to let go.

But he wasn't an idiot. He recognized that he'd never had any idea how to let Joshua go or how to stop loving him. It seemed impossible. Loving Joshua was all he'd ever known.

His phone started beeping, and he pulled it out of his pocket. It was Dr. Peters, of course. He turned it off and threw it across the room. It hit the wall and crashed to the floor.

Neil rolled over, covering his head with a pillow when it kept on ringing.

HOURS PASSED, AND Neil ignored the knocking on his hotel room door and the sound of Dr. Peters calling to him through the thick wood. He couldn't sleep, and he couldn't do anything else, either. He just lay there, scanning through memories from another time, and trying to figure out how he was going to keep on living if he couldn't do his work, if he couldn't block out thoughts of Joshua by diving into nanite research and experiments.

The sound of the privacy settings of the room being overruled brought Neil upright, and his mouth hung open as Joshua walked in, with Dr. Peters on his heels, as well as a few members of hotel security behind them.

Joshua's eyes flashed annoyance and relief at once. Neil couldn't tug his gaze away from Joshua, but he knew he must look a mess sprawled on the bed, his shirt rumpled and his hair rubbed every which way by the pillow. His face wasn't schooled. His emotions were showing.

Dr. Peters was talking, but Neil didn't hear him.

Joshua swallowed and took a step forward, reaching out toward

Neil. "Hey, you had us pretty worried." Joshua looked behind him, waved the security away. They stepped outside the room, but Neil got the impression they didn't leave entirely. Turning back to Neil, he said, "Are you all right?"

"I'm fine." Neil tried to snap the words out, but he didn't think he sounded especially convincing. His voice was breathy and strange. Horrified, he realized that Joshua thought he was a melodramatic teenage genius who was pouting about having lost the funding.

Joshua glanced back toward Dr. Peters, waiting to follow his lead.

Dr. Peters took several steps forward. His tired expression said it all. "Neil, I understand that you're disappointed, but scaring us like this wasn't necessary."

Neil wiped a hand over his face. "I wanted some privacy. That's all."

Joshua looked momentarily startled, though Neil didn't know why. But then he trained his face into an expression of concern again and stepped a little closer. "Look, I'm willing to hear you out. Things got a little uncomfortable earlier, and that was partially on me. How about we let bygones be bygones and give this another try?"

"Why?" Neil asked, standing up to try to feel more on equal footing with them both. His tongue moved and he made words, and as soon as he heard them, he wanted to grab them back from the air. "So that you can soothe the poor kid's hurt feelings? My work will be fine. With or without you."

Dr. Peters threw his hands up in the air and walked out of the room. Clearly, he'd had enough of Neil. Joshua watched him go but didn't follow. Instead, he took a deep breath, shut the door to the room, and pulled up a chair. He turned it around backward and sat down. He eyed Neil speculatively from his shoes to crown of his head, and then sighed, unbuttoning his shirtsleeves and rolling them up.

Neil was speechless. He couldn't take his eyes off Joshua's forearms, the soft hair and skin he exposed. Memories of Joshua's arms under his hands as they'd kissed came back to him. He scrunched up his eyes to shake those thoughts away.

When he opened his eyes again, Joshua had his arms crossed over the back of the chair, and he was studying Neil intently.

"Have a seat. I'm going to be upfront with you," Joshua said as Neil let his legs give out to sit back on the edge of the bed. Joshua licked his lips and then cocked his head a little, his eyes focused intently on Neil's face. "You look a lot like someone I knew once. I suspect you even know you do. It seems like you know an awful lot about me, Dr. Green."

Neil said nothing.

Joshua nodded as though he had, though. "So, we're going to have to deal with that. I didn't give you a fair shot because I…well, I lost my husband two years back. A poorly researched, experimental nanite procedure led to his death. So, that, combined with the fact that you look like…well, you know who you look like. So I got upset. Like I said, I didn't give you a fair shot."

"There was no way to prevent what happened to Lee," Neil said, defaulting to his work. It was safer there. "When your husband started with the nanite treatment, we didn't have a test for the genetic markers."

Joshua nodded. "I know. And you've since developed one."

"Yes," Neil said. "*I* did. I developed it *because* of him."

Joshua blinked. "Excuse me?"

"Well, your husband and about fifteen hundred other people. The future of nanite medicine depended on it. With the tests I've designed, we can be sure it won't happen again. My propositions might be experimental, Mr. Stouder, but I'm not without a conscience. There's always protocol to keep me in line, but I *do* give a damn about human beings. All creatures, really."

Joshua's expression softened, and he said with fondness, "Like I said, I knew someone like you once—he cared about human beings, too. And animals. Maybe a little too much."

"Oh yeah?" Neil asked, his Adam's apple bobbing hard. "What do you mean by that?"

"It got him killed," Joshua said. "Maybe if he'd cared just a little less…"

Neil's breath hitched. "I'm sorry."

"Me, too."

"I'm sorry he died." Neil felt like he was about to be swept from the face of the earth for even daring to say it. "Both of them, I mean. I can't imagine how you felt."

"It *sucked.*"

Neil recalled the expression on Joshua's face when he'd first seen Neil, how much he didn't want to be reminded of him. It reminded him of the torture he'd put himself through watching Joshua's interviews over and over, memorizing every wrinkle, every smile. He thought of the years that he'd spent in Atlanta, growing up with Alice, being so much more than a little kid, and yet never enough to be with Joshua. Too young, too late, too dead. And then Joshua had been too happy, too married.

It was too much.

"I know you grieved for…for Neil. But you had a pretty awesome life after that, didn't you? You were happy." As long as he could remember, he'd wanted nothing but for Joshua to be happy. He looked away. "Well, until recently, that is—"

"Don't talk about Lee," Joshua said, putting a hand up in warning. "Don't even mention his name."

Neil nodded and mimed zipping his mouth shut.

Joshua shook his head. "As for Neil—not that I owe you an

explanation—but I've missed him every day since his death. Some more than others, sure, and eventually it became bearable, something I just lived with the way I'd live with a scar before nanites." He huffed a laugh. "Funny how nanites can't repair emotional wounds."

"Not yet."

"Hopefully not ever," Joshua said. "But I've never once been *happy* that he died, if that's what you're asking."

Neil looked down at the floor and then back up to Joshua's eyes again, wanting to say the right thing. He wanted to tell him the truth, that he'd missed him, too, that he was sorry he'd died, that he wanted more than anything to make it right, but how could he? It would sound absurd. Moreover, it was unkind.

Joshua had grieved him and moved on, not only with Lee, but in every way. It would be the highest act of selfishness to confess to him now, rip his life open again, and ask him to accept something so confounding. He deserved peace. He deserved to find some measure of joy again. Not bewildering madness with a man half his age, if that was even what he wanted. They'd been together so long ago. Nothing had been guaranteed between them even then.

The world had changed. So had Joshua. And Neil would be a monster to try to deny that.

"I know you're young, but have you ever been in love?" Joshua's voice was tinged with some anger, but also soft with compassion.

Neil shrugged. He had always been in love. It was painful and full of despair. It was a terrible way to live.

"Okay, well, then, let me ask you this," Joshua went on. "Have you ever loved anyone at all? Someone besides yourself?"

Neil stared at him blankly, the most inappropriate answer screaming in his mind.

Joshua said, "No? Not even your mother?"

Neil swallowed. "I love my mother very much. But I'm a terrible son."

"Oh, really? Did I just hear you say, Dr. Green, than you are *terrible* at something?"

Neil's lips quirked, and he gazed down at the carpet, unable to look at Joshua as he smiled at the jab. "Just don't let it get around."

Joshua snorted. "I hate to break it to you," he said, drawing air in through his teeth, "but you seem like the kind of guy whose reputation precedes you. I doubt anyone would be surprised to hear that you're a jerk to your mother."

Neil flinched. "I never said I was a jerk to her."

Joshua's head cocked with interest, and he seemed to back down from whatever barb he was going to throw next.

"I said that I was a terrible son. But I don't mistreat her. Is that what you think?"

Joshua's brow furrowed with some confusion. He seemed to understand that he'd hit a sore spot, and, in typical Joshua manner, he was sorry for it now. "Frankly, Dr. Green, I don't know what to think of you."

Neil nodded once to indicate that what Joshua had said was fair enough. He still felt defensive, though. He thought of Alice with her dark brown hair and the kiss she'd planted on his forehead every night at bedtime as his body grew into his mind, and he wanted more than almost anything else to find a way to make it up to her, to make up for having been *him*.

"Are you okay?" Joshua asked.

Neil couldn't believe it. After the ways he'd been hurtful and callous, Joshua was asking *him* if he was okay. Joshua was still such a good-hearted man that it made Neil's chest ache. Simple country boy, with a heart of gold. He jerked his head in affirmation, averted his gaze again, and rubbed his fingers through his hair. He heard Joshua take a sharp breath.

"Yeah, well. I'm sorry about your lover. And your husband,"

Neil said, the words coming out low and tired. "I'm just sorry. For everything."

"I...uh, thank you," Joshua said, sounding confused.

Joshua stood up from the chair and sat down next to Neil on the bed. Not incredibly close, but the weight of him dipped the mattress lower, and Neil could smell his aftershave. It was nice. Different from years ago, but still very nice. Older, somehow; more mature.

Joshua tilted his head down, trying to see Neil's face. "Dr. Green? What's going on here? I feel like there's something you're not telling me."

Neil shrugged. What could he say without cutting Joshua open needlessly? "No, no. Everything is fine."

Joshua nodded. He sighed heavily, and he sat there, so close and so horribly far. Neil's entire body wanted to lean against Joshua, to turn and press him to the bed, to climb on top of him, to kiss him, to smell him, to be near him, and to hold him for the rest of his life. If he could just make himself tear Joshua open with the truth now, they could both lead a very long life. Together. It was excruciating.

Neil stood, kept his back mostly turned, and grabbed his suitcase. He plopped it onto the bed next to Joshua and started to fill it with his few clothes. Coming to Scottsville, seeing Joshua in person...it had been a bad idea. Now he really didn't know how he was going to survive without him, and he hadn't even touched him. He kept his focus down, because if he looked into Joshua's tired eyes, he was going to lose all resolve, and then he'd be responsible for Joshua's pain.

"Dr. Green?"

"I'm sorry, Mr. Stouder," Neil said. "Coming here has been a waste of both of our time."

Joshua sat there, watching. Neil could feel him, but he didn't look.

Finally, Joshua said, "Dr. Green...hey. Listen. Neil—"

A shudder went through Neil to hear his name spoken by Joshua in such a gentle, tender tone.

"Neil, if you need help."

He was being stretched out on a rack. He didn't know how much more of being near Joshua he could take before he came apart. He spat out whatever words he could grab from his mind, so long as they didn't have anything to do with wanting to kiss Joshua's neck, or being reincarnated, or missing him. "Help? What I need is money, Mr. Stouder, and since you're unable to relent there—"

"Fine, fine, forget I mentioned it," Joshua said, standing up. He'd raised his hands in surrender, though there was an undercurrent of worry to his voice. "I'll just get out of your way, and then you can get out of here."

"Maybe, if we're lucky, we'll never see each other again," Neil said, feeling that much closer to tearing in half as he said the words.

"Yeah, if we're lucky."

Neil closed his eyes, letting out a hard breath, prepared to tell Joshua to get out if he had to because he couldn't take another minute of it.

He sensed Joshua's retreat, and his back stiffened as Joshua said from the doorway, "You're right. I had a good life with Lee. I loved him very much, and I miss him every day. But if Neil had lived, I would have had a good life with him, too. A different life, but a good one. And I regret that I didn't get to have that experience. I regret it every single day."

Neil thought that was it, but no.

"I don't know why I'm telling you this," Joshua said. "Lee understood it. Understood *me*. I don't know why I want you to understand, too. It shouldn't matter to me. But it does."

Neil's head bowed as he heard the door shut. He fought the

urge to chase after him, to confess it all, and tell Joshua that he could have that experience with his Neil now, if he wanted. Mastering himself, Neil fell facedown onto the bed.

Sobs wracked him as he tried to breathe through the pain of letting Joshua leave.

Chapter Thirteen

NEIL'S PLAN WAS to leave Barren River, call a car to take him to the Nashville airport, and catch the first flight out to Atlanta. It'd cost an arm and a leg, but what choice did he have but to stay here and travel with Dr. Peters the next day? But cars and taxis didn't come out this far in the boondocks, so he couldn't find a driver to take him to Nashville.

He cursed softly, throwing himself backward onto the hotel bed again. He was trapped here. And he needed to get out. He thought about renting a car—surely this town had a car rental service?—but then he started to laugh, because he wasn't *old enough* yet. Hell, he wasn't even old enough to go downstairs and order a drink at the bar. He was so fucking *sick* of being a kid.

Angry, he stood up, pulled on his coat, and walked out of the hotel room. He didn't know where he was going, but he needed to move, and walking seemed better than pounding his fists against the pillows some more.

Neil realized his mistake as soon as he hit the parking lot. Every lap around the lot was just another circle of the same new, horrible memories: every word he'd said to Joshua, the way Joshua had looked, how he'd smelled, how it had all gone so wrong. He wasn't usually one to call his mother when he was feeling low, mainly because he tried to stay too busy to ever get truly down, but sitting on the bench outside of the resort's main building, he didn't know what else to do.

"Two weeks," Alice said as her greeting. "Two weeks since you called, and I hear from Derek today that you're not even in the state!"

"Mom," Neil said to cut her off, and then he was silent.

When she spoke again, her voice had changed. "Where are you? What's wrong?"

He shook his head at himself, dreading telling her, knowing that this was the stupidest thing he'd done since he'd tried to race a semi-truck to save Magic and lost.

"Scottsville," he said. "I'm in Scottsville." Technically, Barren River was on the outskirts of Bowling Green, but whatever. Close enough.

"Oh." There was a long silence at the other end of the line.

"We applied for that grant. The one I told you about. I failed to mention that the foundation in question was…"

"The Neil Russell Foundation," she murmured. "Did you see him?"

"Yeah." Neil rotated his shoulders like he was trying to shake his mood off. It was easier already, faking it for her. He let a long breath out between his teeth, and said, "Well, it's better this way, I guess. Stupid is as stupid does. My genius card has been revoked."

"Are thinking you're a genius at life when all you are is a genius at science?"

"Gee, thanks, Mom. That's the kind of encouragement I needed right now."

Alice sighed. "You don't need encouragement, Neil. You need to get out of Scottsville before you break your own heart. But I'm sure it's too late for that, isn't it?"

"Yes," he said. His throat grew tight. The bench was hard and cold against his ass, even though the fall evening wasn't too cool, and he could have done without his jacket.

"So you met him, then?" Alice asked. He could hear the hesitancy and the worry.

He didn't speak. He tried, but he had no idea what he could say. Yeah, he'd met him. Joshua was everything Neil had known he would be, and it had felt so *right* and so horribly *wrong*. And Neil had scared the shit out of Joshua. Hell, he'd scared the shit out of *himself*.

"Neil?" she asked.

"He said I reminded him of someone."

"You didn't tell him?" she asked, and the 'surely' was left off, though Neil heard it there.

"I'm an emotional idiot, not a madman," he said. "I mean, sure, I know things that only his Neil could know, but why would I do that to him? He's just gotten over the loss of his husband. Why would I split him open like that again?"

"Oh baby."

Neil let out a soft moan of pain.

"So, how did it go?"

"I'm calling you," Neil whispered.

"Not well, then."

"I need to get out of here."

"Come home."

Neil laughed, and it sounded bitter. "I'm stuck."

She made a strange sound. "You haven't been arrested, have you?"

Neil tugged at his hair and said, "No, but I can't get a cab or a car up here. It's the middle of nowhere Kentucky."

"Neil, do you need me to come get you? I can be there in, I don't know—how long does it take to get to Scottsville?"

"By car? Too long. By plane? Still too long. I think I'm going to lose my mind."

Neil looked up then. A tall, thin man with long, brown hair was walking toward him on the sidewalk from the offices of the resort.

He wasn't looking where he was going, his head down as he pawed around in a giant purse that seemed, as far as Neil could tell from the items he kept pulling out and dropping back, to contain the entirety of a beauty-supply store. A young, butch man dogged his heels, dressed like a stereotypical farmer, and talking a mile a minute.

That's when Neil knew, and he couldn't look away.

"You're going to hold it together, baby. I promise," Alice said fiercely.

"I have to go," Neil said, disconnecting the call.

"Declyn, honey, you're a grown man," Chris said as he paused by the bench where Neil was still sitting to paw through his purse some more. "As much as I want to jump in and save you, you're going to have to figure this one out by yourself."

"I know, but it's just…" The boy groaned and stuck his hand in his jeans pocket. "Wait, that's Nadia calling now. Stay here, okay? Don't go anywhere." He took the call and ducked around the corner of the building, obviously wanting some privacy.

Chris sighed, rolled his eyes, and then looked down at Neil. He was older than the last time Neil had seen a photo of him on Lee's social media, but he didn't look that different. Like Joshua, he'd obviously been able to afford the anti-aging nanite creams, because he was still bright to look at.

Once upon a time, in that other life, Chris had been Neil's friend. One of his only friends.

Neil jerked his gaze away, but it was too late.

Chris plopped down onto the bench beside him and said, "You look lost, sugar tits."

Neil snorted softly, lifted one shoulder, and let it fall.

Chris started up with his bag again, saying, "Argh, *finally*," and brought out a tinted lip balm. He took the lid off, looked at the color, and began to apply it.

Neil didn't mean to talk to him. He meant to stand up and walk away. Instead, he said, "That's not a good look on anyone."

"Gee, thanks, lost stranger, for your input on my lip color." Chris rolled his eyes. "Are you homophobic, too? Because we ain't got time for that around here, as my husband says."

"No. I don't care about your lipstick. Or the gay thing. I meant me. Looking lost. It's generally not a good look on—"

"Anyone. Got it," Chris said. He narrowed his eyes. "You know, it's kind of uncanny how much you look like this guy I knew once." He reached out and took hold of Neil's jaw. Neil flinched back from the touch instinctively.

Chris rolled his eyes. "Let me look at you. Hmm, yes, I see that you're lost, and you're in need of some advice." He grinned and let go of Neil's chin. "Lucky for you, I know everything there is to know about this town, and I'm excellent at dishing up fantastic and unwanted advice. Just ask my son." He looked toward the corner that Declyn had ducked around. "If he ever gets off the phone with that girl. I swear, is it always like this? Do kids always take up with the absolute worst person for them? Of course, my parents love Dale. It's me they hate."

Neil stared at him. Chris was the same. Exactly the same. Talking to anyone like he had a right to, and being unfailingly cheerful even when he was being a bitch. And Chris had remembered him—well, the old him. And he seemed pleased to see the resemblance.

Neil felt like he'd stepped into some kind of strange time-transport device where the people he knew and loved best were older, and he alone was younger. His phone buzzed. He knew it was Alice calling back. He hadn't been very clear when he ended his call. She probably thought he'd been accosted or something. Again, at the rate that his life was going downhill, it was only a matter of time.

"Aren't you going to get that?" Chris asked.

"It's my mother," Neil said.

Chris slapped him upside the head softly. "Like I said, *aren't you going to get that?*"

Neil connected the call and said, "Hey, I'm okay. Gotta go."

"Are you sure?" Alice asked.

"I'll call you later," and he said firmly, and hung up on Alice again.

Chris frowned at him. "So, are you rude to your mother like that all the time?"

"Do you hit strange men over the head all the time? First, that's assault. Second, neurological damage could result from that kind of behavior over the long term."

Chris grinned again. "Aw, that's cute. You think you're a man." He patted Neil's knee in an over-fond way. "Keep eating your vegetables and maybe you will be one day." Neil shot him a look, and Chris laughed. "What's your name?"

He let the corner of his lips turn up. "Green," he said. "Neil Green."

Chris's expression changed, and he grew serious. "Are you... I don't suppose you're any relation to Dr. Neil Russell?"

Neil nearly said, "I'm his son," just to see the reaction, but instead he shook his head.

"No, of course not," Chris said a bit absently, studying his face. "You do look so much like him. It's so odd that you'd have the same name. But no, of course you're not related."

"Coincidence," Neil said softly. "Never heard of the guy."

"Right. Of course." Chris seemed to get himself together, and he smiled brightly again. "So, you're lost. How can I help ya?"

"You can't. I just...need to get to Nashville so I can get back home."

"And where's 'home?'"

"Atlanta," Neil said, though his mind supplied him with a compellingly fresh memory of Joshua's brown eyes studying him with earnest concern.

"And how did you end up here?"

"You wouldn't believe me if I told you."

"Try me."

Neil rubbed his fingers over his eyes and considered blurting out, "Well, it all started when I died beneath a semi truck about twenty years ago." But instead he just said, "I'm a scientist. I was here for an interview with a potential investor." Keeping it simple, if inaccurate.

"No way!" Chris said, staring at him suspiciously. "Are you sure? You look a little young."

"Uh, yes, I'm sure. Graduated early. Yadda yadda."

"It's just so strange how much you're like—"

"Life's strange," Neil said, cutting him off.

"It really is."

"Speaking of, what are you doing here?"

Chris blinked hard. "Working? I'm the office manager."

"I mean here. In Scottsville."

"Oh. That's a long story." Chris smiled and looked off into the distance. "I guess it's obvious I'm not from around here, huh? I grew up in Nashville. A much bigger city. But love brought me a long way from home."

"Are you happy here?"

"I'm happy, yes." Chris turned back to him. "You know what? I think I can help you." Chris glanced toward the corner of the building where Declyn was talking animatedly to his girlfriend. "I know a certain someone who could use a time out, actually."

"Wait, are you—?" Neil asked. "You just met me. I'm a complete stranger, and you're going to have your son drive me to Nashville? I could be a serial killer for all you know."

Chris shrugged happily. "But you're not. And Declyn, my stepson, should get out of Scottsville for the afternoon. It would do him good."

Neil felt a weird rush of anxiety at the thought of being trapped in a car with Chris's kid.

"You remind me of someone I loved who died a long time ago," Chris said, rather cheerfully considering he was discussing death. "And I'd feel like I was doing him a favor if I helped you out."

"That's ridiculous," Neil said, suddenly hot and uncomfortable, because Chris *would* be doing his Neil a favor, and the layers of weirdness were suffocating.

"Yep," Chris agreed. "You sound just like him. Okay, hold on. You stay right here, Neil. Wow, that sounds so weird to say. I'll be right back with Declyn."

Neil watched Chris grab the phone from Declyn, tell the girlfriend something that looked rather unpleasant, and then disconnect the call. Declyn's hands on his hips and shocked face gave away that he wasn't too pleased by his stepfather's behavior. Part of Neil wanted to stay and see how it all played out, curious about the man he'd once cared about. But another part of him could think of few more disastrous ways to end this already dreadful day than getting into a car with Chris's stepson.

He darted back inside the Barren River Resort before Chris could stop him. He prepared himself to face Dr. Peters at least long enough to blow him off again. He'd spend the rest of the evening and night in bed.

With any luck, the blanket that Joshua had touched would retain his scent, and Neil could torture himself all night long with that, before he headed back to Atlanta with Dr. Peters the next morning as planned.

NEARLY TWENTY HOURS after landing back in Atlanta, and fifteen hours after convincing Alice that he would be happier returning to campus, Neil's body was exhausted, but his mind wouldn't shut down. He'd worked in the labs, trying to keep away from painful, wrenching thoughts of Joshua by focusing on his project before their cash flow dried up, but it was useless. After he'd given up, he stalked home to the apartment irritable and wrung out.

He glanced around at Derek's mess, the half-eaten bowl of cereal on the table and the litter of food wrappers around the couch. He muttered "I live with an animal" under his breath and stalked into his own room, where he kicked off his jeans and pulled his T-shirt over his head. Neil rubbed a hand over his face and then jerked down his boxer shorts.

Without a word, he walked from his room into Derek's, startling Derek out of a pretty sound sleep. But Derek didn't stop him, only whispered "Yessssss" as Neil flipped Derek onto his stomach and yanked Derek's sweat pants down to his ankles, revealing his round, tight ass.

Neil might not have been able to concentrate on work, and he might have felt like he was about to come apart from the intensity of the renewed pain and unresolved longing for Joshua, but he could drown that out for now with a good, long fuck. Derek was a messy roommate who was annoyingly close with Neil's mother, but his body was pliable, eager, and always open for business.

Derek looked over his shoulder, while Neil grabbed a condom and rolled it on. Derek's blue eyes were wide with lust, and his mouth gaped. Neil was grateful he didn't ask questions.

Neil squirted lube onto Derek's hole, lined up, and roughly shoved inside. Derek's head fell forward as Neil slid into him hard and fast, with no time for adjustment or warming up.

"Jesus," Derek gasped, clenching at the sheets and biting his pillow. "Fuck, Neil."

Neil closed his eyes, concentrating on the tight, gripping pull of Derek's ass on his cock. The hot slide in and out was almost enough to block the aching, horrible pain that seemed to have opened in his chest since seeing Joshua in person.

Neil pounded into Derek roughly, leaning down to sink his teeth in sharp bites along Derek's shoulders and neck, feeling the delicious response of Derek jerking and tightening around Neil's plunging dick. He didn't let up, angling to hit Derek's prostate and burying his face in Derek's already sweat-damp hair, as Derek shivered and crooned beneath him.

It felt good to fuck Derek. He was in control of *something*, at least, as he drove Derek to the edge of orgasm and then held him there, not quite pushing him over into it. Derek writhed and begged, and Neil felt a surge of reassuring power. He couldn't be with Joshua, but he could fuck Derek, and he could make Derek scream, and he could feel something besides pain. He rubbed Derek's back, knowing by the way that Derek moved that he was going to come, and sensing Derek's shock and even fear at the intensity of the orgasm about to slam through him.

Neil grabbed a fistful of Derek's hair, used it for leverage, and fucked Derek impossibly harder. Derek made wild, animal noises as Neil rode him, and then Derek scrambled against the sheets in a desperate and yet half-hearted attempt to get away from Neil's cock, before Derek's straining movements popped the fitted sheet off the mattress, and he jerked beneath Neil in shuddering surprise.

"Fuck!" Derek cried, his asshole clenching rhythmically as he shot his load without even touching himself.

Neil continued to fuck Derek's spasming ass, and he ran a soothing hand through Derek's hair, vaguely grateful for Derek's willingness as he fought his own orgasm, holding it back, preferring to keep on screwing so that he didn't have to remember how Joshua had looked at him, or the sound of Joshua's voice saying his name.

Derek jolted and squirmed underneath him, crying out every time Neil stroked in and raked against his prostate, obviously too sensitive, but it wasn't long before Derek was thrusting back, up on his hands and knees, calling out for harder and faster. He fell forward onto his elbow as he screamed and jerked his cock to orgasm again, his asshole clenching so hard that Neil had to momentarily stop his thrusts to ride it out.

"Holy shit," Derek gasped when Neil started pounding him again, and he melted into the mattress, a limp body taking Neil's cock without resistance, and Neil grabbed Derek's hips, hauled him up a little for a better angle, and didn't let up.

Derek drooled and occasionally convulsed in pleasure, his eyes rolled back in his head. Neil carried on, delaying his own orgasm for as long as he could, before finally shoving into Derek all the way to the root. Falling onto Derek's sweat-slick back and shaking as he finally filled the condom, he saw nothing but Joshua's brown eyes.

The pain that swallowed him was enormous. Desperately, Neil pulled the condom off, tossed it on the floor, and rolled on another. Shoving into Derek's slick, spasming hole while his cock was still sensitive from orgasm hurt, but it was better than the emotional pain that engulfed him when he stopped. Derek whimpered but didn't ask him to pull out.

Neil fucked Derek until they were both too fatigued to move. They lay panting and twitching helplessly, both of them covered in sweat and Derek's come. As Neil rolled away, exhausted and hoping to fall asleep, he noticed that Derek was smiling deliriously, high as a kite from the intense fucks. Neil, though, was drained of strength, and instead of Derek's happy humming, he heard Joshua's angry voice, saying, "You're just a kid!" as he dropped into an exhausted, miserable sleep.

Chapter Fourteen

FOR THE THIRD time in as many days, Joshua's night was peppered with wakefulness and anxiety. His bed seemed far too big. His dreams, when he did manage to fall to sleep, were a hodgepodge of frustration, grief, and old, thwarted desire.

Joshua ran his hand over the pillow beside him, remembering the last few months of Lee's life, when they'd thought the experimental treatment to stop the damage the nanites had wreaked on Lee's vascular system had worked. There had been a lot of joy, a sense of pardon, and Joshua's dreams had seemed innocent enough.

During that time, he'd had a reoccurring one of a beehive dripping with honey. The hive had swarmed, and the bees danced in the air around him when he approached, greeting him cheerfully with their secret message-bearing movements.

Later, he remembered that historically it had been believed that bees took the message of a person's death to the gods. He wondered if somehow his subconscious mind had known that they were in the middle of a honey-sweet reprieve and that Lee was on his way out of life despite the apparent success of the treatment. It certainly explained his lack of surprise when Lee had collapsed during breakfast, his face going white as he'd bled out internally, dying in only minutes, while Joshua had held him and whispered to him not to be afraid.

Joshua groaned and rubbed the heels of his hands over his eyes, remembering how Lee had apologized to him as he died. At the last,

Lee had remarked with a kind of surprise, "I'm so cold, babe," and then he'd been gone.

Even now, Joshua didn't know for sure what Lee had intended with his apology—sorry that he'd been so enthusiastic about the nanite procedures? Sorry that he was leaving Joshua alone just like Neil had, or sorry that he was dying in Joshua's arms? Whatever he'd meant, Joshua had told him it was okay. "It's okay, I love you, don't be afraid." He'd said it urgently, over and over.

After Lee was well and truly gone, he'd managed to call 911. The paramedics had arrived, and Joshua had held Lee's lifeless body tight for a last moment before the paramedics had asked him to move aside. They worked uselessly while Joshua watched, tears streaming down his face.

He hadn't dreamed of bees again until the night after he'd met Neil Green.

It took forever for him to fall asleep, his mind replaying every moment of his conversations with Dr. Green and presenting him again and again with the uncanny resemblance to his Neil. The piercing blue eyes, the jawline and long neck, the way his fingers were shaped, and the color of his hair, the hold of his lips, and even the tense barbs that seemed to fly out of his mouth before he could think them through. How many times had Joshua heard him talk that way to lab assistants when he was angry?

As Joshua finally dropped off, his fingers fisted into the sheets on Lee's side of the bed, seeking comfort from the memory of his husband, he found he was walking toward a honey-dripping beehive. Unperturbed by the buzzing of the bees around him, he knelt by the hive and let some of the honey drip onto his finger. He tasted its sweetness as the bees danced by his head, waiting for him to tell them something to take back to the gods.

The peace of the moment evaporated as Joshua searched deeply for words and couldn't find them. There was something important—a message, yes, but maybe it wasn't for him to deliver; maybe it was for him to receive.

Joshua listened to the buzzing as hard as he could. He felt the tickle of the bees landing on his ears and crawling into his ear canal, buzzing, buzzing, urging him to take what they had to give him, but he couldn't decipher it. He didn't speak their language.

Then Joshua woke in a panic, scratching at his ears to shake the buzzing noise away. Impotent and frustrated, he was lost and alone.

Two days later, he still felt the same way. The dream kept coming back whenever his body succumbed to exhaustion. He'd just woken from it again, and the room was barely lit with dawn.

Joshua sat up, stretched, and closed his eyes as he thought of Neil Green's mouth. His cock throbbed with his usual morning wood, and he resisted the urge to reach down to jerk off. His resolve only lasted a few moments, though, as his mind went to the length of Neil Green's throat and his familiar eyes.

What did it hurt to imagine? If only for a few minutes?

Joshua clenched his jaw as he palmed his cock, and then gripped it firmly, imagining Dr. Green's challenging expression. In his mind's eye, Joshua grabbed Dr. Green by the hair, tugged him forward into a kiss that was searing and hot, and then forced him to his knees. He could show Dr. Green a better use for his runaway mouth.

Joshua imagined Dr. Green eagerly opening his lips to suck Joshua in. The wet, hot slickness of his tongue and cheeks engulfed Joshua's cock, and he didn't last after that, coming hard enough that his ejaculate hit his chin and he was left gasping for air. In his imagination, Dr. Green looked unbearably smug and far too pleased with himself.

Even that made Joshua's cock twitch again.

"Crap," Joshua muttered, wiping the come from his chin with one hand. He brought it up to his mouth, sucking his own fingers clean.

He wished it was just the unexpected lust that he felt for Dr. Green that was eating at him, but it wasn't. The resemblance was so overwhelming, the familiarity so unexpected and intense, that Joshua hadn't been able to stop his mind from asking questions ranging from the improbable to the impossible.

Joshua showered and headed into his offices at the lumber company, determined to flip through the hard copy of the information sent to him from Emory one more time before calling to check with the Private Investigator in Atlanta.

Adair Pimberton came at the recommendation of one of his oldest contacts, so Joshua felt certain of her competence. She'd see to it that Joshua would know what kind of soap and laundry detergent Dr. Green used within twenty-four hours. She was that good.

Joshua hadn't intended to go so far as to have Dr. Green investigated, but after the first sleepless night, he'd been unable to put his questions aside. He'd started looking over the proposal again, and it wasn't a bad one necessarily—if he could put his doubts to rest on the nanite project, and satisfy his need to know more about Dr. Green at the same time, then it was a win/win endeavor.

Joshua justified it to himself by telling the board of the Neil Russell Foundation. "I'm still unresolved on the funding of the Emory nanite grant proposal. I just need a little more information on the kid who's running the whole thing. He struck me as a potential loose canon."

The fact that his need for information came mainly from his inability to stop wondering just who the kid really was, and if he was related to Neil or not, wasn't something he felt the need to share.

In his obsessive thoughts about Dr. Neil Green, Joshua had even gone so far as to wonder if Neil had once been a sperm donor.

While Neil had never seemed to express an interest in having children during the time he and Joshua had known each other, Joshua didn't think it was outside of the range of possibility that Neil's ego could have led him to donate his genetic material for the betterment of the future. Joshua couldn't even completely dismiss the idea that Neil would have willingly donated to a childless woman he admired. He'd been a very loving man to his friends.

And then there were the other thoughts—the ones that no amount of liberally applied logic or daylight could dispel, making Joshua conclude that he'd gone around the bend, and was, at the very least, not entirely sane. Those thoughts all boiled down to one thing: somehow Dr. Green *was* Neil. Not someone like Neil, not a relative to Neil, but actually Neil himself. It was ludicrous.

Joshua sat down at his desk, unlocked the middle drawer, and pulled out the file folder again. It contained the written proposal as drawn up by Dr. Neil Green, and it was, strangely, a rather amusing read. Dr. Green was seemingly incapable of not inserting parentheticals such as, "Translation of all those big words in the previous sentence: nanites repair brain damage, people get better, hooray! Life extended! Now they can party into even older age." Obviously, Brian Peters either had no control over the kid, or he hadn't seen the final draft sent in to the foundation.

"Joshua," his assistant, Rebecca, said from the doorway. Her new bob cut framed her middle-aged face. "You okay? You've been a little out of it lately."

Joshua looked up from Dr. Green's description of the anticipated dissolution of the nanites within the body, the most concerning and important part of the entire study to Joshua, and forced a smile. He took the time to notice how strong and tall Rebecca stood now, without even a hint of the limp she'd had before the nanites had completed their work on her curved spinal cord two years ago.

Despite what had happened to Lee, Joshua saw living proof in front of him (as well as within him, in his better-than-ever skin and health) of the importance of nanite technology. He wasn't entirely against the application of it; he simply demanded more rigor in the testing if he was going to fund it. The belated realization that certain genetic markers could predict the failure of nanite dissolution was something that could have been avoided, as far as Joshua was concerned, had scientists been more cautious from the beginning.

"Yeah," Joshua said. "I'm fine. Just tired."

Rebecca nodded. "I guess it's hard around this time of year, huh?"

Joshua cocked his head. "What do you mean?"

"Pete reminded me of it last night when I mentioned that you seemed down."

"I'm not following. Pete reminded you of what, exactly?"

"They both died in fall. Your partners: Neil and Lee, I mean. I guess that must make autumn seem… Well, it must be kind of hard every year."

Rebecca and Pete hadn't even known Neil, and yet, thanks in part to Lee, and how he'd insisted that no one forget, they'd noticed a connection that Joshua hadn't even seen until now. How had he not considered that Lee and Neil had both died in the fall? And it was autumn again now. Maybe that explained his unusual reaction to Dr. Green. Maybe both the long-ago trauma and the more recent one were playing with his mind.

Enormous relief flooded him at the thought that it was possible Dr. Green didn't look so much like Neil at all. Maybe it had all been a trick of Joshua's imagination brought on by a wave of unconsciously triggered grief. It tended to come and go. Joshua knew that from long experience.

His short-lived relief was crushed by a heavy thought: what if Neil Green wasn't his Neil after all?

Joshua hoped he kept the rollercoaster of emotions from his face. "I'm going to be okay, Rebecca. Thanks for checking on me. Why don't you go ahead and go home early. I'm closing up shop here, myself."

Rebecca smiled kindly, moved as though to leave, and then paused. "Oh, and by the way, there's some private stuff that came from that P.I. in Atlanta in your email. The flags on it notified my calendar that they were urgent. So, just a heads-up." She gave a little wave and then hurried off to take advantage of his suggestion that she go on home.

Joshua's throat went dry, and he waited until he heard Rebecca get her things to go, before ditching the file he'd been examining and accessing his email instead.

Pulling up the documents, Joshua skipped the accompanying write-up for the moment and moved on to the part that most immediately interested him. Adair had included three short videos of Dr. Green taken within the last fifteen hours, and Joshua opened those files with his heart in his throat. He didn't know what he hoped to see—part of him longed for the videos to put an end to his obvious insanity, and another part of him felt unbearable grief at the idea that he'd been delusional all along.

The first video showed Dr. Green in a small coffee shop, grimacing over a steaming mug, while a young man with dyed black hair chattered at him. "Basically, what I'm trying to explain, is that Iron Brian was part of the mythopoetic men's movement, and—"

Neil interrupted him. "You lost my interest at 'mythopoetic.'"

The kid didn't seem bothered and talked right on. "—that's sort of relevant, because it's rooted in Jungian psychology—"

"Jungian bullshit—" Dr. Green muttered.

"—and neopagan shamanism, which seems kind of quaint now, doesn't it?"

"If you say so," Dr. Green said, taking another sip of his coffee and frowning. "What is this crap?"

"The computers have been overheating the coffee all week."

"Hey," Dr. Green called toward the counter that Joshua could just barely make out in the background of the video. "I want my account credited! This isn't coffee—it's diesel fuel."

The black-haired kid snorted. "Oh my God, freak. He probably doesn't even know what diesel fuel is. Like, didn't they stop using that—"

"Six years ago, not last century. Idiots. Everyone."

"Grumble-grumble! You need some mythopoetical neoshamanism in your life, and you'd cheer right up." The kid sparkled at Dr. Green, who seemed oblivious to his charms, and then the kid sighed and rolled his eyes. "Maybe you also need a good—"

"I'll tell you what I need—" Dr. Green called over his shoulder again, "Credit my account, or I'll go over your head and make sure someone else gets the illustrious job of sitting on their ass and watching coffee machines spit out crude oil."

"You know, you're never going to make friends this way," the black-haired kid said, looking unperturbed. "Were you like this before? I mean, how did you get anyone to even fall in love with you back then?"

"I wasn't like this."

"Why not?"

"I wasn't so fucking angry."

"Ah." The kid tilted his head. "You're sure angry now. Do you want to tell me why?"

"No." Dr. Green grimaced. "Yes. This coffee. That's why I'm mad."

"Right. Okay." Dr. Green's friend shoved the black hair behind his ears and studied him. "I'm here if you want to talk."

Neil shrugged. "It won't fix anything."

"I know but...I do care. For some reason. I don't even know

why. Because you're a dick."

Neil smiled a little, and then said, "Tell me more about the neoshamanism crap."

"Why should I?"

"Because it's important to you, and I should stop being an asshole and listen."

"Aw, it's almost like you're learning to be human!" The friend reached out and mussed Dr. Green's hair.

"Believe me, I've got plenty of practice in that."

And the video ended.

Joshua bit his lip, any thought that he'd only imagined the resemblance to Neil had been dispelled. Dr. Green looked more like Neil than ever, complete with eye rolls and hand flourishes that made Joshua's stomach knot.

The second video was uncomfortable to watch. It was of Neil and a dark-haired woman, someone who looked a bit older than Joshua himself. But given the expense of the nanite creams, it was possible she was younger than Joshua and had never been able to afford the benefit of them. She and Neil sat on the bumper of her car, a newer model with autodrive from what Joshua could tell, so she couldn't have been in *terrible* financial shape.

"You have to let it go, Neil," the woman said, her eyes dark with sadness. Joshua wondered how Adair managed to get such good film without being spotted. He supposed that's why she got paid the big bucks. "It's time to move on. Find someone new. Like I did after Marshall died."

"Because that worked out so well for *you*," Dr. Green said.

The woman sighed. "Yes, Jim was a mistake. I was young and pregnant. I acted in desperation. But you're nothing like me. You'll make the right choice."

"Exactly, Mom." Dr. Green sighed. "I'm not like you."

He stood up and walked away from her, heading toward a

building that looked like some old-fashioned university student apartments. They reminded Joshua of the old dorms that MTSU had torn down a few years ago to replace with more up-to-date accommodations.

Dr. Green's mother didn't follow him, only buried her face in her hands. Joshua didn't know if she was crying or was just in despair.

The third video was the shortest of all. Dr. Green walked toward a campus building, a frown etched onto his face, and before opening the door, he rubbed his fingers over his eyes in a move so incredibly Neil-like that Joshua couldn't breathe. Dr. Green swallowed hard, shook himself, and said softly, "Damn it, Joshua. I'm losing my mind here." And then he opened the door to the building and went in.

Joshua watched the final clip three times. He licked his lips and said under his breath, "Me, too, Neil. Me, too."

Chapter Fifteen

JOSHUA SAT ON the bench outside of Barren River Resort staring at his phone.

According to the report Adair had sent, Neil Green had been born a few months after Neil Russell's death, on January 17, to one Alice Green Martin, girlfriend of the deceased Marshall Green, and wife to Jim Martin—though she later divorced the man when Neil was eight, almost nine. The report indicated that Dr. Green had been an odd child—neighbors and teachers were on record saying that he was 'eccentric,' 'tiresome,' and—the description Joshua found most unnerving for some reason—'like an angry, middle-aged man in a child's body.'

Dr. Green had graduated at the top of his college class at the young age of fifteen and immediately started a fast track through medical and engineering school at Emory, achieving his MD and PhD in record time. And while there were opportunities for which he was suited outside of academia, he was quoted in the school digi-paper as saying, "I'm difficult and strange. The people here are used to me. I can get what I want from my career by staying. Why leave?"

In the same article, the college reporter asked him about having time for a personal life, and Dr. Green had said, "Yeah, I don't do personal lives. I tried it a long time ago. It ended in a wreck." The reporter had managed to rather respectfully scoff at the idea that the boy-genius had ever had any romantic prospects, and he'd asked Dr.

Green, "A long time ago? When you were, what, twelve?" Dr. Green had declined to dignify that with a response. Joshua, however, didn't find it scoff-worthy at all. He'd found it chilling.

Adair's report also revealed that there was a rumor—not a big one, because Dr. Green was not someone targeted by a lot of gossip—that Dr. Green had a standing order in at all the local paper-book collectors for journals, articles, and books discussing reincarnation. That, too, had left Joshua sitting at his desk, staring into space, feeling as though his heart had been cut from his chest.

Could Neil have been reborn? Did Joshua even believe that was a possibility? And if it was possible—did Neil remember who he'd been, what he'd been to Joshua, and was that even something that could happen? Joshua didn't know anyone he could ask without sounding completely insane. His mother would be no help; she'd pat him, and call him 'baby,' and worry. Chris's eyes would get all concerned, and he'd suggest Joshua take more time away from work, and probably tell him it was just grief for Lee talking. Sam didn't need the burden of wondering if his big brother had lost his mind, either. Paul would suggest a therapist, and whether or not he *should* engage one, Joshua didn't intend to do so. Which left Joshua to his own counsel, alone on a bench near the place he'd last seen Neil Green.

Joshua didn't know where to start or what to do. But he couldn't do nothing. He couldn't just sit and wonder. He glanced toward the door to the hotel. There was a bar in there. He imagined the soothing, obliterating bite of alcohol in his throat. It could wash all the obsession away.

Joshua rubbed his forehead and cleared his throat.

"Hey there, partner." Chris's voice was cheerful. His long brown hair was braided, and he was dressed in a bright orange sweater with a fall pattern on the arms. He carried a steaming thermos, and he dropped onto the bench beside Joshua. "What's going on?"

Joshua smiled at his welcome company. He, at least, would be a distraction from the tempting fantasy of getting wasted. "You a cowboy now?"

"Nah, but you're my partner."

"In what?"

Chris's bright smile nearly blinded Joshua in the midst of his angst and gloom. "Friendship! Life!"

"Oh, of course."

Chris leaned closer. "Plus, we shared Neil once, remember. That's something we never talk about."

Joshua tried to smile, but the mention of Neil had hit him like a punch to the solar plexus, and he couldn't breathe. He hadn't heard Chris say Neil's name in years. He'd almost started to think Chris had forgotten him. But Chris wasn't one to cling to grief. He moved on from life's difficulties with determination.

"Speaking of Neil," Chris said, not seeming to notice how close to coming undone Joshua already was, or possibly thinking that indulging in memories of old times might cheer him up, "I saw this guy last week—right here on this bench, well, on *that* bench—" He motioned across the way. "And he looked exactly like Neil. Talked like him, too."

"You saw someone who looked like Neil here? On that bench?"

"Yeah, looking lost as all get out. I thought I was being ridiculous, but then when his mouth opened? Boom! All Neil—just pouring out. It was wild. And kind of creepy."

Joshua's heart thumped in his chest. "What did he say?"

"Oh, I don't know. He said he needed to get back home to Atlanta. I offered to have Declyn drive him to Nashville to catch a plane. He seemed weirded out by that suggestion." Chris laughed. "But then he was gone. Just disappeared into thin air like a ghost."

Joshua blinked. "While you were watching? He vanished right

in front of you?"

"Oh! Of course not! No! Don't be silly!" Chris laughed again. "No, I was over around that corner rounding up Declyn, and when I came back, the little booger was gone. Did I mention the guy was young? Like, I don't know—a teenager. Younger than Declyn. And such a smart mouth on him. I sure hope he has some brains to back that mouth up."

"Oh, believe me, he does," Joshua muttered.

Chris leaned closer, his hazel eyes sparking with interest. "What? You know him?"

"Kind of."

I know him, Joshua's mind insisted. *I know him like I know myself—less and less, and more and more.*

"Doesn't he look just like Neil?"

Joshua could only nod in agreement, not trusting his voice.

Chris drew close enough that his thigh pressed against Joshua's, and Joshua could smell the coffee on his breath. "It's bizarre, isn't it? Who is he?"

"A doctor—well, researcher. From Emory."

"Neil was a researcher." Chris frowned, like he was putting it together.

"Yeah."

"So how do you know this guy?"

"He applied for grant funding for nanite research. Like Neil."

Chris's eyes bugged out. "Okay. Seriously?"

"What do you mean?"

"I mean, the kid claimed not to know who Neil was when I asked him, but he was obviously holding something back. And I mean, *come on,* Joshua." Chris shoved a stray lock of hair behind his ear. It blew gently in the wind. "Look at him, you know? So, what's the real story? Is he related to Neil or what?"

"I—"

Chris didn't wait for an answer. "I'm trying to remember. Neil and I didn't talk about his family a lot. Hell, I did most of the talking. He just listened to me yammer on about all the guys I was screwing and sometimes he'd get up the nerve to hit on guys at the clubs. Or we'd watch baseball at his place and shout at the television together." Chris tapped his front teeth with his index finger. "Did Neil have a nephew? Or a brother? Or—never mind—I doubt he had a kid of his own. He'd have told me."

"You think?" Joshua asked.

"Yeah. I can't imagine he wouldn't have told me if he had a kid somewhere out there. That's a kind of big deal, isn't it? And, besides, Neil was *really* gay." Chris elbowed Joshua. "But you know that."

Joshua grimaced. He didn't know it nearly as intimately as everyone assumed, or as intimately as he'd have liked. "Yeah. But maybe he donated sperm?"

"Hmm. I could see Neil doing that. Is that what happened?"

"I don't know. Maybe. I…have no idea."

"But I thought you knew the guy from the bench. Can't you just ask him?"

Joshua shook his head. "'Fraid not."

He couldn't ask Neil Green anything. He could barely even think about calling him without shaking so hard that he had to hold on to something. He glanced toward the entrance to the resort, longing for the bar again.

"Why?"

"It would seem like a conflict of interest. For the grant funding." He never lied and now he'd done it twice in a week. But he wasn't going to tell Chris the truth either.

"Ah," Chris said, like that made sense. "I wish I'd gotten to talk with him longer. What was his name? He told me, but I forgot."

"Dr. Green."

"Right. That's it. He was scrawny, just like you know Neil would've been."

"I'm not sure Neil would have appreciated that description."

Chris grinned. "Probably not. Still, I haven't been able to stop thinking about Neil since I saw that kid. I miss him, Joshua. He's been gone a long time, but he gave me a safe place to go when I needed one. And I'll always be grateful for that."

Joshua swallowed hard. Could a person be brought back to life? In another body? In a body that was exactly like the one they'd been in before? He rubbed a hand over his face. "Yeah, me, too. He gave me a safe place, too."

Chris seemed to clue in to Joshua's grief at that moment, and he leaned closer, touching his arm. "Joshua, are you okay? I know you're probably still missing Lee. But it gets better. I promise. We both know that."

"I do miss Lee, Chris, and I know it will ease over time," Joshua said quietly, reminding him with his tone that he'd grieved hard for Neil for a long while, but had gone on to have a good life after that. "And it's not Lee. It's...." He trailed off. What could he say? That he'd become convinced that Dr. Green was Neil incarnated into a new body? Chris would call his mother, and she'd have them take him into the hospital for an involuntary commitment if he said that.

"It's what? You know you can talk to me, Joshua. I'm here for you."

Joshua forced a tight smile. "You know, Chris, I think this is something I have to deal with alone."

He frowned. "You're never alone, Joshua. You know that, right?"

Joshua patted his friend's hand and forced more brightness into his smile. "I know. Thanks."

That night, after tossing and turning for hours before finally falling to sleep, Joshua woke up sweating and sick to his stomach. He reached for the side of the bed Lee had slept on and grabbed the pillow, holding on tight.

In his dream, he'd been sitting on the bench outside Barren River, handwriting notes in a paper journal, when Neil sat down beside him.

"Oh my God! It's you!" Joshua said, just like always.

Neil looked the same, love and affection shone in his eyes, and a small smile tugged just on the corners of his lips, almost like it was involuntary.

Joshua embraced him, feeling Neil's sharp shoulder blades under his hands, the solid, wiry frame of him, and he was so full of joy that he almost couldn't stand it. He pulled back to tell Neil that he was so glad he was there. They could finally do all the things they were meant to do together. But instead of Neil, his Neil, he was holding the young Dr. Green, who stared at him with Neil's eyes. Joshua jolted with confusion.

"Recognition is governed, in part, by the fusiform gyrus," Dr. Green said.

"What?" Joshua asked.

"Joshua. Wake up. You know who I am."

"*What?*" Joshua asked again.

"Wake up," Dr. Green said. "This doesn't have to be a dream."

Wake up.

Chapter Sixteen

N EIL'S HANDS SHOOK as he left the meeting with Brian Peters. It was one thing to have to exist in this world without Joshua while knowing he was out there, alive and completely out of reach, but it was another to try to do it without the benefit of his work as a distraction. And, as of fifteen minutes prior, he was out on a forced sabbatical. Sure, it was only twelve days for now, but it was twelve days of pure hell as far as Neil was concerned.

The cherry on top was that it was *Joshua* who had gotten him into this situation.

Neil didn't wait to get back to the apartment before putting in a call to the Neil Russell Foundation. After haranguing someone named Rebecca, he was finally transferred to Joshua's cell, and as the sound of the ring hit his ear, he nearly doubled over, suddenly nauseous with nervous anticipation that almost blanked out his rage.

"Dr. Green?" Joshua's voice answered, sounding every bit as overcome as Neil felt. "Can I help you?"

"You sure as hell can," Neil said, his tongue feeling thick, and his head swirled with lightness and blue dots. "You can call off your investigations, Mr. Stouder."

"Excuse me?"

Neil tasted a surge of anxious bile in his throat. He didn't know what he was saying. Words just came out. He held on to the side of the bike rack he stood next to and listened to them tumble from his lips like a sickness.

"I know you don't support nanite projects since your husband died, but the collateral damage here is too much. I'm not going to let you screw me over in a grudge against nanites or against me. I'm ethical and honest. I do the best work there is in this field and taking me out of the game isn't going to result in better nanite outcomes. I need my job, Mr. Stouder. Not for money. Not for glory. And, believe it or not, not for my ego. I need it for my sanity. And if you had any clue at all why that is, you'd leave me to my work in peace. Are you listening, Mr. Stouder?"

"Yes. I hear you, Neil," Joshua said.

Neil's knees went weak, and his chest felt like it was being crushed in. "Then why? Why call Peters? Why ask him about my questionable hobbies and my activities? Which are, for the record, *no one's business*. Not yours. Not his. I didn't cause your husband's death. If people had listened to me from the beginning, it wouldn't have happened. But no! Who listens to a kid? No one."

"I do," Joshua said. "I'd have listened to you."

Neil's throat felt tight. "The hell you would have. And what could I have said? 'Mr. Stouder, believe me. I'm twelve. I know what I'm doing.'"

Joshua made a strange noise, and then Neil spouted off more. "Do you have any idea how important this work is to me? Do you know what it means when a massive donor calls a project head and basically implies with his questions that they might be interested in funding an immense nanite project, except for the pesky kid with a big mouth and weird hobbies?"

"Maybe you could try controlling your mouth, Neil," Joshua said, and his tone when he said Neil's name was full of meaning. "Or you could try telling me more. About yourself. About your hobby. Why do you read all those books on reincarnation? That's a strange topic for a scientist, don't you think? Or maybe you want to tell me where you came from. I mean, where you *really* came from." Joshua sounded almost panicked now, like he was on the verge of some sort of emotional freak-out himself.

Neil's dread ratcheted up in the face of it. Was this a trick? Would he say something that would incriminate his sanity and get him blacklisted from credible nanite research for life? "Are you…are you trying to sabotage my career?"

"No, of course not. I'm worried about you." Joshua sounded like he wanted to say something else, but had settled on the closest thing he could admit to.

Neil scoffed. "Worried? About *what*, exactly?"

"After I denied the funding, I felt concerned about your mental health. I worried that you might…hurt yourself."

"Hurt myself? Are you kidding me? I'm not going to go put a bullet in my brain because you aren't giving me money. I've had more reasons to off myself than that and made it through."

"Well, that's comforting," Joshua said in a tone that made it clear that it was not. Then he seemed to steady himself, and he came back sounding more professional and more in control. "Listen, as a potential donor to your project, I have every right to be concerned for your mental welfare."

"Oh, please. You're not donating, so let's call off this charade."

"I actually haven't decided yet."

"Why? You've made it more than clear that you despise my work, that you believe I'm a bad risk, even implying that—" Neil *was* freaking out now. He was lost without his work, and this was too much. Pushed off the project in hopes of wooing Joshua as a donor, and trapped in this young body in the wrong time and place. Fucking Derek at night would never wipe this clean. He could feel everything closing in around him. He was in the middle of the road again, Magic's leash just out of reach, with a truck barreling down on him.

Joshua interrupted his babbling. "Will you just shut up for a second? You run your mouth when you really should listen, okay?"

"Fine. Why are you considering funding a project that goes against everything you've believed in since your husband died? Everyone knows you've blamed nanites for his death. That you—"

"Shut up. For once in your short, privileged life...just shut up."

"Short and privileged. That's hysterical."

"Listen—" Joshua fell silent for a moment, clearly gathering his thoughts. Finally, when he spoke, he sounded like he was hedging on the truth. "You remind me of someone. I'd feel guilty if I didn't try to help you."

"I don't need your guilt, and I sure as hell don't need your—"

"What? You don't need my money? I'm pretty sure you do, actually."

Neil's heart raced hard, panic rushing through to own him, and, spontaneously, he disconnected the call. His legs trembled, his breath came in short, terrified pants.

He sat down on the sidewalk to stop himself from falling over. He'd been a fool to apply for that grant. He'd been an even bigger fool to meet with Joshua in person. But calling him now had been the biggest mistake of all. He wanted to find a hole and crawl inside it. He wanted to go home to Alice and bury his face in her lap and cry. He wanted to tear off his own skin and grow it back as the man he used to be. Hell, he'd wanted *that* his whole life.

Neil snorted. Maybe Joshua had good reason to worry about his sanity. Maybe everyone did.

He didn't know how long he sat there, but when the call came in from Brian Peters telling him that the Neil Russell Foundation was going to back the project, so long as Neil was in charge, and so long as Neil answered directly to Joshua himself, he found the strength to stand up and start walking back to the labs.

Neil didn't know if his overwrought nervous system had finally kicked in enough endorphins to override his emotional pain, but he felt as though every nerve and synapse was firing at once, leaving him with a single, atypical thought: "This is what the saints called ecstatic pain. Funny, because it's feels like hell."

Hope. He couldn't afford to have it. But it was there like a flare in his chest, burning hot and bright, promising phone calls with Joshua, promising pain, and maybe something more.

Chapter Seventeen

November 2032—Bowling Green, Kentucky

THE MORNING AIR was crisp in the lingering dawn, and Joshua adjusted his scarf before shoving his gloved hands deeper into his pockets. The cemetery was empty, as usual, but it seemed occupied in a different way by the low-lying fog that rose from the dewy grass.

Joshua hadn't visited in a while.

At first, he'd come almost every day, just to remind himself that Lee was buried there and not away on some business trip or an extended vacation that Joshua could hop on a plane and join him on. But after awhile he'd stopped. He remembered the day that he chose not to go anymore—alone in Earl G. Dumplin's, watching high schoolers jostle each other, ready to head out into their day filled with techno-babble that Joshua failed to understand. Just living their ordinary lives, in their ordinary ways.

Joshua had swallowed hard and understood that that would be every day from now. Every day would go on without Lee. No amount of going to the cemetery or talking to his gravestone would change that. After that moment, Joshua hadn't gone again for a long time, just like he'd eventually stopped talking to Neil. Life moved on, and whether or not it was fair, he was still in it, and so he had to move on, too.

But the dream about the bees had overwhelmed him again in the night, and after he'd gone back to sleep, he'd dreamed of Neil and Dr. Green again. He'd woken up sweaty, sick, and desperate, but he thought he finally knew what he had to do. First, though, he needed to talk to Lee, and so he stood by the completely ordinary grave with a completely ordinary gravestone, with his hands in his pockets and a terrified lump in his throat.

Lee Michael Fargo
B. December 5, 1984 D. November 28, 2030
Beloved Husband and Dearest Friend

He remembered the discussions he and Lee had had about death during the illness caused by the nanite damage.

"I don't want to be cremated," Lee had said, a dark look on his face. "It's not logical, but I was in a fire, and I survived it. I don't want to put my body in one again, even if I'm not really there to feel it."

Joshua had agreed easily. "Whatever you want." And worry pulled at him, not for the first time, over his decision to have Neil's body cremated. He'd done what he thought Neil would have wanted at the time, but there had been no way to know for sure.

In the end, Lee's body had been laid to rest in a plot that Lee had chosen himself, in the middle of Crescent Hill Cemetery, without an empty spot beside it.

"Because you should be cremated, babe," he'd said. "That's what you've always wanted, and that's what you should do. I know you love me. Whether your body's ashes are in the creek with Neil or buried in the ground next to me doesn't change that."

Joshua had changed his will after Lee's death to dictate that half of his ashes should be dumped into the creek on Stouder Farm close to where he'd poured Neil's remains, and the other half interred with Lee's grave. Laid to rest with both the men he'd loved.

Despite himself, and thinking of Dr. Green, Joshua wondered if he'd have to change his will yet again.

"So, look," Joshua said, his voice quavering with the puff of condensed heat that left his mouth, "I think I've gone and lost my mind. And it's safe to say it's your fault. If you were still here, I'm sure you'd keep me grounded and all of this wouldn't have happened. You'd laugh at me, and I'd accept that it was just a delusion."

Joshua's gut churned with the lie.

"Okay, so, maybe not. That's the thing, Lee. This is the most real thing I've felt since you died. It doesn't make sense, and I can't tell anyone, but he's my Neil. I know he is." Joshua blew out a slow breath, tightness inside him making it hard to speak. "I think he knows he is, too."

A blackbird cawed from a tree near the edge of the cemetery's boundaries, and Joshua looked up to the sky, seeing the rapid brightening from the east.

"I talk to him by phone every day. It's been three weeks now, and I can't go twenty-four hours without calling him. I get the shakes if I don't hear his voice—he sounds just like him. And ever since he's softened toward me, I can tell our conversations scare him, too."

Joshua remembered the day before, how his hands had trembled as he'd called Neil to 'check in' on the progress of the protocol development. Neil had already told him it would take a few weeks to design the specs so that everyone would be satisfied, and yet Joshua called daily with the excuse of making sure that things were going as planned.

"Yes, we're still on track," Neil had said as a greeting, his deep, gruff voice sounding annoyed and yet indulgent at the same time. "Yes, it's all in the same place as yesterday. Yes, I will not rest until I have everyone's signature. Yes, that's a lie, because I slept four whole hours last night. Anything else, Mr. Stouder?"

Joshua had chuckled softly, his stomach wrestling itself in excitement and nerves, just like every time he spoke to Dr. Green. His brain had tripped around looking for another reason to keep Neil on the phone, though. And just when it had seemed like Neil would disconnect the line if he didn't speak, Joshua asked desperately, "How's your mother?"

There'd been a small hesitation before Neil had said, "Fine. Why the small talk, Mr. Stouder? If you have something to say, just say it. I don't have time to pretend like you give a damn about my family."

"I give a damn," Joshua said, remembering Adair's video of the woman with her face in her hands. "I know you're an only child, and I'm keeping you busy. Just wondering if you've called your mother lately."

There was a snort from Neil, and Joshua could imagine the eye roll that accompanied it. "I'm trying to get a project off the ground so that the asshole providing the big bucks for it will get off my back. I've been a little preoccupied. But, for the record, I spoke with her this morning, and she's still alive and kicking, and for some strange reason happy that I am, too."

Joshua barely refrained from admitting that he was happy about that, as well, and that talking to Neil, hearing his achingly familiar voice, so long gone and yet suddenly right there in Joshua's ear again, made him believe impossible, ridiculous things.

"Now." Neil had sighed. "I have things to do. If you could leave me alone for ten minutes, I might actually accomplish some of them."

There was something in Neil's tone, though, that made Joshua think that he didn't really want Joshua to leave him alone, that he really wanted Joshua to find another reason to stay on the line, and Joshua sought frantically for one.

"Maybe I should come down and see what's happening for myself," Joshua had said. "After all, we're talking about a lot of money."

"No!" Neil had exclaimed, causing Joshua's head to rock back in surprise, and his warning flags to rise. "We've got it covered. Your input will just…mess everything up. You wouldn't even know what you're looking at. Either you trust me or you don't, Mr. Stouder. Make up your mind."

The panic in Dr. Green's voice had sewn through Joshua like a golden yanking thread, and he'd listened to the silence of the disconnected call for a few seconds before hopping into motion. Within minutes, he'd set up a schedule with the pilot to fly down to Atlanta the next day.

"So, here's the deal: I'm going down there. In two hours, I'll be on the plane," Joshua told Lee's gravestone. "It's unreal, I know, but I have to see him again. I have to know, Lee." Joshua hesitated, feeling like he was betraying Lee by saying it, but he needed to admit it all the same. "I've missed him so much, and I've wanted him every day since he died. If it's him…if somehow this is real, and it's really him, then I have to go be with him. I need him, Lee. I need him so much."

Joshua stared in amazement down at where his feet mashed the grass at the edge of Lee's grave and swallowed a lump in his throat. Crawling on his leather shoe, despite the onset of early winter, despite the frost and the morning cold, was a black-and-yellow bee. Joshua watched as it arched and thrust its stinger into the leather, delivering its message, before flying away to die alone. Joshua's eyes filled with tears, and he bowed his head.

"Thank you," Joshua whispered. "Thank you for understanding me."

NEIL POKED AT the lines of code, messing with the commands

again, trying to tweak the acceleration rate down a bit in order to lower the risk of damage to the cell membrane. He groaned and rubbed a hand over his face. He hadn't slept, but at least he'd been able to bury himself in the work enough to put aside the nervous excitement of the prior day's phone call with Joshua.

Neil didn't know how much more his adrenal system could take—each day was a jolt of fear, joy, nerves, love, and anger. He didn't even know how to sort through everything he felt when Joshua called, but he knew that he wished Joshua wouldn't call, and he knew that he'd suffer beyond his ability to endure if Joshua didn't.

The previous afternoon, during a fifteen-minute coffee break, he'd listened to Derek rattle on and on about a new poem that he was picking apart for another literature class, and he'd nodded at the right moments, keeping up the appearance of giving Derek any attention at all. He truly didn't give a damn about how well words hung together, or what they might mean if twisted in different directions, and if various lenses of wishful thinking and subjective analysis were applied. But he liked Derek and wanted to keep him as a friend, so he put up with the nonsense.

"Neil," Derek had said eventually, a hint of frustration in his voice. "Are you listening? I mean, I know you don't care, but are you at least absorbing my words?"

Neil had nodded, but the truth was he'd been obsessing over Joshua's threat to come check out the project in person. The thought of seeing Joshua again, shaking his hand, smelling his aftershave—it was too much. Neil couldn't even consider it without feeling so full of *everything* that he wanted to yell, strip his clothes off, and race around the campus naked and wild with primal energy he couldn't begin to contain. Joshua needed to stay away. Neil couldn't live through seeing him again, not unless he could have him for real. And he wasn't banking on that.

"Listen, Neil," Derek had said, "I don't know what's going on with you, but it's like you're not even here. I don't expect a lot from you, and I know we're not dating, but I care about you, and—you know what I mean?"

Neil hadn't been entirely sure, but he assumed that Derek meant he'd been a lousy friend lately. He'd gritted his teeth against the waves of stomach-tingling nausea that kept rushing through him every time he thought of Joshua's phone call and focused on Derek. "I wasn't listening. I'm sorry. It's the project. I can't stop thinking about it. But I'm listening now." He'd gestured with his hand for Derek to go ahead.

It hadn't even been a full minute before Neil had fallen into thoughts of Joshua again, and when he'd broken off to head back to his work at the lab, he'd noticed that Derek's eyes looked a little hurt. He hadn't apologized. He hadn't even known what to say. Derek should find a real boyfriend; he deserved that. Neil could learn to live without having someone to fuck.

Tired and hungry, Neil put aside his work and checked to make sure his phone was working properly. Joshua hadn't called yet, and it was getting late in the day. He'd usually phoned by now, completely destroying Neil's productivity until he'd had time to calm down, which was why he'd taken to spending a lot of nights in the lab.

There was still nothing. Neil checked all messages—text, email, and digi-center—and there was nothing from Joshua. He cursed himself for having told Joshua to leave him alone the day before, suddenly worried that Joshua would do just that. He'd meant it at the time, mainly because he'd been shot through with intense adrenaline and felt like he was going to burst out of his skin. Now, though, he thought he'd burst out of it if Joshua *didn't* call.

He considered calling Alice, but it would worry her if he called two days in a row. He considered calling Joshua—he'd never done that since the funding was approved, actually. He'd never had to. But it occurred to him that he had Joshua's number; he could invent a reason. He could say that he wanted to get Joshua's approval before moving forward with the decompression work, or, if he could figure out the code for the acceleration rate, he could claim that he was 'reporting back' to Joshua regarding that resolution.

He rubbed the bridge of his nose and shook his head hard, trying to get his mind back in the game, but it was no use.

Neil shut down all the applications and hung up his lab coat. There was always lunch at the apartment, and if he got there before Derek left for his afternoon class—or whatever it was he did at that time of the day—he could take some solace in Derek's ass, too.

It was weird, though. Since Joshua had started calling regularly, fucking Derek wasn't as good as it had been. Neil had started feeling a weird guilt about it, like he was betraying Joshua in some way. He forced himself to shake it off because it was ridiculous, and fucking was one of the few real pleasures of his life. And yet the orgasms didn't seem to pay attention to his justifications. His cock just spit out his spunk with less satisfaction than he'd ever known before. It was annoying.

Regardless, Neil was too tired, anxious, and hungry to get any more work done. He decided to head home. Maybe, if nothing else, he could manage to nap.

Chapter Eighteen

ATLANTA WAS BROAD and big compared to Scottsville, but with skinny little roads that people seemed to travel down recklessly with little concern for traffic rules. Joshua felt lucky to have escaped an untimely death as his rental autocar pulled into the parking lot in front of the student apartment building.

Adair had given him Neil Green's address on Emory University's campus. Joshua had decided to start there, despite a nagging part of him that insisted that it would be more appropriate to go to the building housing Neil's office and labs, or to at least phone ahead. But another part of Joshua was curious about how Neil lived and wanted to see something more intimate than he'd get from what was essentially Dr. Green's office space. And besides, if he called Neil first, then he'd miss the element of surprise and only see what Dr. Green wanted him to see. That wasn't what Joshua was after at all.

Joshua walked up the set of outside stairs, noting the apartment numbers as he went. He untucked his shirt, undoing a few buttons at the top, and wiped a hand over his forehead. It was hot in Atlanta, even though it was November. Almost eighty degrees. Joshua wished he'd worn a short-sleeve shirt instead of his usual business button-up, but he hadn't anticipated this kind of weather in the middle of autumn.

Besides, he'd wanted to appear...he wasn't sure. He'd told himself that he wanted to look professional, and that still held true, but he also wanted to remind himself of the power dynamic between them. With all of the outrageous thoughts Joshua had been having, the hopes, and the unreasonable speculation, Joshua felt like he could easily be overpowered if he wasn't careful to keep in mind that he was the older person and the one with the money. He repeated a mantra under his breath as he reached the top of the steps. *You hold all the cards.* He ignored how that felt like a lie.

Joshua stood in front of Neil's apartment and took a long breath of strangely muggy air, pulling it through his sinuses and trying to get a good grip. He reminded himself that no matter what this Neil said, no matter what he looked like, or what he did, he was just a kid, not a ghost. It seemed less true than ever, though, and he turned his back from the door, saying under his breath, "Come on, Joshua. Be tough. You can do this. Be strong."

The door opened, and he swung around, not really prepared to see Neil but expecting it all the same. Only, it wasn't Neil at all. It was a young guy about Neil's age with dark hair, a sleepy smile, and big bag of trash. The same guy from the video in the coffee shop.

"Oh, uh, hey," he said to Joshua, looking around outside the door like there might be someone else to explain who Joshua was and why he was there.

"Hi," Joshua began, sticking his hands in his pockets and looking past the guy into the apartment. "I'm looking for Neil?"

"Oh, Neil, yeah…um, he's at the lab. Didn't come home last night. Do you…I mean, can I help? Or do you wanna come back later?"

Joshua looked around, there had been rain earlier and steam came up in waves from the black asphalt in the parking lot below. "Could I maybe wait for him here? It's an awfully hot day to wait in my car." The kid looked apprehensive, so Joshua went on, "Or should I go to the lab? Meet up with him there?"

The guy stepped aside and pushed the bag of trash back into the apartment. He waved with a hand. "Naw, come on in. He'll be back soon, I bet. He'll be hungry, and they aren't allowed to keep food in the lab."

Joshua stepped in, looking around, as the guy continued to talk. "They've had some big breakthroughs lately," he was saying. "Neil's been staying all night at the lab a lot." The kid gestured to the room and said, "Make yourself comfortable. It's all clean, I promise. Neil makes me vacuum every day."

Despite the kid's insistence that the place was clean, it looked like a typical student abode. There were pizza boxes with the crusts still inside strewn about and some empty soda cans. The guy shoved a longish strand of dyed black hair out of his eyes and said, "So, want a Coke while you wait?"

Joshua smiled politely and asked for water instead.

"Sure, no problem. I'm Derek by the way." He turned to the kitchen—which did, Joshua had to admit, look pretty clean for a college kid's place.

Handing the drink over, Derek frowned. "So, I can't promise that Neil will be back. I mean, he should be, but...he's in and out. You should text him or call. I used to know his schedule pretty well, but he's been really busy lately. I don't see him as much."

"The best kind of roommate, right?" Joshua said, trying to relate, but he felt old standing in this apartment with a scrawny little kid gawking at him from underneath his stupid statement hair.

"Nah, I wish he was around more," Derek said. "He's cool in his own way. When he's not bitching me out for talking to his momma too much or freaking out about my messes."

Freaking out about my messes. Joshua remembered Neil's fastidious apartment, how diligent he'd been at cleaning up Magic's fur, and the way he'd stare skeptically at Paul's piles of dishes.

"Oh?" Joshua asked, thinking that he must not appear as weird as he felt, or else the kid would have kicked him out by now. "So, you like him, then?"

"Yeah, well…yeah," the kid said, his face turning slightly red as he looked away.

Joshua's eyebrows went up, and he had to close his mouth quickly. He had no idea why the relationship hadn't already occurred to him, but it hadn't. He'd thought Dr. Green was probably gay, but Joshua had admitted to himself that it might just be part of his delusion that he thought so. Now, though, he had a bit of proof—Dr. Green *was* gay. And living with this guy. Another student, someone his age. The same kid as in the video; yes, the one Joshua had written off as just being a friend, but now…now it was clear that there was something more here.

Joshua felt like he might be sick. Disappointment and fear roiled through him. He'd been so close. Could this guy actually be what kept him away from Neil? Or was Joshua just lost in delusion after all?

Joshua asked, "You're Dr. Green's boyfriend?"

"Oh, no." Derek blushed even harder, then, though. "Neil doesn't do boyfriends. A boyfriend is more than he has the time or inclination for. He's too busy, what with being the biggest genius to grace God's green earth in a few decades." The kid smiled. "I mean, he's got two of the profs' classes to teach and this new massive dream-come-true study to run. He's a busy guy."

Joshua swallowed and decided to take the plunge. "I don't mean to be nosy, but doesn't he research reincarnation, too? On the side?"

"Yeah." Derek started to frown a little, looking Joshua up and down. "How'd you hear about that? He's private about it." Derek paled. "Wait, you look an awful lot like… Who are you, anyway?"

"Joshua Stouder," Joshua said, putting out his hand. Derek's eyes went wide as he shook.

"Derek," he said. "Derek Matthews."

"Right, you said."

Derek's eyes were huge. "Wow. Okay, so...you're here. He actually met you." Derek looked like he might laugh, or cry. He looked exactly how Joshua felt. "Did he totally piss himself or what?"

Joshua's heart thumped in his chest, but he wanted more. He wanted something explicit. Proof. "I'm sorry. I'm not following."

"Oooh, so he didn't tell you. Of course he didn't. What am I thinking? I mean, what's he going to say?"

"What's he going to say?" Joshua repeated, dying to hear Derek's response, willing him to mention something about reincarnation, about a truck, about Magic, about Dr. Neil Russell, about how his outlandish delusion was true.

Derek stared at him, clearly caught in a place where he didn't know how to respond.

The key sounded in the lock, and Derek's eyes flashed strangely. He cleared his throat and said, "He's home. I'll just...um."

Neil came in, stopping dead in his tracks when he saw Joshua.

Joshua took in his piercing blue eyes, the length of his throat and prominent Adam's apple. He looked at the black jeans Neil was wearing and the black button-up shirt. He took in Dr. Green's curly hair that was exactly the same color as his Neil's had been, and Joshua crushed the urge to grab him, hold him close, and make it real.

Joshua's head spun.

Derek picked up the bag of trash. "Going to the Dumpster and then...for a run? And then over to Mary's to shower and, uh, stay?" He said it all like it was a question, like he was waiting to see if this was what Neil wanted him to do.

Neil nodded vaguely, his eyes not leaving Joshua's face. Derek had to push past him to make it out the door with the trash bag. He paused for a minute and looked between Joshua and Neil, his eyes welling with tears. But he only said, "So, uh, I'll see you tomorrow,

Neil. I'll just…stay with Mary tonight."

"Later," Neil said. His gaze hadn't left Joshua's face.

Neil had to move out of the doorway so that Derek could shut the door, and the motion seemed to wake him from his surprise. He looked thinner than Joshua remembered, and Joshua briefly wondered if he'd been eating enough.

"What are you doing here, Mr. Stouder? I thought we had an understanding—you either trust me, or you don't. Or is that the problem? Are you here to pull the plug on the whole thing? Or just to check up on me again?"

"I'm not. I'm…not sure why I'm here," Joshua said. How could he explain that he'd dreamed of bees every night, and that the bees had urged him to seek out Neil? Or that his long-dead lover had come to him in his sleep and turned into Dr. Green beneath his palms, in the middle of a kiss? How could he say what he suspected was true? "I came to see you," Joshua said lamely.

Dr. Green tensed and rubbed a hand over his eyes. "You must have a better reason than that. I know I'm a good-looking guy, Mr. Stouder, but not so good looking that you'd fly down here to stand in my living room and stare at me."

The comment was so Neil-like, so much older than the person who stood in front of him, that Joshua didn't know what to do with it.

"So, let's have it. If you're here to argue more with me about the compressing units, I've already told you, I have the protocol designed to shave off that snag, and even though hearing your voice rise in anger is kinda hot, I've barely had any sleep and don't think I can deal with trying to school you on advanced nanite engineering right now."

"Some people say that arguing is a kind of flirting," Joshua said, feeling as shocked as Dr. Green looked when the words came out of his mouth.

"Or foreplay," was Dr. Green's rejoinder, obviously uttered on instinct and the force of his personality.

They continued to stand and stare at each other for a few moments, a frisson in the air between them, until Dr. Green said, "So...what? You came down here to, uh, 'argue' with me some more about the compressing units because, what? You're that hard up?" His lips turned up in a small smirk. "If I recall correctly, you've always gone for a slightly older guy, Mr. Stouder. I'm not exactly your type." He gestured at his own body. "You're no chicken hawk."

Joshua took a sip of the water he'd nearly forgotten he was holding. It was refreshing, cool against his hot throat, so he took another while waiting for an explanation to come to him, some reason to explain why he was there that wasn't completely ridiculous.

"I keep dreaming about you," Joshua said. That was not the explanation he was searching for.

Dr. Green went very still, except for his fingers that seemed to tremble against his leg. "Gotta admit, didn't see that one coming," he said, his voice low and quiet, almost intimate.

"What? I caught the great Neil Green off guard?"

Dr. Green's eyes narrowed a bit, and his lips pressed into a nervous, familiar line that Joshua had seen on his Neil more than once, usually when they were discussing something that both thrilled and terrified him.

Dr. Green said, "I know it's a bit warmer than you're accustomed to at this time of year, but are you suffering from heat stroke, Mr. Stouder? I'm expecting Screamin' Jay Hawkins' 'I Put a Spell on You' to start playing any second now."

That song was already old when Joshua was a kid. He remembered Neil singing it one day, waggling his fingers around, and joking, "You've put a spell on me; it's sickening." Joshua felt a creeping, crawling sensation down his back, as he stared into Neil's blue eyes, sharp and exactly the same.

"Did you?" Joshua put the water down on the side table next to him and stuffed his hands into his pockets. "Did you put a spell on me?"

Dr. Green blew an annoyed raspberry. "What are you talking about? I'm a scientist, remember? Spells aren't based in science. And don't even start on those ridiculous spells cast by Wiccans or whatever they're calling themselves this generation, because—"

This generation. Joshua's hands were sweaty, and his legs felt weak. "I don't mean an actual spell, Neil," Joshua said. "I'm talking about nanites. You can program them to do anything. You've said so yourself. Did you program nanites to make me dream of you?"

He had been clinging to this last shred of semi-sanity—even it was a stretch, because how would Neil have introduced the nanites to his blood stream? How would they have bypassed the blood-brain barrier, when that was part of what Joshua's funding was going toward developing? But it was his only hope—otherwise, he'd either officially lost his mind, or Dr. Green really was Neil, and he couldn't deal with how much he wanted the latter to be true. He *needed* it to be true.

Dr. Green seemed to react to Joshua calling him by his first name. He grew a little more still, and he looked a little more fragile, less full of brass and balls. Joshua tried it again: "So, did you, Neil? Did you use nanites to make me dream those things?"

Joshua felt cold through and through thinking that Neil—no, Dr. Green would do that to him. "Did you mess with my mind that way? Are you trying to make me think I'm crazy? Was it some kind of payback—?"

"Mess with your mind? Nanites to make you dream about me? Even if that were possible, Mr. Stouder, why would I want to do that? Payback for not initially funding my project? That makes no sense."

"I don't know you." Joshua's stomach was tense and felt full of swarming bees that buzzed into his veins, setting him vibrating.

"Yes, you do," Neil said, with a certainty and intensity that was undeniable. "You know me. Look at me and tell me you don't know me."

Joshua felt dizzy. He was too hot, and he wiped at his forehead again. The room felt like it might be moving, and he felt Neil's hand on his elbow, steadying him.

"I don't know you," Joshua said again, fixed and slow, his tongue feeling thick with the lie.

Neil simply shook his head, and Joshua couldn't look away. His blue eyes were intense, piercing, and his expression angry and yet soft at the same time. He moved closer to Joshua, his hand going to Joshua's elbow, and Joshua shuddered when Neil tipped his head back to get a better look at Joshua's face and sidled up to him, seductive and incredibly present. Joshua felt young. So damn young. He hadn't felt this way in a long time. In nearly twenty years.

"I'd never hurt you. I'd never—even if the technology existed, which it doesn't—though, yes, it could. I could make it happen. But, it doesn't matter, I'd never use nanites to hurt you. As for the rest..." Neil spoke quietly, soothing and strong in his words. "I can't explain it to you. It doesn't make sense to me, either. How I came to be here, how I even know who I was before? It's been hell. But I'd never hurt you, Joshua. I've always wanted you to be happy."

Joshua felt the cry of denial rip from him. "I don't believe you!"

"Yeah, you do," Neil said, touching his face softly. Long fingers traced Joshua's cheekbone before cupping his face gently. "You don't want to, and I can't blame you. But you do. You know it's true."

Joshua wavered on his feet. He felt himself giving in, falling forward, it was like gravity and he couldn't stop it from happening. His eyes burned, and his lashes felt wet. He blinked and trembled. Neil's mouth was full of need, like he'd been waiting his whole life to kiss Joshua.

And just like that, Joshua knew that he had.

Chapter Nineteen

"WE SHOULDN'T BE doing this," Neil said, his mouth wet with Joshua's spit, his hands unbuttoning Joshua's shirt, seeking skin and contact and everything he'd ever wanted his whole life.

"Yeah, we shouldn't," Joshua said, diving in for another breathtaking kiss, his hands pulling at Neil's hair, his hard cock pressing into Neil's hip, and his breathing coming in desperate pants against Neil's lips. "It's nuts. I don't do this sort of thing."

"I know. I remember."

Joshua shuddered in his arms, burying his nose in Neil's neck, breathing there. "You smell the same. This is impossible. I'm insane."

"You're not insane."

"Even if all of this wasn't delusional, I'm…your donor," Joshua muttered, his mouth moving on Neil's neck with a sweet sensation.

"History repeats itself," Neil said, his mouth on Joshua's again. "Always with the excuses and delays."

"God, this is intense, Neil. Is it really you?"

"It's me. Wanted you forever," Neil babbled. "Wanted you since you opened the door in your towel back in Nashville. No, no, wanted you before that. Wanted you from the second or third time I laid eyes on you. By the mailbox. Getting your mail."

Joshua made a broken noise and dove for Neil's mouth again.

When Neil came up for air, he found he'd steered Joshua to his bedroom, the bed still unmade from the morning before. The towers of books, which he'd carefully stacked and sorted after his freak-out, shook as he slammed the door behind them.

"This is a bad idea," Neil said again, helping Joshua with the button on his jeans, noting that Joshua's hands were trembling. Neil pushed them aside, hushing Joshua's panic with a gentle, "Let me, let me."

Joshua's hands went to Neil's hair again, then under his T-shirt to push it over his head. He skimmed down his back in firm, wanting, grabbing strokes that Neil responded to eagerly with grabbing strokes of his own. He glided his hands down Joshua's chest, tugging on hair, and then tweaking Joshua's nipples.

"Don't wanna lose you," Neil muttered. "But you're here, can't turn you away, I'd be an idiot, and we know I'm not an idiot—"

"Except for that truck thing," Joshua whispered.

"Touché," Neil agreed, kissing Joshua's collarbone, tasting his skin, a floodgate of memory opening in him. "Do you remember your apartment? That ratty old sofa, and you tasted just like this. Your roommate came in, and I wanted to murder him, because you'd had your hand on my cock through my pants, and Christ, I *wanted* you. What was his name?" Neil asked, urgently, kicking his own jeans off and away, while helping to shove Joshua's down.

"Paul." Joshua moaned. "I can't believe it's really you." Joshua gazed at Neil with wide, shocked eyes. His mouth was open and red from their kisses. "How? Is this a dream? Really, Neil, honestly. Tell me—am I losing my mind?"

"I don't know—maybe. I ask myself that question all the time." Neil knelt at Joshua's feet, and ran his hand over Joshua's stomach. The chest hair thinned to a line under his navel that ran to the top of his underwear, and Neil licked his lips, wanting to get beneath them. "We can't do this," Neil said.

"We shouldn't. It's too fast," Joshua agreed, pushing his underwear down, his cock bouncing up looking achingly hard and rosy.

"Christ," Neil said again, pushing his own off, too, watching Joshua's eyes go impossibly wider at the sight of Neil's cock. "Hey, hey." Neil grabbed Joshua's hands. "This can stop any time. We can slow down."

Joshua nodded. "Yeah, slow down."

And then things went completely out of control.

Joshua grabbed handfuls of Neil's hair, guided him forward, and pressed his dick into his mouth. Joshua's cock tasted like heaven on Neil's tongue, and he sucked eagerly, desperately, before rising up again to push Joshua back onto the bed, kissing him, as they moved against each other in a frenzy of clutching, grabbing, and grinding. A swell of moans and whispers and cries rose in the room.

Neil clutched the condom in his hand, his fingers trembling as he rolled it on. "If we do this, there's no going back. I don't want you to regret it. Just tell me to stop."

"Please, Neil," Joshua said, his voice rough and vulnerable, his legs spread and his cock throbbing visibly against his stomach. Pre-come pearled on the head, and his thighs trembled.

Neil met Joshua's lust-filled gaze, eyelids heavy and mouth bruised with kisses. The hair on Joshua's chest didn't hide the flush of red up over his skin and up his neck. Joshua was open and begging for him. It was more than Neil had dreamed of his entire life, more than he thought he'd ever have. He couldn't stop now. He should. He should stop it before it all went to hell. Neil growled, grabbed his own cock roughly in one hand, and managed not to come.

Neil threw Joshua's legs up to his shoulders, lined up, paused, staring at Joshua's small, quickly lubed hole and the thick head of his big cock. He hesitated again. "This isn't how I wanted it. Not back then. Not now. Wanted it to make sense—for you to understand. This isn't how I wanted it."

"Me, either. But I'll take what I can get," Joshua said, reaching for Neil's ass and pulling him in.

Neil's eyes rolled up against his will—dammit, he wanted to see Joshua! He wanted to see it all! Joshua's asshole trembled and opened, stretching tight, so damn tight, around his cockhead.

Joshua's noise of shock brought Neil's focus back to his face, and he watched as Joshua's eyes and mouth scrunched with the effort to take Neil in. In that moment, Neil knew Joshua hadn't done this since his husband's death. The knowledge was unsurprising but intense all the same, and he breathed deeply to try to control his own urge to shove inside the only man he'd ever loved and wanted like life itself.

"Shh," Neil soothed, backing out all the way, only to have Joshua grab at his ass again and haul him forward with a deep grunt. Neil pushed against Joshua's hole and moaned as he sank into the hot, velvet grip of him. He kept his eyes on Joshua's face, watching in amazement as Joshua's eyes told him everything—the intensity of Joshua's emotions, the moment pain turned to pleasure, and the shock of the girth of Neil's cock putting pressure on Joshua's prostate.

"Oh my God," Joshua breathed, using his grip on Neil's hips to still him with his cock half-buried inside. "I've never...oh my God."

Neil held himself steady, bending low to kiss Joshua's collarbone, to tongue his nipples and press kisses to Joshua's heaving chest. He licked his soft chest hair and breathed in the sweetest scent he'd ever known—Joshua's skin. And then he moved, a shallow thrust. Joshua grabbed Neil's face, pulled him down, and the wet, slick slide of the kiss and the tight grip of Joshua's ass around his cock was *perfect*. Tears stung his eyes. Joy and a deep sense of rightness swept through him, followed immediately by nearly excruciating fear.

"This can't happen," Neil said, because he'd never thought he'd have Joshua. "We can't do this. You need time. I need to explain. You'll want to be sure."

And yet he was doing it. He was rolling his hips and fucking Joshua with intimate, intense, deep strokes, and Joshua was staring at him, mouth open, eyelashes fluttering with each thrust. Completely out-of-control noises issued from Joshua's throat, shocking noises of want, physical ecstasy, and desperation.

"So big," Joshua whimpered when Neil bottomed out inside him and then withdrew, a long, sweet pull from Joshua's clinging, tugging heat.

Neil meant to say that he could stop, that he'd pull out if it was too much, but he shushed Joshua and murmured, "You're doing great. You feel so good."

"Better than I ever knew," Joshua said in awe.

"Yes," Neil agreed. "So good." It didn't even begin to cover it. He felt like his heart would stop, or like it might beat out of his chest. He felt like his brain had stopped ruling his body, because by all rights he should be still clothed, they both should, and instead they were moving together, sweaty and entangled, emotions pouring from them in waves.

Joshua's legs scraped along Neil's sides, and he rocked up to meet Neil's thrusts, his ass convulsing around Neil's cock. His fingers twined into Neil's hair like he was never letting go.

"Can't take it," Joshua grunted, his body tensing and then shuddering under Neil. "Too much."

Neil tried to slow down, to pull his cock free, but Joshua squeezed him in tighter with strong thighs and moved his hands from Neil's hair to grip tightly at Neil's ass cheeks, keeping him inside, as his hole clenched on Neil's cock to hold him in place.

"Oh God," Joshua cried, and his head tossed on the pillow. "Is it really you? Tell me it's you, *Neil*."

"It's me," Neil agreed, staring down at Joshua's face, watching every expression as it moved across his features. A jumble of emotion and confusion, and underlying it all a vibrant joy that seemed to drive Joshua from within, as he strained beneath Neil, trembling all around him, and clinging to him with everything he had.

Neil kissed Joshua's wet lips, sucking on them as they fucked and pulsed together, scrambling at each other, gripping and sweating, until Neil noticed that a tear was running down the side of Joshua's temple. He touched it with his fingers, bringing the liquid, salty wet to his mouth and licking it.

"Hey, hey, you're okay," Neil said. "You're okay, Joshua. I've got you. I'm here."

Joshua's face crumpled as he hiccupped a soft sob, his legs wrapping around Neil's lower back to hold him inside his ass. His arms were all the way around Neil, strong and desperately pulling him so tight and close that Neil almost couldn't breathe. For a moment, he felt claustrophobic, and then he felt Joshua's pulse beating along the length of his cock, buried so deep inside Joshua's tight body, and the feeling disappeared. He was in Joshua, and he'd never wanted to be anywhere else.

"Don't leave me again," Joshua whispered, sounding shocked by his words, like he still couldn't tell if any of this was real. "I don't care if this is true. I just need you. I need you, Neil."

"It's true. It's true, Joshua. Shh, I'm not going anywhere." Neil thrust, feeling Joshua jolt under him as he fucked into him. "Feel me? You've got me. Feel me in you?"

"God, yes," Joshua gasped. "You're huge."

Neil kissed Joshua's eyebrows, his eyelashes damp with tears, and his mouth, before saying, "I've loved you for you twenty years, dammit. You're an idiot if you think I won't love you at least twenty more."

And then he fucked him without holding back, pounding into his ass as hard as he could, making Joshua cry out, and twist, and scream for more. When Neil wormed a hand between them to grip Joshua's cock in his palm, squeezing in rhythm with his unrelenting thrusts, Joshua's face contorted, and he sounded shocked and overwhelmed as he shot a thick, heavy load of come between them.

Joshua jerked and trembled, crying out as Neil didn't let up the thrusts, not until he felt the rush of orgasm in his own balls, and he buried himself as deeply as possible. Shaking and staring down at Joshua's wide brown eyes, he came so hard it was agonizing, his entire body lighting up with unbearable pleasure. He didn't know or care what Joshua heard or saw in that moment; giving over to the intensity of his orgasm was all he could manage. When he finally shuddered his way to the end of it, he'd collapsed on Joshua's chest, drooling as he jerked gently under Joshua's soothing, petting hands.

Carefully, after his breathing had settled and he could hear that Joshua's heart rate had slowed, too, Neil pulled out of Joshua's embrace, holding onto the base of the condom as he withdrew from Joshua's ass. Neil didn't look at Joshua's face, afraid of what he'd see there. Regret? Anger? Neil didn't know for sure. Having sex like this wasn't how Joshua operated—at least it never had been before. Neil was suddenly terrified that even though everything Joshua believed was absolutely true—he was Neil Russell, despite all logic and scientific explanation—somehow Neil would screw it up, and Joshua wouldn't believe him anymore, or, worse, after having lived so long without him, Joshua would find he didn't love him after all, much less *need him*, as he'd claimed mid-fuck.

As the head of Neil's cock popped past the tight ring of Joshua's anus, Joshua gasped. Neil glanced up to see if it was pain that had forced that noise from Joshua's throat. He met Joshua's eyes, and tears prickled at the sight of the soft, hopeful, slightly terrified adoration he saw there.

Quickly, he examined Joshua's hole—he'd been rough at the end—and found that it was gaping a little but was otherwise fine. It would be tight and tiny again within minutes, and yet Neil knew from Derek that gaping like that felt empty, and he didn't want that sensation for Joshua. So, he sucked on three of his fingers, and pushed them into Joshua's slick, hot ass, feeling the velvet softness of the inside of Joshua's body against the pads of his fingers. He'd pull them out one by one until Joshua wasn't hungry for them anymore.

Joshua sighed, and Neil slid up next to him, keeping his fingers inside, moving them in slow, pumping motions that seemed to soothe Joshua, who relaxed as Neil rested his head on Joshua's shoulder, gazing up at his face.

"Okay?" Neil asked.

"No," Joshua said, a freaked-out chuckle underscoring his word. "I just had sex for the first time since Lee died with someone I think is the reincarnation of a man I was in love with years ago. And I just had the most intense orgasm I've ever experienced. But you are my Neil, I know it, I can feel it—and I am really not okay."

"Me, either," Neil said.

"Yeah?"

"Yeah." Neil kissed Joshua's shoulder. "If you panic now, I don't know what I'll do. I'm a mess. I've been a mess since I saw you in Scottsville. It's been hard enough living without you all these years. If you freak, and leave, and I have to do this without you—oh God, listen to me. Or don't. Don't listen to me. I sound like a maniac."

Joshua's ass clenched on Neil's fingers as he let out a soft chuckle. "Look, considering I'm basically having the same thoughts, only replace 'freak and leave' with 'wake up to find myself in a mental hospital,' I'm a little relieved to hear I'm not alone in this."

Neil's heart thumped, and he said, "You're not alone."

Joshua snuggled in closer, and Neil found Joshua's prostate, moving his fingers over it automatically.

Joshua groaned and writhed. "Oh, God," he said, and Neil rubbed harder, watching in avid fascination as Joshua's face crumpled in reaction. He forgot all about taking his fingers out of Joshua's ass and instead poured more lube over Joshua's hole. As Joshua whimpered and said his name in an awed voice, Neil grabbed another condom and moved over Joshua, pushing back into his tight, throbbing slickness. He moaned as Joshua's ass seemed to grab at his cock and suck him in.

"Neil," Joshua breathed, his hips angling up to take the slow, gentle, rolling thrusts. "Don't stop."

"Couldn't stop if I wanted to," Neil said. "You're everything I knew you'd be. No—more."

They fucked slowly, kissing and whispering confessions.

"I never stopped loving you," Joshua said, his eyes full of vulnerability and an urgent need for Neil to know. "Do you believe me? Even when I was with... When I was married, I loved you. I was ashamed, but it was true. I dreamed about you." Joshua angled up for a kiss. "Tell me you believe me," he breathed against Neil's lips.

"I believe you," Neil said, but it didn't matter now. Lee was gone. Neil was here. And he had his cock so deep in Joshua that Joshua seemed shaken apart by the sensation of it. The past didn't matter to him. He'd never thought he'd have this, and now he did. Nothing else made any difference.

"Never stop," Joshua said as Neil thrust into him and then pulled mostly out again. "Never leave me."

Neil knew that he'd have to stop fucking Joshua at some point, if only to get some food and water, but he readily agreed to Joshua's demand. He rested his elbows on either side of Joshua's face, tangled his fingers in Joshua's short hair, and watched Joshua's face shift with each thrust against his prostate—surprise, pleasure, need. And as irrational as it was, Neil felt a stab of smug pride that his cock was apparently bigger than Lee's, apparently bigger than anyone Joshua had been with, because Joshua seemed continually awed by the size of it, breathing shallowly at times, and then whimpering about how good it felt, how intense the stretch.

Suddenly, mid-thrust, Joshua reached up and grabbed Neil's face in both hands, staring at him, "You look so young. Like a kid. But when I look at you, all I see is Neil."

"I'm old," Neil said. "Believe me. Older than you. Older than this body will ever be." Neil turned his head, kissed Joshua's fingers, and sucked one into this mouth, watching Joshua's eyes roll up a little. Then he guided Joshua's hand down his back, spreading his legs enough to give Joshua room. He dropped his head back with a groan as the tip of Joshua's finger pierced his tight hole. So good— so right—a circuit between them. In and out, and in again, Joshua moved his finger, as Neil thrust his cock into Joshua.

Neil sucked at Joshua's sweaty neck, and listened to Joshua's sounds—noisy and desperate, grunts, whimpers, words of love and amazement. Each of them ricocheted within him with an answering lust. He'd known Joshua would be vocal in bed. He'd been right.

"Can I fuck you?" Joshua asked, and looked shocked by his question.

Neil swallowed. He barely remembered ever being fucked—a few times in his previous life, but never in this one—and he realized that he wanted Joshua to do it. He wanted Joshua to be the first. "If you want that," Neil said, feeling the strength of Joshua's limbs, wondering if he'd have the urge to fight Joshua off when he was penetrated as he remembered he had with the one man he'd let do it in the past. The only way to know was to see.

"Now?" Joshua asked.

Neil groaned, forced himself to pull free of Joshua's body, and then passed a condom to Joshua, watching him slide it on. Neil prepared his own ass with a couple of fingers, some lube, and a few good twists. Joshua's cock was hard and Neil wanted to feel that hard length press inside of him, take him in a way he hadn't been taken in this lifetime. It would be the physical manifestation of just how owned he was by Joshua, and had been for his entire life.

Joshua's chest heaved as he held his cock steady, and Neil realized that he'd been so involved in fucking Joshua, *feeling* him, that he hadn't had a good look at his body—his toned abs, his tight nipples, and still-youthful build. Nanites had kept Joshua young, and while Neil was pretty sure he'd have felt this intense attraction and need for Joshua no matter how old he'd become in the time it took Neil to grow up again, the additional life-span overwhelmed Neil with a sense of gratitude and desperate joy in his work. Nanites would keep Joshua with him until Neil was able to let him go.

Neil straddled Joshua's hips, gripped Joshua's shoulders, and stared into his eyes as he pushed against Joshua's cock. His asshole stretched and burned, and then clamped down. He cried out, freezing in place, his body rebelling against the intrusion. Joshua's hands moved on his lower back, soothing, rubbing.

With trembling thighs, Neil tried once more. His cock jerked and spurted a shot of pre-come as the delicious sensation of Joshua's cock filling his ass rocked through him.

JOSHUA FELT PULLED in every direction. His ass ached with an empty, thudding need for Neil's cock, and his own dick was enveloped in the tightest, hottest, slickest clench he'd ever known. His heart felt on the verge of exploding with joy, lust, and ecstatic disbelief that bordered on mania. He couldn't stop marveling at the young, scrawny, commanding kid riding him. Neil was so self-assured that he'd taken full control, swiveling his hips and holding Joshua steady with surprisingly strong hands as he powered them both toward orgasm again.

And yet, despite Neil's unlined face and underdeveloped body, there was no doubt in Joshua's mind that the kid was Neil. *His* Neil, returned to him by the sheer force of Neil's will. It was the only explanation that Joshua could understand.

Joshua didn't know if it was lust, or the shock of it all, but it took him several long, violently good minutes of being ridden like he was a mechanical bull before it occurred to Joshua that there was something about the determined set of Neil's mouth, and the way his body moved almost desperately, that said Neil had probably never done this before—at least not in this life. Joshua put his hands on Neil's slim hips and forced him to slow down, bringing his knees up to cradle Neil from behind, and hold him more firmly still.

"Hey, hey, take it slow," Joshua said.

Neil's eyes sparked with pride and a bit of determined anger. "Don't treat me like a virgin, Joshua. I've got it. I can handle it."

"Don't hurt yourself."

Neil snorted. "Hate to break it to you—you feel great—but you're not *so* big that my flexible orifice can't take you on."

Joshua ran a hand slowly up Neil's chest, tweaking his small nipples, before gripping him around the back of the neck and pulling him down for a kiss. "You've proven that," he said against Neil's lips, suddenly understanding Neil's vulnerability, his need to show Joshua that he was worth the twenty-year wait. He almost laughed, but he kissed him slowly and lazily instead. "Slow it down. I waited for this—for you—and I want to feel you from the inside for a long time. If you keep riding me like that, I'll come in seconds."

Neil's eyes flashed, and he whispered, "*You* waited? I had to grow up again. It's been agony."

But it got deliriously good after that, with Joshua grinding into Neil's body as they kissed. He whispered in shocked amazement that this was real, this was happening. Neil made small, urgent noises with each thrust, and Joshua wrapped his arms more firmly around him, using his larger frame to roll them so that he was on top of Neil.

Neil's eyes were blown wide, and his lips were wet and trembling as Joshua gazed down at him, watching his face change with every pump of Joshua's hips.

"Christ, Joshua," Neil whimpered.

Joshua gripped his hands, holding them above Neil's head, and rocked harder and faster into his delicious, hot, tight ass. The sweet pull drove him wild. Joshua kissed Neil, trembling as their tongues met, and they tangled together—Neil's thin arms and legs wrapped urgently around Joshua's body, his heels banging against Joshua's ass cheeks. His tongue and lips twisting with Joshua's, as Joshua's cock slammed into his ass, and Joshua's stomach rubbed against Neil's hard cock.

Suddenly, Neil lurched, and with surprising strength in his limbs, he pushed Joshua over, and rode him again for several long moments, before pulling off Joshua's cock. Joshua groaned, but Neil kissed him quiet, as he rolled another condom onto himself, and then shoved Joshua's legs up.

"Gotta get in you again," he said, as he pushed into Joshua's ass, his head flinging back and his scrawny, long-limbed body flexing all over as he pumped and fucked Joshua with abandon.

Joshua's cock still wore the condom, and Neil shocked him by occasionally pulling out and then climbing up and sliding down on Joshua's cock to ride for a few minutes. Then he'd climb between Joshua's legs to lose control fucking him again. Both of them clawed at the sheets, clawed at each other, and when Neil finally yelled and came hard, he bit down on Joshua's shoulder, leaving a mark that he lathed with his tongue as he jerked Joshua off several shaky minutes later.

"We should talk," Neil said breathlessly. "You'll want to talk."

Joshua nodded mutely, but neither of them said anything, staring at each other, touching, and kissing. It wasn't more than a few minutes before Joshua, shivering as Neil licked his nipples while putting on a fresh condom, moaned in disbelief as Neil pressed inside *again*. Neil's hard cock throbbed like a pulse in Joshua's tender ass.

But Neil barely moved, settling in on top of Joshua, kissing his mouth, whispering in his ear words that Joshua believed despite the absurdity of them, and when Neil said what Joshua had waited twenty years to hear—*I love you, I'll never go away again*—Joshua almost started crying, until Neil noticed and fucked that urge away.

Chapter Twenty

I F NEIL HAD been asked how it would go if he and Joshua ever did manage to come together during this lifetime, he would've first said that was an impossible dream. But if it wasn't impossible for some reason, then it would be a long, arduous process of explaining everything he knew about reincarnation, telling Joshua everything he remembered from his prior life, and eventually winning Joshua's trust and belief.

He had never been so glad to be wrong. Even if everything seemed precarious and delicate, he could see in Joshua's eyes that there was no regret—at least not yet. Also, they couldn't seem to stay clothed at all. An hour earlier, Neil had finally rolled out of bed, insisting that he needed to call in to cancel work on the project at least for the rest of the day, arrange for a substitute to teach his professor's evening classes, and, at the very least, check his email. Instead, he'd barely gotten to his feet before Joshua was sucking his cock, and then Neil had shoved Joshua back onto the bed overcome with the need to press into Joshua's body again in every way that he could.

"I love you," Joshua said now, still panting, kissing Neil's neck and ear. "I do. I love you."

Neil smiled, his cock pulling out of Joshua's ass as Joshua rolled over onto his back. Neil rested his elbows on either side of Joshua's head and ran his hands over Joshua's hair, threading his fingers through it and tugging softly. Joshua grinned up at him.

"That's a little sudden, don't you think, Mr. Stouder? Last time, I recall you needed...*time*. Lots and lots of time. Don't rush things on my account. Though, given *this*"—Neil gestured to their naked, come-covered bodies—"I guess it's a little late to say we're going to take it slow."

Joshua's eyes shaded darker. "When I lost you, I figured out that taking things slow is pretty stupid."

Neil ran his thumb over Joshua's lips.

Joshua took hold of his hand and moved it away, squeezing. "I didn't do things slow for a long time after that. I worked as hard and as fast as I could, and when I met Lee...."

That brought all kinds of weird feelings to the surface. Neil didn't want to seem jealous. He wanted to be gracious, accepting, but some part of him still wanted Joshua to have always been his, even if that wasn't right and wasn't fair. He didn't want to be that guy, though, so he prompted, "When you met Lee...?"

"Well, when we started dating, anyway...I didn't wait very long. A few days." Joshua sounded guilty.

"Good," Neil said, and it was easy, because seeing Joshua look ashamed, like he'd done something wrong or like he was afraid Neil would be angry over his choice to be happy made him want to wipe that fear away. "Sparing a man the blue balls I suffered could only be a kindness."

Apparently, that was the wrong thing to say, though, because Joshua looked devastated.

"Hey, what? I was joking. Why do you look...?" Neil waved at Joshua's face, and he felt his own expression bending into the newly familiar shape of panic. "Don't do that. Whatever you're doing—don't."

Joshua shook his head, and his eyelids fluttered a little, and Neil was horrified when a tear slid down one side of Joshua's face.

"No," Neil whispered. "That's not...."

Joshua put a finger to Neil's lips. "I'm not the same Joshua, you know?"

Neil shook his head, a sudden fear ripping through him. What if he'd mucked it up already? "I don't care," he said. "I just want *you.*" It would sound ridiculous to him in any other situation, but the extenuating circumstances imbued his next statement with undeniable truth. "I've only ever wanted *you.*"

Joshua looked horribly sad, and Neil felt like everything that had been so easy, so right just moments ago might crumble. He didn't know if he should scramble to salvage it, or freeze and hope nothing else happened to make it truly fall apart.

"There's been too much time between then and now," Joshua said. "Too much has happened to both of us to not take it seriously, Neil."

"I know. It's...it's what I do when...I don't know what else to do."

Joshua nodded. "It is."

"I love you," Neil said. "I've always loved you. And I'll love you...." He trailed off and swallowed hard. Joshua's hand came up and brushed against the side of his face before moving into his hair. "I can't ever stop loving you. I tried. It didn't work."

Joshua's expression went impossibly softer, and he pulled Neil down for another kiss.

Neil was urgent in his relief. He'd felt like there was a moment when it had crossed Joshua's mind that this, what they had now, might not work. That maybe too much had happened, too much had changed. And those were fears Neil *could not let cross Joshua's mind ever again*, not even for a minute, because the idea of going back to a life without Joshua's physical presence in it was entirely unfathomable now.

When he grabbed another condom from the roll on the bedside table, Joshua moaned a little and said, "Neil, I'm too sore. I don't think I can."

Neil kissed his mouth as he pressed the condom into Joshua's hand. He felt Joshua's response under him, shaking with anticipation as understanding dawned. Neil didn't have many regrets about fucking Derek for two years, mainly because it had refreshed his memory of sex and how to make it good, but right at the moment he regretted that he couldn't in good conscience let Joshua screw him without a condom. He was almost certain he was free of STDs, but he couldn't risk it.

Joshua whispered, "Let me get you ready."

Neil nodded and let Joshua rise up to flip him over, surrendering to Joshua, giving himself over, and he hoped that Joshua would understand. He loved him. He didn't know what else to do.

Another hour later, Neil passed a plate with a PB&J sandwich on it over the kitchen table to Joshua. He thought Joshua had gotten his message loud and clear, because there hadn't been even the smallest hint of doubt on Joshua's face since that slow, passionate joining. Neil closed his eyes, remembering vividly how the pressure of Joshua's cock against his prostate had made him feel like he had to have a hand on his cock or he'd die, and the way he'd jerked himself off frantically as Joshua had fucked into him, taking his time. Joshua hadn't been able to come again, but he'd kissed Neil with so much tenderness and love that Neil had nearly lost it, still feeling vulnerable and open from being fucked, and from his fourth orgasm of the day.

They still hadn't talked about what they were doing, what happened next, or anything like that. Neil wasn't sure when they would, but he knew the subject had to be broached. The sooner, the better. They were both busy men and had people who relied on them. They couldn't live in this in-between world of discovering each other for long.

Neil sat down gingerly on the opposite side of the small table and took a bite out of his sandwich, ravenous.

Joshua smiled at him. "Still have terrible table manners, huh?"

"What are you talking about? I'm the epitome of politeness."

"Right." Joshua cleared his throat and took a sip of water. "So…I guess we should talk."

Neil nodded, taking another bite of sandwich. He spoke around the wad of peanut butter and bread, "Sure. But let me warn you—I don't have a clue, either. I mean, I was born this way. That's all I know." Neil shook his head, feeling frustrated that he didn't have more to offer Joshua than that.

"Who knows about this? Aside from me—and Derek," Joshua's voice held a strange note, and Neil looked up, curious.

"My mother. That's it."

"Your mother. Of course." Joshua nodded, but his eyes were off to the side. "You must have a lot of faith in him—Derek—to tell him something this strange." Joshua's tone was one of forced casualness, and Neil blinked.

"He's my friend. Probably the only friend I've ever had. This time around, anyway," Neil said. "But that's all he is."

"A friend," Joshua said, taking a bite of his sandwich and looking around the apartment. "And that's it?"

Neil felt a flutter of anxiety in his chest. He frowned and said, "You only just showed up on the scene today. I didn't expect you here today, much less naked in my bed, so…yes. I messed around with my roommate." His voice pitched up nervously, betraying him. "Is that going to be a big problem?"

"Neil, I just…I need to know—"

"You're the only one I want," Neil said in a rush. He wasn't about to play coy now. That would be ridiculous. "He's my friend, but if it's between you and him, or hell, you and anything in the world, I'll take you. Every time. I've waited my whole life to be with you. I've wanted you forever. I can't be more clear, Joshua."

Joshua looked shell-shocked again, and then he leaned forward and said, "I need to know everything. Start at the beginning."

"Well, it all started out with the Big Bang, and after a few hundred thousand years, galaxies started to form—"

"Neil."

"Honestly, that about sums up what I know. It's all so much mumbo jumbo." Neil smiled and felt a bubble of laughter in his throat, and he was relieved to see it echoed in Joshua's expression. "But, okay, give me a starting place. What do you want to know?"

"Did you always know?"

"Yes."

Joshua's eyebrows went up. "Really? Always?"

"Always. My first memory from this life is from before I could walk. I was angry—enraged—wanting you, knowing how scared you must be, and wanting to get back to you."

"Oh my God." Joshua's voice was quiet.

"Yeah. Tell me about it. Alice—my mother—she had it pretty rough dealing with me growing up. I wasn't normal. She put up with a lot."

"I'm sure she loves you."

Neil shrugged and was surprised when Joshua reached out and took hold of his hand where it rested on the table. Neil relaxed a little, letting his lips turn up at the edges. "She does. Surprisingly. I sometimes even think she likes me."

"Of course she likes you, Neil. She's your mother."

"But I'm not her son," Neil said seriously, voicing a thought he'd never shared before. "I've always been me, Joshua. And she had no part in who I am. I don't look like her. I don't think like her. There's nothing in me that she influenced."

"That's not true. You don't live with someone for twenty years and not take in some of who they are," Joshua said. "I'm different because of Lee. I'm stronger, and more peaceful. I know I'm worthy of being loved—and of being loved really well."

Neil's stomach twisted. He wanted that for Joshua, and he could see that it was true. Yet he'd wanted to be the man who taught him that. Instead, the job had fallen to someone else.

"Good," Neil said, keeping it simple, thinking that Alice would be proud of the control he was exerting over his mouth.

"So, she taught you something."

"How to make the best of a sorry situation," Neil said.

Joshua let out a puff of annoyed breath.

"If you're expecting rainbows and puppy dogs from me, you'll be disappointed," Neil said. "My mom ate Ramen Noodles to send me to a private school for bratty geniuses and never got the thanks she deserved. Being my mom didn't pay dividends. Not in happiness and not in affection from me. I do my best, but it's not something I'm good at."

Joshua narrowed his eyes. "You seem plenty good at it to me."

"That's sex, Joshua. It's different."

Joshua rolled his eyes and sighed.

"I don't hug and kiss on her. She's a physically affectionate woman, and she never got what she needed from me. I'm hoping she'll meet a man. She deserves that kind of happiness."

"I remember physical affection from you," Joshua said, looking uncomfortable. "From the you before."

Neil shrugged. "I can't help touching you. You're some kind of magnet for everything weak in me."

Joshua covered his face and took deep breaths. "Oh my God, oh my God, oh my God."

"If you freak out, I'm going to freak out," Neil said, his voice going high and choppy.

"I think we can both freak out. I think that's okay. I think we're allowed."

"Okay. You go first."

Joshua looked up at that and started to laugh, a delirious, crazed sound.

"What?"

"Is that how it works? We take turns?"

"I think so. I mean, you'd know better than I would. You did that relationship thing for a long time. I've screwed my roommate for two years, and had some regular fuck buddies in my prior life that I might have passed off as relationships but really weren't, so I think you probably have a leg up on me here. But I'm a fast learner, and I don't think you'll find it a problem. This is sink or swim, and I'll swim. I'll swim the Atlantic Ocean if that's what it takes. The Pacific! And you can count on that."

"You are so freaking out," Joshua said, his laughter still hiccupping in a panicky way in his throat.

"I am. Yes."

"I think I should get to go first. You've had twenty years to get used to the idea that you're reincarnated. I've had a few weeks if we count the time when I just thought you *might* be my Neil."

"Okay, then. Have at it."

They stared at each other over the table, and Neil's heart thudded in his chest waiting for *something big*. And then Joshua picked up his sandwich and started eating.

"What?" Neil asked.

"You go first. It's kind of entertaining."

Neil blinked, shook out his hands, rotated his shoulders, and turned back to his own sandwich. "I'm too hungry now. Maybe later."

Joshua nodded, grinning with a crinkle in his nose. "Yeah, maybe later."

Neil felt a warmth in his chest, a rush of unfurling love that shook him deeply, and he reached out to grab Joshua's hand. And they sat and the table and ate like that, fingers entwined.

MORNING LIGHT PEEKED through the blinds in the window of Neil's room. Joshua rubbed his hand up and down Neil's sweaty back, feeling the knobs of his spine, and the sweet dip where his tailbone led down into the crack of his ass. He fingered Neil's hole gently, pressing inside, and then pulling out to rub the pad of his finger against the puckered edge, and then pushed back in again.

"Mmph," Neil said into his pillow.

Joshua murmured some kind of nonsense in response, in a daze from multiple rounds of sex. He didn't know the last time he'd been this fucked out. Probably the early years of his relationship with Lee. No, not even then. They hadn't had the stamina.

Joshua kissed Neil's freckled shoulder and gazed at the chestnut hair that curled with sweat at the nape of Neil's long neck. He wanted to bite along the side of it, lick into Neil's ear, and push his cock in again, but he just couldn't get his body to agree with him. His dick was limp and still twitching against his thigh.

Joshua jumped when the door to the bedroom jerked open. Derek barged in clutching a bag of takeout from the OK Café. Shock broke over his face as he took in the scene.

Neil yelped and rolled over fast, knocking Joshua off of him. He was surprisingly strong for being so wiry. Standing up, naked as the day is long, he barked, "What the hell?"

Derek's eyes flew between Neil's nakedness and Joshua under the covers, and then he dropped the bag on the carpet and shut the door.

Neil rubbed a hand over his face and cursed under his breath.

"Is he upset?" Joshua asked, getting out of bed and finding his underwear. Though it was a rhetorical question. Obviously Derek was upset.

"Hell if I know," Neil said, though he obviously knew, too.

As Joshua dressed, he watched Neil process the situation. For once, Joshua felt a weird disconnect. Whenever Joshua looked at Neil, all of Neil's knowledge and experience over the last two lifetimes seemed to overlie his features, making Joshua see him as much older than his body claimed. But at that moment, naked and worried, he looked every bit of twenty.

Joshua pressed a pair of underwear and some black jeans into Neil's arms. "I know he's not your boyfriend, but you had something going on with him. I'm sure he feels hurt."

Neil cursed again softly and shook his head, like he was trying to change or deny the situation with that movement alone.

"You should talk to him," Joshua said. "And I should probably go back to my hotel."

He'd checked in the day before after his plane landed, and he'd left his bags in the room, but he hadn't made it back. He probably had messages waiting for him on his phone, and work issues to deal with, too. He definitely needed clean clothes.

Neil dropped the clothes on the bed, and hauled Joshua in close. He jolted at the sight of pure fear in Neil's eyes. "Don't go. Don't leave me."

"Hey, it's okay," Joshua soothed. "I'm just trying to...."

Just trying to what? He didn't know. He was covered in come and he was unbelievably exhausted, physically sated, but he was still hungry for more of Neil. He was also terrified that this was some kind of dream, or something more sinister than that. Yet he also knew that if this was real life, then there were things to be handled—phone calls he and Neil needed to make, people who relied on them to make decisions, sign paperwork, and help them do their jobs. Some kind of sanity had to be patched together out of this madness. And the outside world was already intruding on them now. It couldn't wait.

"You're going." Neil's skin went so pale that freckles Joshua didn't realize he had stood out.

Joshua covered his face with his hands. He needed to get his head around this.

Neil pulled Joshua's hands away, ducking to get a look at Joshua's face.

Joshua smiled softly, putting on his 'big boy' pants, and doing the right thing. "I'm just going to my hotel." He put his hands on Neil's shoulders, gazed into his eyes, and went on. "You're going to talk to Derek. And then you're going to make the calls you need to make."

Neil swallowed and nodded.

Joshua kissed his mouth, pulled back. He ran his hand through Neil's soft, curly hair again. He was afraid to leave, too. But he supposed he had to test it. He had to rip the Band-Aid off. They had responsibilities, and they couldn't stay in Neil's bed forever.

"All right?"

Neil nodded again, before glancing toward the door. They could hear loud, aggressive music coming from Derek's room.

"I never led him on," Neil said.

"I'm sure you didn't," Joshua said. "You've always been honorable. Even before."

Neil's eyes went up to the ceiling like he was trying hard not to freak out, and then he nodded and stepped back from Joshua. "All right. We'll do this your way."

"You think?"

Neil nodded again. "Yep. You've got more experience at it than I do, so okay. You can be in charge of this part of...this."

Joshua watched as Neil pulled on his pair of black jeans and grabbed a clean, black T-shirt from his drawer. They should shower. He knew they should. But if they did, then Joshua had no doubt they wouldn't make it away from each other. He had to leave now if he was going to go. Neil seemed to understand.

Music blared from Derek's room as Neil walked Joshua to the door. They lingered there for a minute, and Joshua stroked his fingers down Neil's determined face. It struck him as ridiculously cute that Neil had to steel himself almost as much as Joshua did for this, and yet seeing that made him go deeply and suddenly calm, too.

Neil put his hand on Joshua's cheek, too. "If I don't see you again, I'll understand. You shouldn't worry about me. I love you."

Joshua didn't know why his reaction to that miserable statement was to laugh softly, but he did. He pressed his cheek into Neil's hand and cupped Neil's neck with his own. "Neil, you're ridiculous."

Neil's lips curved a little.

Joshua kissed him, and Neil held onto Joshua's face, a hint of desperation in his grip. Joshua understood. He couldn't believe he was going to walk out the door. He took another look at Neil. "Do what you have to do, because if this is going to work, we have to face reality. And I want it to work, Neil."

Neil touched his cheek again, and then Joshua stepped out into the unseasonably warm Atlanta mid-morning. He looked back twice. Neil lingered in his open doorway, barefoot and looking incredibly young, watching him go.

Chapter Twenty-One

THE SHOWER WAS hot, and Neil leaned into the stream. He didn't know how to process what he was feeling emotionally, so he concentrated on his body. His ass was sore, his arms ached from the positions he'd held himself in to fuck Joshua, and his legs trembled in exhaustion. He thought they'd probably slept for less than two hours the night before, so lost in each other's bodies and in making sure it was really real.

Neil had never felt anything like the sex they'd had, the love they'd made. He knew that's what Joshua would call it. Hell, he knew that's what it was. It was an intense, wholly emotional experience that had blown his mind. He'd enjoyed fucking Derek. They'd had really good sex. But with Joshua, it was like all inhibitions broke away entirely, and he wanted to be in him, over him, and around him all at once. He'd never known desire like that before.

The *thump-thump* of Derek's music rattled the bathroom wall, and Neil rinsed the suds of shampoo from his hair and scratched a soapy hand over the dried come on his stomach and stuck in his pubic hair. He hesitated before washing it away, a sense of loss descending on him. Aside from the messed-up bed, the plates in the kitchen sink, and the possibly hurt feelings of his roommate, he'd just watched the evidence of the most important thing in his life go rushing down the drain.

"Get a grip," he muttered to himself. But when he closed his eyes, he saw Joshua's smile. As he shut off the shower and toweled dry, he had to talk himself out of getting a car to take him to Joshua's hotel.

And that was when he'd remembered that he didn't know where Joshua was staying. His heart hammered wildly. What if Joshua didn't return? What would he do then?

He'd follow him back to Scottsville, that's what.

The song from Derek's room changed tempo and speed. The new music was a melancholy, slow piece sung by a drugged-up-sounding man. Neil pulled on fresh clothes, ran a comb through his wet hair, and noticed in the mirror for the first time the dark, red hickey that Joshua had left on his neck, and he touched it. A stupid smile turned up his lips. Joshua would be back. He'd said as much. Neil believed him.

Neil sat down at his desk and made the necessary arrangements for the project. He notified Peters and the graduate students that he'd be out for a few days for personal reasons and outlined how to proceed in his absence. And then he called in a favor with a fellow grad student named Eric Johns to get a sub for the next week of classes for him.

He had to concede that Alice had been right. She'd suggested that he help Eric out with his classes the prior spring when he'd been laid low with mono. The extra money Neil earned—all of which went to pay off the final debt that Alice had owed the private high school Neil had attended—was the deciding factor, but now Neil made a note of how handy it was for Eric to owe him. With one fast text, Neil was able to give over the reins of his professor's classes without any worry.

When another sad song started from the bedroom next door, Neil sighed. He couldn't escape it any longer. Joshua had specifically directed him to talk to Derek, and later Joshua would want to know how it had gone. Assuming Neil was right to believe in him, and he didn't freak out and board the next plane to Nashville. Neil shook that thought away. It was something he couldn't contemplate or *he'd* freak out and start searching every hotel in Atlanta.

Neil knocked on Derek's door. He didn't wait for Derek to open up, though, twisting the knob and walking in.

Derek was stretched out on his bed. His eyes looked a little red, but he was reading something on his touchpad and otherwise looked okay. He looked up at Neil in surprise.

Neil waved toward the door. "See how I did that? It's called knocking." Neil sat down in the chair opposite the bed. Normally, he'd have crashed down next to Derek, and the sex would have started immediately. But that was never going to happen again.

"Yeah, sorry." Derek brushed his long hair out of his face. "I didn't think he'd still be here when I got back. I figured he'd be gone, and you'd be in there moping. I thought I was gonna have to cheer you up." His mouth quirked up and his lips quivered. "Funny, huh?"

"No. It was smart. The best, most logical conclusion. What actually happened was unexpected."

"Is he gone?"

Neil nodded.

"Oh. Wow." Derek sat up, put aside his pad, and wrapped his arms around his knees. "So. Was it...." Derek shrugged. "I mean, is he gone-gone? Or just gone? Are you okay?"

Neil looked up at the ceiling. 'Okay' was something he didn't think accurately described the place where he found himself. He didn't know a word that did. "He's gone to his hotel. He said he'd come back."

Though Neil wasn't sure Joshua had said that at all. He'd said he wanted to make it work. Whatever that meant.

"So, you told him?" Derek peered at him intently. "And what? He just said, 'Okay' and dropped trou?"

"No." Neil didn't want to talk about it. It was raw, personal, important—the most important thing that had ever happened to him.

"But he knows?"

Neil nodded.

"And he's not going anywhere, is he?" Derek said. "I mean, he's really accepted that you're…him? And he's going to be with you? Be part of your life?"

"I hope so," Neil said. It was a massive understatement.

"Right. Wow. So I guess there isn't one last fuck in this for me?"

Neil pursed his lips and shook his head.

Derek smiled and shrugged. "Oh well. Bound to have ended one day."

Relief swept through Neil. Maybe he and Derek could still be friends.

Derek glanced shyly up through his lashes. "I have a question, though?"

Neil waited, his knee jittering up and down, a horrible rush of missing-Joshua replacing the blood in his veins.

Derek went on, "Can I keep your mom? I mean, as my friend."

"This isn't a breakup. We aren't dividing our things. We just aren't screwing anymore. We're still friends. I mean—aren't we?"

"Of course." Derek shrugged. "Right. Well, cool. I'm happy for you." Derek stood up, arms wide. Neil leaned away as Derek hugged him, and then, with relief, Neil submitted to it.

Derek laughed. "Damn, man. Who would've thought? Way to prove us all wrong, Neil. And, hey, I'm really happy for you. I am. Truly." Derek pulled away, kissed Neil's forehead with a sticky pop, and then said, "You'd better tell your mom. She'll be pissed if she hears it from me."

"Then keep your mouth shut."

Derek dropped down on the bed, picked up his pad again, and said, "Yeah, you know me. That's not gonna happen."

Neil stared at Derek until he was sure the conversation was over, and then he went back to his own room, thrilled by the rumpled, sex-messed sheets on his bed. He dropped down into them, smelling Joshua all over.

He finally made the call, clinging to the pillow that smelled of Joshua's shampoo and skin. "Hey, Mom," he said, when she answered. "He's here. Or he was. I think...I think I'm going to freak out now."

AT THE HOTEL, Joshua stripped out of his clothes. He sat down on the bed. He looked down at himself and at the clumps of dried come in his chest hair, and he started to shake.

He closed his eyes as images rushed through his mind.

Neil's eyes rolling up as he'd ridden Joshua's cock. Lee wiping grease from his hands and smiling when Joshua walked into the back of the shop. Neil hooked up to life support, blood caked in his hair, and the light gone out of his eyes. Neil standing barefoot by the door of his apartment, watching Joshua go. Lee smiling and splashing water at him in the Stouder creek, Lee's scars winding over his arm and body. Neil's eyes gazing at him with amazed adoration.

Joshua curled up on the bed. Covering himself with a blanket and clutching a pillow, he tried to wait out the tumble of emotions. There was no one to talk to. No one to call. How could he ever explain? He needed Lee now. Lee would understand.

Joshua started to cry. He gave himself some time to grieve and marvel, and had only just gotten himself together again, deciding that a shower had become a necessity, when his phone alerted him that Neil was calling. His stomach flip-flopped, and he hesitated, a sudden surge of worry rushing through him, followed immediately by a tidal wave of excitement and joy.

"Hey," Joshua answered.

"Where are you?" Neil asked.

"At my hotel."

"Are you…are we…? Yeah, here's the deal—I need to come see you."

"Miss me already?"

"Yes."

Joshua smiled at Neil's gruff, frank response. "I'm not going anywhere."

"What are you talking about? You already went somewhere. I've done my work. Which hotel? I can take a car and be there in less than an hour."

Joshua stretched and told Neil the name of the hotel. He sniffed his armpits, and said, "I need to shower."

"Okay. I'll be there in twenty. Which room?"

"312."

"Right. Don't go anywhere."

"Just the shower," Joshua said, a rush of adrenaline pulsing through him.

"Whatever. I like you dirty. Or clean. Just…be there."

"Neil, I'm not going anywhere. I promise." Joshua grinned, amazed by the certainty that filled him from the inside. "I want to be with you." It suddenly occurred to Joshua that was true no matter what—even if it turned out they were both delusional.

"I'll believe it when I see it."

Joshua could tell by the ambient noises behind Neil's voice that he was outside, moving quickly.

"Then come see it," Joshua said. "Did you call a car?"

"Yeah, before I called you. It'll be here any second."

"Then I really have to shower." Joshua struggled to find the words to end the call.

"Okay," Neil said. "I'll be there."

The call disconnected, and Joshua felt the drop like a physical thing in his gut. He groaned as he got up from the bed, every muscle in his body sore from the physical exertion of the last twenty-four hours. He touched the water with his hand before stepping under the stream.

He scrubbed himself quickly, every nerve ending in his body alive and straining for Neil. It was almost as if Joshua could feel Neil's approach, and with every second he felt more and more lit up from the inside. He started to hum as he washed. When he turned off the water to grab a towel, he decided that if this was insanity, he didn't want to be sane.

Chapter Twenty-Two

November 2032—Atlanta, Georgia

NEIL LAY ACROSS Joshua's chest, feeling the thunder of Joshua's heartbeat under his hands. He greedily watched as Joshua gathered his composure. They were both sweaty and smeared with come again. Joshua's eyes drooped; he was completely wiped out. It was a cute look on him, and Neil smirked in amusement.

"I hope you get old fast," Joshua panted. "Or you're going to kill me."

"You're keeping up pretty well. For an old guy."

Joshua huffed but grinned, and Neil felt like he'd won something better than the Nobel Prize just for getting to see that smile aimed at him again.

It had been a week since the madness had started, and they'd been out of each other's company for no more than ten minutes at a time. Neil was surprised to find that he was just as needy and clingy as Joshua—if not more so, because despite how weird everything was, Joshua seemed committed to accepting it and moving forward into a new reality with Neil.

"I was looking at houses," Joshua said. "There's one not far from the university. Four bedrooms. Two baths. A spacious kitchen. Lots of light."

"What would we need four bedrooms for? Variety?"

Joshua said, "One for your office, one for mine, because your mess is too much to deal with. How you can be such a neat freak everywhere else but in your office, I don't know, but I need my own space."

Neil had offered to move to Scottsville, but Joshua had dismissed the idea immediately. "No," Joshua had said. "You've got your work here, and I've got good employees at the lumberyard. It can practically run on its own. Scottsville is my home, but it's got lots of memories attached to it—good ones and bad. I want a fresh start. Just you and me together."

Neil hadn't argued. He'd considered it, but the idea of trying to go to Scottsville, not just for visits or family weddings, but to live in the shadow of the years Joshua had belonged to Lee, didn't appeal. Neil felt grateful and glad that Joshua seemed able to let all of that go.

"And that extra room?" Neil braced himself, visions of nurseries dancing in his head. It was a little soon to be planning for that in Neil's opinion. They'd only just found each other again.

"A guest room," Joshua said. "For when my family comes to visit."

"Oh," Neil said. He didn't know if he was relieved or even more horrified. A baby would've been too much to even consider right now, but Joshua's family was very real, and from what he remembered, very conservative.

"What?" Joshua looked worried. "Why do you sound that way? I thought you wanted to live together? Are we rushing it? We can slow down." Joshua sounded like slowing down was the last thing he wanted. "I mean, this house I saw is great—perfect—but there will be other houses."

Neil rolled his eyes. "Get the house. And slowing down isn't an option. I've waited twenty years for you. Get a house, get a dog— definitely get a dog—just don't go anywhere."

"In any other circumstance, statements like that would seem pretty controlling," Joshua said.

"Yeah, well, we're unique."

"You can say that again."

Neil rested his forehead on Joshua's chest, rubbing his nose into Joshua's chest hair, smelling him and kissing his nipples softly.

"So," Joshua said, shoving him off. "Don't you even want to look at the place first?"

Neil shrugged. "Sure. The extra room will be nice for my mom, too. If she wants to stay the night at Christmas or something. She'd probably like that."

Joshua's eyes sparkled, and Neil cleared his throat, suddenly nervous. He'd talked to his mother every day since she'd advised him to call Joshua and go to him at the hotel immediately. "Don't miss your chance at this, Neil," she'd implored. But he still hadn't introduced her to the man himself. It felt too much like letting the streams collide. It was simultaneously too real and too unreal.

"I want to meet her, Neil," Joshua said. "Today."

Neil rubbed a hand over his face. "Were you always this bossy?"

"No."

"Huh. I guess you've matured."

"And you've immatured," Joshua said, tweaking Neil's side.

Neil laughed.

"What's up? Are you afraid she won't like me or something?"

"She'll love you," Neil said vehemently. "And that'll be the problem. She'll call you up and talk to you on the phone, and ask you if I ate my vegetables, and if I'm taking vitamins, and if I've smiled enough lately."

Joshua's eyebrows went up.

"Trust me," Neil said. "She will."

"She called Derek," Joshua said knowingly.

"She still does." Neil sighed. "She says he's got a boy he's seeing already, which is great. He's needed a real boyfriend. He's basically a sex maniac, and without me, well... He was probably hard up the last few days, and I just hope he didn't choose an idiot."

Joshua's mouth hung open a little. "*He's* a sex maniac?"

Neil shot Joshua a look and said, "Yes."

"You're not going to distract me," Joshua said after a moment's hesitation. "I want to meet your mother. And I want to meet her today."

Neil sighed. He was trapped. There was no way he was going to get out of it. If Joshua couldn't be distracted by his lingering jealousy of Derek, then he wasn't going to be distracted at all.

Unless....

Neil started to kiss his way down Joshua's body, heading for his cock, when Joshua shoved him away. "Ugh. No. Enough sex."

Joshua climbed out of bed, calling over his shoulder, "I'm going to shower. You arrange something with your mother."

ALICE SAT BY the window of the diner with the menu clenched tightly in her hands. She wasn't hungry at all. She was far too excited and nervous to think about food.

She glanced down at the picture of Neil's usual order—veggie burger, fries, onion rings, and a strawberry milkshake. He'd ordered the same thing every time they came since he was five years old, and he'd been able to stuff in the entire meal since he was twelve. She put down the menu and pressed her fingers to her lips.

She felt strangely like everything was coming to an end. Like this was goodbye. Neil had his life back—the one he'd been born searching for, and Alice suddenly realized that she didn't know how she would fit in now.

Alice opened her purse and got out a mirror, double-checking her face. She wanted to look her best, and she definitely didn't want to embarrass Neil. She analyzed the small wrinkles around her eyes and the deeper ones around her mouth.

She was looking so much older lately. Neil had insisted that she stop working so much, but she hated taking his money. Of course, he wouldn't take no for an answer and had started wiring it directly to her bank account.

She put on a little more lip-gloss and sighed. Neil had tried for years to convince her to use nanite creams to reduce the effects of aging, telling her she needed to stay hot for when he was finally out of her life and she could move on, find a man, and make a 'real kid.' Reasoning that did nothing but make her angry with Neil for continually making himself out to be a burden on her instead of the most important thing in her life.

But when her vanity had won out, and she'd finally given in, they'd run the requisite tests to make sure her vascular system could handle it, only to find she hadn't been a candidate anyway. She'd told Neil that it was a good thing she'd refused him all of those years, because the last thing he needed was to blame himself for her death, and she knew that's what he would've done.

Alice closed her eyes and lifted up a small prayer.

When she opened them again, she glanced out the window and saw the most amazing thing: Neil walking next to Joshua Stouder. She'd know the man anywhere after years of seeing photos and videos of him. Neil's hand was on Joshua's lower back, guiding him toward the restaurant. For his part, Joshua had his hands stuffed into his jean pockets, and his head was tipped down. Though his eyes were on the sidewalk, a bashful sort of smile dimpled his cheeks.

Alice bit down on her lower lip, a surge of bittersweet joy clenching in her chest.

Joshua said something, and Neil's face broke into a quick, lightning-bright smile that didn't disappear right away. Instead, it lingered as a soft curve of his lips. Neil turned his head toward Joshua, who looked back with a shy expression. Then Joshua bumped Neil's shoulder.

They stopped walking. Neil's hand came up to Joshua's cheek, and Joshua, despite being taller and older, somehow seemed younger than Neil, looking at him through his lashes with an uncertain expression. Neil leaned forward and kissed him, full on the mouth, and Joshua kissed him back, pulling away with a grin so bright that Alice felt its reflection on her own face.

Neil gestured toward the restaurant door, and Joshua's expression flashed apprehensive for a moment, but he nodded, and they turned to enter.

Alice cleared her throat, twisted her napkin in her lap, and then stood up, tossing the napkin on the table. She didn't know what to do with her body as Neil and Joshua approached.

Neil's eyes were intense as he gazed at her, full of so much that Alice understood immediately: *This is him. He's everything.*

"Mom, this is Joshua." Neil stood protective and proud, like he was presenting the greatest thing he'd ever accomplished to her.

Alice had never seen him so at home in himself. He was relaxed in his skin, and she suddenly saw the man he would become, and could easily imagine the body he'd grow into over the next few years of his life.

"Mrs. Green," Joshua said, putting out his hand.

Alice took it immediately and squeezed it. He was beautiful. And looked years younger than her, despite being forty-three to her forty-one. His eyes were a gentle brown that looked at her with respect and hope, and she smiled at him, saying, "Alice, please, Mr. Stouder."

"Then you have to call me Joshua," he said.

"Of course, Joshua." She shook her head in amazement. "I can't believe it. He's talked about you since he was just a baby."

Neil grimaced. "And the embarrassing childhood stories begin. Can't we sit down and get the food ordered before we start on tales of my diaper years?"

Joshua smiled and put his hand on Neil's shoulder, shaking him lightly, which didn't take much effort since Neil was still too thin by Alice's estimation.

"Ah, come on, Neil, just because you're like a grumpy old man doesn't mean you weren't cute once."

"What are you talking about? I'm cute now." Neil huffed, pulling out a chair. "Sit. I'm starving."

Joshua grinned and looked like he might kiss Neil immediately, but instead sat down in the chair Neil had pulled out for him. Alice retook her seat, grabbing Neil's hand when he started snapping his fingers in frustration at a waiter.

"Behave," she said.

Joshua's eyes twinkled like he was fighting off a laugh as he turned to the menu.

Neil grabbed it from his hand, saying, "The veggie hamburger is the only safe option. Or the grilled cheese. I'm telling you this because if you take half as long to choose your food as you did last night, I'll keel over dead. Then we'll be in a real mess, since I'll probably be reincarnated somewhere in Japan and have to go through being a kid all over again, and you'll be really old by that time. Not to mention, I'd really stick out like a sore thumb over there with this hair and complexion."

Joshua's eyebrows were up near his hairline. He rolled his lips in, obviously trying not to laugh.

"He rants when he's hungry," Alice said.

Joshua grinned. "Or when he's nervous, or angry."

"Oh, come on, for the love of—" Neil said, when the waiter stopped two tables over and whipped out a digital order pad. "They got here after us."

Alice sighed heavily and said, "Neil, stop. Joshua is going to think I raised you like this."

Joshua wrinkled his nose and said, "Nah, he was always like this."

Alice brought her hand to her chest. Joshua understood, and he accepted, and he believed. Which, yes, Neil had already told her on the phone, but it was something else entirely to see it in his eyes and to know that it was true. What was even more shocking, though, was how she suddenly felt like she wasn't so alone. The world opened up a little bigger with Joshua here.

"I can only imagine how much waiter-spit he's ingested in the last two lifetimes," Joshua said, making a face at Neil who rolled his eyes at him.

A different waiter, not the one who Neil had annoyed, appeared and asked for their order. Neil got his usual, and Joshua requested the grilled cheese. Alice ordered a salad with dressing on the side while Neil frowned at her.

"Mom, I have two words for you."

Joshua looked at Neil, and another grin broke over his face.

In a weird way, Alice felt like crying again. It was clear that Joshua thought her son was adorable. She almost couldn't believe it.

Neil went on, "Salmonella. Poisoning. But if you want to puke your guts out for hours later today, go right ahead. No one's stopping you."

"Thanks for your permission, honey," Alice said.

Joshua snorted, and Neil's arm came up to rest on the back of Joshua's chair. He relaxed again now that food was ordered. Alice smiled softly as Joshua leaned toward Neil, like some unseen force was pulling him. They weren't leaning against each other really, just angled in such a way that they seemed a unit, an already solid thing. Between them there was a palpable, almost visible tug of rightness. Alice thought if she put her hand out and into the small space between them, she'd be able to feel it—love, attraction, warmth, need, protection, and everything all at once.

"Well," she said, shifting her napkin a little in her lap. "So...where to begin?"

"How 'bout this," Joshua said, leaning forward in a conspiratorial way. "In exchange for you giving me good blackmail material on Neil here, I'll tell you about the Neil I knew, and some stuff about myself, too."

Neil sat back and looked around the room, his eyes straying back to Joshua occasionally, but he seemed unperturbed by Joshua's suggested conversational topics.

Alice nodded. "You go first."

Neil flashed a grin at her. "That's my girl, Mom. Put him on the spot."

Joshua shrugged. "What do you want to hear about first?"

Alice took a sip of her water. "What about your family? And...your husband? I was sorry to hear about that, by the way. I'm sure that was hard."

Joshua glanced toward Neil at the mention of Lee, and Alice almost regretted bringing him up. Neil had often seemed jealous of the man over the years, but he'd been a large part of Joshua's life. It was important to her that her son be realistic about the man he was involved with. This wasn't a do-over. This wasn't living the life he could have had. This was uncharted territory.

Joshua said, "Thank you. It was very hard. I loved him a lot."

Neil moved his hand from the back of Joshua's chair to his shoulder. He squeezed gently. "Go on. Out with it. It's not like he doesn't deserve to be talked about."

Joshua looked a little uncomfortable. "It's just this..." He motioned between them. "It's fresh, and I don't want to drag all that into it."

Neil made a face. "I won't lie and say that I didn't spend years in seething jealousy, but I'm not an absolute jerk, either. He was good to you. You loved him. I'd be an ass to resent that."

"He always respected you," Joshua said softly. "Your place in my life."

Neil seemed to struggle with something for a moment, and Alice had to resist the urge to reach out and take his hand. She knew he was pushing down his possessiveness, his urge to win, to be the only one Joshua ever wanted or needed, and she knew it was vital that he do so. She also saw the exact moment he conquered himself.

"And now it's my turn to respect him. Tell my mom how you met Lee. She'd like to hear about him." Neil gazed at Joshua warmly and added, "I would too."

Joshua eyes filled, and he leaned over to press a kiss to Neil's lips. Then he blinked his tears away. Neil gave a small smile, and Joshua's eyes glowed right back at him.

Alice leaned back in her seat, her throat tight, and she felt so damn *proud*.

She didn't know how, but Neil had done it. He'd found Joshua again, won his heart, and he was going to be so *good* at this. She just knew he would. He was good at everything he really wanted to be good at, and he loved harder than anyone else she'd ever known.

It was going to be okay. It was wild, unbelievable, and no one would ever believe her if she told them the story, but watching Joshua and Neil together, she knew without a doubt that love never dies.

Chapter Twenty-Three

S WEATY AND STICKY, with Joshua's come all over his chest, Neil ran his hands over Joshua's thighs and up to his nipples, pinching gently. Joshua shuddered and clenched on Neil's cock, and Neil smiled, loving the view of Joshua riding him, flushed and shaking after his orgasm.

"Alice loved you," Neil said.

Joshua collapsed on him, pressing his face against Neil's neck. "Don't talk about your mother right now."

Neil chuckled. He didn't really expect Joshua to understand how he felt about Alice. Despite being the best person Neil had ever met, aside from maybe Joshua himself, he'd never been able to really feel the appropriate mother-son connection. He loved her, but mentioning her at a time like this felt more like bringing up a close friend. Now, his first mother? Sharon Russell? He'd never want to think about her during sex. That would just be disgusting.

They'd returned to Neil's apartment after their lunch with Alice, ostensibly to collect some clothes and things for Neil, but they'd ended up having a delicious, hour-long love-making session amidst the towers of books on reincarnation.

"God, Neil," Joshua whimpered. "Making love with you is so good."

Neil hid his smirk in Joshua's hair and then pressed a kiss to the crown of Joshua's head. "I'll tell you a little secret."

Joshua lifted up to see Neil's face. "What?"

"Last time around? I wasn't this big. I mean, I had a good cock, but this one is a humdinger."

Joshua sputtered. "Are you telling me you're exactly the same *except your cock is bigger?*"

"What? You don't believe me?"

Joshua laughed. "Neil, I used to feel that thing through your pants when we made out on the sofa in your apartment. It was terrifying. Why do you think I was so scared to have sex with you?"

Neil scrunched his face. "Uh, because you were all tied up over your parents' conservative religious beliefs?"

Joshua laughed again. "Well, there was that, too. But the size of your cock wasn't exactly reassuring."

"Really?"

Joshua pinched him and then kissed his mouth. "Really."

Neil thrust up into Joshua slowly, feeling his come squelch out of Joshua's ass and slide down over Neil's balls. "Feel that?" he asked.

"You know I do," Joshua murmured, his breath coming in soft gasps as he started to ride again.

Neil moaned and settled back, enjoying the view. He loved the feel of his cock, raw and slick with his own come, in Joshua's tight ass.

They'd stopped using condoms after only a few days. Joshua had basically begged for it, wanting to feel Neil's come in his ass, and Neil had been so madly turned on just by hearing Joshua say those words that he'd agreed as soon as they could be certain it was safe.

The tests for STDs no longer took the time they had years ago in his first life. Neil was profoundly grateful for that as they'd hustled over to the health clinic, both of them twisted up with lust and urgency, and both of them walking out with clean bills of health. They hadn't even made it to Joshua's bed at the hotel, before they'd stripped each other and fucked raw and wild on the floor just inside the door of the room. Both of them had been deliriously turned on by the intimate sensation of skin on skin.

Neil loved everything about fucking Joshua raw. He loved the sweet push inside and the sensation of Joshua's velvet-soft insides against the tight, engorged flesh of his cock. He loved how he could come in Joshua and not stop to change his condom, just fuck on through the over-stimulation, and watch Joshua go wild at the squelching noises as the come worked its way out.

His favorite thing about fucking Joshua without a condom, though, was after. He loved to watch Joshua *lose his mind* as Neil licked and sucked the come back out of him. The first time Neil had done it, Joshua had protested that it was too dirty, but when he'd finally agreed and Neil had dove in, the complaints had died away into delirious cries of need. Joshua had basically suffocated Neil by shoving his face into his ass harder and harder, and in the end, Joshua had frantically jerked himself to a shocked and flailing completion while Neil's tongue had wriggled in his ass.

Now Neil did it as a matter of course, and Joshua still went out of his mind every single time.

"Get off me," Neil said, and helped Joshua flip onto his stomach.

"Oh God," Joshua moaned, his face in the pillow, and his hips lifted in invitation.

Neil smirked. He crouched down between Joshua's spread legs, pulled his cheeks apart, and smiled at Joshua's clenching hole, still wet from having been fucked. He leaned in and just *breathed* on it, watching it spasm in reaction. Some of his come dribbled out.

Neil licked it away, and Joshua whimpered, cursing into the pillow. Neil waited.

"Please," Joshua whined.

"I thought this was too dirty," Neil teased.

Joshua spread his legs more and lifted his ass toward Neil's face, saying nothing, just begging with his body.

Neil pressed a finger in, and Joshua grunted. Neil grinned, leaned forward, and went to town—eating, licking, slurping, biting, tonguing.

Joshua writhed on the bed, gripping the sheets and scrambling away and back again, cursing and whimpering. Neil urged Joshua up to his knees so that he could get a hand down to his cock and begin a desperate, fast-paced jerk.

Neil wrapped his own hand around Joshua's balls, pulling down a little, keeping him on the edge of coming, until he was ready. And then he released his hold and licked frantically at Joshua's clenching hole. Timing it from the rhythm of Joshua's hand and Joshua's stuttered breathing, Neil raised up, aimed his dick, and thrust inside with a thick, insistent push just as Joshua threw his head back and came hard. His ass squeezed convulsively around Neil's invading cock as he yelled his release.

Neil grinned into the sweaty hair at Joshua's nape and kissed his neck as Joshua shuddered through aftershocks, still pinned on Neil's cock.

As Neil wrapped his arms around Joshua, he heard him mutter, "Promise you'll never leave me again."

"Never," Neil agreed.

He couldn't help but chuckle, though, amused at how Joshua turned even the filthiest thing they did together into so much love. And what was even more amazing—Joshua was right. Neil's tongue in his ass, felching out come, *was* about love, and need, and how they would never be apart again. Never.

Leave it to Joshua to know that.

When their breathing regulated, Joshua sat up. "We should get out of here before Derek gets back."

Neil rolled his eyes. Despite everything, Joshua was still a little insecure about Derek. Neil considered delaying just so that Joshua could see for himself that there was nothing there to fear. Derek was a great guy, a good kid, and Neil's only friend. He didn't really want to give that up.

"I know," Joshua said, reading Neil's expression. "He's just a friend."

"Yeah."

"It's wrong to be jealous, I know," Joshua said. "But I don't like that what we just did—everything we just did—you've done with him. I don't like having that in common."

Neil sighed, pulled Joshua back down, and reached down low to rub his finger against Joshua's hole. Another shiver went through Joshua at his touch.

"I haven't done everything with him. I didn't eat come from his ass."

Joshua's eyes went wide. "Really?"

"Really."

"Why?"

Neil shrugged. "I only want to eat come out of *you*."

Joshua's face lit up, and the reaction was ridiculous, but Neil felt too warm and soft and schmoopy inside to tell Joshua so. He was just glad that Joshua was smiling again. He wanted to make sure Joshua smiled all the time. The way he saw it, Joshua's smile was his calling. The desire for it was what had propelled him into this world again, and seeing it was like a drug—addictive and necessary.

"I love you," Neil said.

Joshua grinned. "I love you, too."

Chapter Twenty-Four

November 2034—Paris, France

NEIL WOKE UP and snuggled into Joshua's side, breathing in the hollow between Joshua's shoulder and neck. He curled his fingers into Joshua's chest hair and let the images from the dream wash over him. He had the dreams less and less these days, but they always left him feeling profoundly grateful.

Joshua rolled toward him, gathering Neil into his arms and smiling in his sleep. Neil gazed at his face and felt an answering lift in his own lips. The hotel room around them was lush, with thick bedding, and a view of the Seine out the window. Still the dream vibe lingered.

Neil never told Joshua about the dreams. He sometimes wondered if he should, but Joshua seemed untroubled by their life together. He didn't seem to want or need any reassurance about their relationship—except for the occasional promise that the age difference between them wasn't important. As Neil pointed out, he was actually older than Joshua in most ways, and between the nanite creams and treatments keeping Joshua's body young and Neil's adamant refusal to do anything to prevent his own aging, they'd be peers before they knew it.

The dream always started the same way. Neil would be working in the lab, and he'd be right on the edge of a massive breakthrough, something huge, when the sensation of someone next to him would break his concentration. He'd turn, annoyed, ready to tell off whoever it was for interrupting, and then stop short.

"Hey," Lee would say.

Neil remembered that when the dreams first started, he'd felt a weird wave of guilt, like he'd been caught fucking Joshua, and his husband had just walked in the room. But he didn't feel that way in the dreams anymore. Now, he just experienced a kind of realization that, oh, he was dreaming, and, hey, Lee was here to check on Joshua again. He didn't mind it.

"You could just ask him yourself," Neil had said in the particular dream he'd just woken from. "I'm not his keeper."

"Sure you are," Lee answered. "Besides, I like asking you. Keeps you humble."

"What's that supposed to mean?"

"I'm a reminder that he wasn't always yours—even though he was, you know. Always yours."

Neil shrugged. "He had a life with you. He loved you."

"Yup." Lee leaned against the counter, and Neil refrained from telling him not to jostle anything. It was just a dream, after all. "So, how's he doing?" Lee asked.

"Great. He's happy. I mean, he seems happy. He smiles a lot."

Lee's own smile was always brilliant. It made Neil feel like he was a kid in the presence of someone much older and much braver. Someone who had a hell of a lot more knowledge than he did about the most important thing in the world to Neil.

"Good. Keep it that way. It's not hard to do. Just love him and let him know that you do. That's all it takes."

"I know that."

Lee had rolled his eyes. "Of course. Anyway, it's good to see you again. You're looking pretty happy yourself."

"I am," Neil had said. He was the happiest he'd ever been. Happier than he'd known possible.

"Okay, well, I have to go. Heaven calls and all that."

Neil had snorted at the joke. "Don't know how he put up with your bad sense of humor."

"You're one to talk."

Neil put out his hand, and they shook. Lee's fingers were strong, and even after waking he could still feel the ghost of that touch as he stroked Joshua's chest hair.

Joshua shifted, and his eyes fluttered open. A grin broke over his face, and Neil touched his lower lip with his thumb.

"Neil," Joshua said, his voice tremulously happy. "We're in Paris."

"Yup."

"And you've never been here before."

"Nope."

Joshua's eyes were full of light, and he rolled Neil over, framing Neil's head with his elbows. An even bigger smile spread over his face. "I'm going to show you *everything*."

Neil smirked. "Yeah, maybe you can fit that in around the day of conferences Brian's set up for us."

Joshua threaded his fingers into Neil's hair and pulled a little, a physical reprimand. "I have it on good authority that we'll be in a meeting for less than two hours today and three tomorrow. And the rest of the time is ours."

"Paris must not be very impressive if you can show me everything in only two days."

"Neil," Joshua said, with one scolding eyebrow raised. "We're going to have a good time. Don't try to spoil it for me."

Neil kissed Joshua's beautiful mouth. "Wouldn't dream of it."

The knock at the door made Joshua groan almost as loudly as Neil, who threw himself back on the pillows. He let Joshua be the one to grab a complimentary robe and answer the door.

"Just remember, you invited her," Neil said, grinding the heels of his palms into his eye sockets and willing away the hard-on he'd been on the verge of doing something about.

"Shh," Joshua said, glaring at Neil. He opened the hotel room door to greet Alice. "Good morning!"

She stood there wearing a lovely dress and fresh makeup applied on her face. Joshua made a move to invite her in, but Alice shook her head.

"I'm heading out for some sightseeing. I didn't want you to worry about me if you couldn't find me later."

"Because I'm all about keeping tabs on you, Mom," Neil said, trying to figure out just why his mother was wearing lipstick.

Alice rolled her eyes. "Dr. Peters has offered to take me to breakfast and then he says I simply have to see the Bouguereaus at the D'Orsay…"

Neil narrowed his eyes. He could have sworn his mother had just *blushed*.

"And then he said he'd take me out to lunch." She bit her lower lip and looked positively giddy. Neil gritted his teeth and sat up.

"Dr. Peters said you and Neil had the meetings covered, Joshua?" She gazed up at Joshua with hopeful eyes, obviously dreading the possibility that Joshua might say he didn't feel comfortable running the show, or capable of keeping Neil in check during the presentation.

"Sure," Joshua said, putting his hand on her shoulder and squeezing. "Have fun."

Alice smiled like a dazzling magazine cover model, and Neil sat all the way up in the bed. "Why is Brian taking you out? Can't you go by yourself?" Joshua shot him a sideways look, but Neil went on. "You realize he's divorced. With three kids. And he's got a beard. On his face."

Joshua looked like he might laugh, but he shook his head at Neil, obviously trying to shut him up.

Alice's smile flattened into a tight line of annoyance. "His children are all grown up, Neil. They're older than you—"

"Well, not really, but—"

Alice ignored him. "And he's a kind man. A *nice* man. He's smart, and he makes me laugh. Not to mention, he likes my kid. You're always telling me what a rarity that is, Neil. And it's *Paris*. Let your mother have a little romance in her life. Aren't you the one always telling me to meet someone?" She clucked her tongue at him. "Someone might think you were *jealous* and didn't want to share your mommy."

Joshua laughed under his breath.

Neil started to stand up but realized he was naked. He sputtered. "That's ridiculous, I—"

"You're going to tell me to have a wonderful day, and that you'll see me later," Alice said, her arms crossed over her chest and her dark brown eyes boring into Neil like he was eight again and arguing with her about the mess of his experiments on the kitchen table.

"Have a wonderful day," Neil said with a scowl. "But don't tell me later about how scratchy his beard is. I don't want to hear about it."

Alice laughed. "And what makes you think I'd want to tell you about something like that? Seriously, Neil, you're being a big baby."

She turned on her heel and left the room. Joshua shut the door behind her, his expression full of barely suppressed laughter.

"What?" Neil asked. "She's too good for him. He's a workaholic, and not nearly smart enough for her. Besides, he'll...slobber on her. She's a fine woman, and—"

"You love her."

"Well, yeah. She deserves the best."

Joshua locked the door, sat on the edge of the bed, and said seriously, "Brian's a pretty great guy. His wife left him because she likes women, not because he mistreated her. They raised the kids together, and then she went on to do her thing."

"And you gleaned all this when?"

"On the airplane, while you were drugged out and sleeping."

"I get airsick!" Neil said, defending his vulnerability.

"Believe me, I remember." Their first trip together out to California had involved a lot of vomit. "Plus, I've known Brian for years."

"Well, fine. Okay. She can date him."

Joshua laughed harder. "I'm sure she'll be so happy to have your permission."

Neil threw a pillow at Joshua, laughing at himself.

Joshua pounced on him. They wrestled on the bed, elbows and knees connecting in uncomfortable ways, but once it all came down to skin on skin, Neil *was* happy. Happier than he'd ever been. Happier than he'd known was possible.

Only one thing could make him even happier.

JOSHUA STOOD WITH Neil at the top of Sacré-Cœur, looking out over the lights of Paris. They'd climbed the slick granite steps up to the top earlier and watched the sun set with a rosy glow. Now, the wind whipped around them, slightly chilly, but not too miserable between their coats and scarves. They weren't the only ones at the top of the basilica. There were several other couples and a family or two, still watching as the night fell.

Joshua fingered the velvet box in his coat pocket. His stomach twisted with nerves, but it was time. He'd been living with Neil for over a year, and he wanted to put a ring on his finger, to call him his husband. He wanted to make sure that everyone knew that Neil was with him.

It had been an amazing year full of ups and downs, sure, but mostly ups. At first, Joshua had been obsessed with satisfying his curiosity about all the details of Neil: his favorite color, his original parents, his life since he'd been born this time, how he liked his eggs, and so much more.

In return, Joshua had told Neil everything, too. He'd talked about the people who had benefited from Neil's organ donations, including Lee. He'd told Neil, in detail, many stories from the life that he and Lee had shared together, and was honored that Neil didn't mind. Sometimes Neil even referred to Lee with affection and warmth of his own, saying, "He took good care of you. I'll always owe him for that."

It had taken almost a month of them being unable to get their hands off each other long enough to accomplish anything of any worth, but Neil had eventually returned to work full time at the project. They weren't able to keep their feelings for each other on the down low, though, and within an hour of Neil being back in the lab full time, with Joshua there 'observing,' Brian Peters had confronted them about their relationship.

Joshua leaned against the thick stone wall, looked up at the night sky, and laughed under his breath as he remembered Brian's expression of extreme confusion when Neil had said, "Listen, if you tell me it's the project or Joshua, let me just say that I've been there and done that. Joshua wins every time."

As it had turned out, Brian didn't have a problem with Joshua and Neil's relationship, especially when Joshua said that he'd be moving to Atlanta and bringing more of the Neil Russell Foundation resources with him. "We want to have the best, most advanced, and thorough nanite research facility in the world," Joshua had told Dr. Peters. "And Neil's the only one I trust to run it."

Away from work, they'd bought a house that became their refuge, and they spent almost every evening there. Including a cozy Christmas, with just Alice and a brightly lit tree that Joshua had hauled in from a corner lot near the university.

It had been Joshua's first Christmas away from Scottsville, and he'd only gotten a little choked up when he opened the gift his mother had sent him. It was a little angel ornament that had been his favorite on the family tree for his entire life. The note included read: *I thought you might need this on your tree in your new home with your new love. Mom*

Joshua's heart still clenched when he remembered how, seeing Joshua's sadness, Neil had suggested that they spend every other Christmas in Scottsville. Alice had agreed that it was only fair. And Joshua, of course, insisted that Alice would come with them if they did indeed make the trip to Kentucky for the holidays.

"Oh, no," Neil had said. "She should just stay right here. She might not be able to escape the Scottsville vortex. I mean, look, it took you over forty years! And it trapped Chris there too!"

In the end, though, it had been decided that of course Alice would go with them.

Joshua touched the velvet box in his pocket again and put his arm around Neil, gazing at the cut of his profile against the backdrop of Paris at night.

"Are you sure about this, baby?" Chris had asked him over the phone. Joshua had called to tell Chris about his plans after he'd chosen the ring a week before their trip. "I know you say you're happy...but we miss you at home."

Joshua had known this was code for many things, one of which was his skepticism and confusion over Neil Green.

Cautiously, Chris had added, "Dr. Green's nothing like Lee, and you two were such a good pair."

"Yeah, we were," Joshua had agreed. "And I loved Lee a lot. But I love Neil a lot, too."

"He's quite a bit like our Neil," Chris had said gently. "So I get that. But—Joshua, he's awfully young. What do you even have in common?"

"You'd be surprised," he'd answered, certain that Chris would probably join the rest of the world in thinking it was all about sex. Let them think what they wanted. The truth was impossible to explain.

The official story they'd spun for folks back home was that Dr. Neil Green was Dr. Neil Russell's long-lost nephew, and hey, isn't life strange? Love will find a way.

Chris, though, had stayed skeptical, saying, "Joshua—is there something you're not telling me? Because he is *so much* like Neil. Are you sure he's not Neil's son? You know, through a sperm donation or something? Because, while it might seem sort of weird if you were in love with Neil's child, compared to other things that have happened in this world, there's really nothing to be embarrassed about. You shouldn't have to make up stories, partner."

Joshua had stuck to the official line, though. Neil agreed it was the best course of action. Their predicament was so unbelievable, and both of their reputations would be compromised if they attempted to explain the truth.

The only person Joshua had been honest with was Lee. When he'd finally been able to bring himself to leave Neil and Atlanta in order to return to Scottsville and break the news of his move to his family, he'd stopped by the cemetery. It was the middle of December by then, and freezing. There were Christmas wreaths with red or green bows on a lot of the graves, and Joshua had brought a big one for Lee's.

He'd knelt in the snow, getting his pants wet as he'd put the wreath on the gravestone carefully and brushed the snow away from the letters of Lee's name and the inscription that followed.

"Hey," he'd said, a lump in his throat. "I love you. You gave me such a great life, and I'm so happy I got to have that with you. That will never change."

He'd waited for an answer, and he'd gotten one—a sense of

warmth, affection, and happiness filled him. Inexplicably, it had tasted like Lee.

"So, look, you already know what I'm here to tell you. The thing is, I'm going to Atlanta to be with Neil. I love him. He makes me happy—he always did."

Joshua had paused and then said, "One day, part of me will come to be with you here forever. Until then, Lee...." He'd trailed off. He hadn't known what to say, and his throat was clogging with tears. He'd patted the headstone and nodded firmly.

He'd stood up, stuffed his hands in his pockets, and walked toward the skinny figure standing by the hired car at the graveyard's edge. Neil's hair had been a burnished chestnut in the afternoon sun, and Joshua's heart had thumped wildly in his chest at the still-surprising sight of him.

Even now, at the top of Sacré-Cœur, with Neil grumbling about the mayo-infused sandwich he'd had to choke down at the café where they'd grabbed a bite, Joshua's heart beat faster just looking at him.

"So," Neil said, waving his hand at Paris below. "It's impressive. But let's get back to the hotel. It's too cold to be out here much longer."

Joshua grabbed Neil's hand and held it. "Wait. There's just one more thing."

Neil's eyes were so blue, and his mouth so perfect, and Joshua loved him so much. He was unbearably grateful for whatever force had brought Neil back to him. Joshua dropped to one knee, and he felt more than saw all the heads of the other tourists near them turn his way.

Neil's eyes narrowed, and he shook his head. "You'd better not be proposing to me, Joshua Stouder."

Joshua's stomach lurched, and his heart fluttered anxiously in his chest. "Shut up, Neil." He cleared his throat. "Neil Joseph

Green, would you do me the honor—"

"No!" Neil said.

"What?" Joshua said, surprised outrage rocking through him. He hadn't thought Neil would be *enthused* by a romantic and public proposal, but he'd thought Neil would say *yes* for sure.

Neil groaned, rolled his eyes, and then said, "I mean, yes. You've ruined it, though. I had a whole... Dammit. Fine. Yes, I'll marry you."

Joshua frowned. "I haven't even asked yet."

"Well, do it. I had strawberries and champagne and a *plan*, but you've gone and started it now." Neil rolled his hand. "So finish."

Joshua stood up. Leave it to Neil to ruin a perfectly good proposal. "What are you *talking* about?"

"This!" Neil said, gesturing between them, and then down where Joshua had been kneeling. "I was going to ask you. Tonight, at the hotel. I had it all planned. I was going to wow you. You have *no idea* how hard it was to plan this, and now you—" He blew out a rough breath. "So, go on then. Ask. The answer is yes."

Joshua crossed his arms over his chest. "You are such an ass."

"And?"

Joshua turned around, irritation welling up in him. If Neil was going to be a jerk, he had no intention of—

Neil grabbed his arm, and said, "Hey, hey, wait a minute." Neil's voice was rough and soft now. "Just...wait a minute."

Joshua did wait, his arms still crossed, as he blinked at Neil in frustration. The other people at the top were starting to get curious about the seeming lover's quarrel, and several came around the tower to watch.

Neil rubbed a hand over his face, rotated his shoulders like he was working out some kinks, and then nodded firmly. "Okay. I'm ready. I'm sorry. Let's try it again."

Joshua shook his head and started to turn away, but then Neil grabbed him and fell down on his own knee in front of Joshua.

"The rings are in the room," Neil said. "But Joshua Stouder, I've loved you for two lifetimes, and—"

Joshua put his hand over Neil's mouth, and he got down on his knees, too. A few 'awwws' and excited whispers started around them. "Dr. Neil Green, I love you—past and present and future—even when you're a total ass. Will you be my husband?"

"Will you marry me?" Neil asked when Joshua moved his hand away so that Neil could answer. "Yes, Joshua, I'll marry you."

Joshua leaned in, pressed a kiss to his lips, and said, "Yes, I'll marry you, too."

There was a spatter of applause as they kissed, and Joshua let Neil help him up, before they kissed again. As they pulled apart, Joshua grabbed the ring box from his pocket and brought it out.

"Do you want to wear it now? Or when it's official?" Joshua asked.

"Now," Neil said, letting Joshua slide the ring on his finger. "Not bad, Mr. Stouder," he intoned, looking at the band in the light of the platform. "Not bad at all. They're almost identical to the ones I bought."

Joshua felt a mix of joy and satisfied anticipation. When another American tourist walked by and clapped Joshua on the shoulder, saying, "Congratulations," before moving off, Joshua glanced around at the happy expressions of their impromptu audience. "I think everyone's glad you said yes."

"Nah, they're thinking, 'Those drama queens deserve each other,'" Neil said, looking at everyone with suspicion.

Joshua laughed. He had to agree.

As they walked back to the hotel, joy rose in Joshua that couldn't be denied. He held Neil's hand tightly and fairly floated.

"You know what I want?" Neil asked.

"What?"

"A puppy."

Joshua laughed. "You do?"

"Yeah, I've wanted one since I was a kid, and it's about time I had another one. Magic was a long time ago."

"What kind are you thinking of?" Joshua's heart sang.

"Oh, I don't know. A big black one."

"Neil…"

"What?" he asked coyly.

"Don't you think that's tempting fate?"

"It's not like we'd name her Magic." Neil squeezed his hand and grinned. "We'd name her something totally different. Like Abracadabra."

Joshua turned and grabbed Neil, nearly lifting him off the sidewalk, and then kissed him, passionately, desperately, happily. The entire past and present and future wrapped over and through him, piercing him and surrounding him with so much love and happiness that he couldn't contain it.

Joshua broke the kiss first, his back against the wall of a random café, and Neil pressed solidly against him. "You're the only one, Neil," he whispered. "God only knows how you got here, how it is that you're here with me. But you're everything to me."

Neil took Joshua's chin in his gloved fingers, the leather cold against Joshua's skin. "No, you've got that backwards. You're the one who's everything. I wouldn't have come back to this miserable earthly plane for anyone else."

Joshua laughed, giddy. "I don't know why you feel that way, but I'm glad you do."

Neil's eyes were warm as he gazed at Joshua, always greedy, always with a hint of gratitude underlying it all. "There's nothing in this world—not my work, not nanites, not a single human being—who is what you are to me. You're the reason for my existence. Joshua, you're my everything. I'll find you in any given lifetime.

Never forget that."

"Neil," Joshua started, overwhelmed by the truth. Sometimes it still hit him hard all over again. Neil had come back for him. He'd loved him that much. Even now, he wondered how it could be true.

"Save it for our vows. Because, Joshua, I think just being here with you should prove beyond a shadow of a doubt the depth of my commitment to you."

Tears rose, and Joshua blinked them away.

"That was part of my pretty speech," Neil said. "The one I'd planned for the hotel, but you ruined it by stealing my proposal."

Joshua shook his head, laughter pushing past his tears. "Neil!"

"I know. I'm an ass." He smiled. "Let's get back to the hotel room. I want to have hot, passionate, newly engaged sex with my fiancé. Also, I'm starving."

Joshua kissed Neil again, feeling the heat of him under his palms. As they walked through the Paris night, hands entwined, Joshua looked up at the sky, wondering at the universe where this was his life.

How impossible. How beautiful. How mysterious. How 'God only knows.'

And despite all the pain they'd been through to get there, he wouldn't change a thing.

THE END

LETTER FROM LETA

Dear Reader,

Thank you so much for reading *Any Given Lifetime*! Be sure to follow me on Amazon, BookBub, or Goodreads to be notified of new releases. And look for me on Facebook for snippets of the day-to-day writing life, or join my Facebook Group for announcements and special giveaways. To see some sources of my inspiration, you can follow my Pinterest boards or Instagram.

If you enjoyed the book, please take a moment to leave a review! Reviews not only help readers determine if a book is for them, but also help a book show up in searches.

Also, for the audiobook connoisseur, several of my books are available at most retailers that sell audio, all narrated by the talented Michael Ferraiuolo or John Solo.

Thank you so much for being a reader!
Leta

Gay Romance Newsletter

Leta's newsletter will keep you up to date on her latest releases and news from the world of M/M romance. Join the mailing list today.

Leta Blake on Patreon

Become part of Leta Blake's Patreon community in order to access exclusive content, deleted scenes, extras, bonus stories, rewards, prizes, interviews, and more.

www.patreon.com/letablake

OTHER BOOKS BY LETA BLAKE

The River Leith
Smoky Mountain Dreams
Angel Undone

'90s Coming of Age Series
Pictures of You
You Are Not Me

The Training Season Series
Training Season
Training Complex

Heat of Love Series
Slow Heat
Alpha Heat

Co-Authored with Indra Vaughn
Vespertine

Co-Authored with Alice Griffiths
The Wake Up Married serial
Will & Patrick's Endless Honeymoon

Gay Fairy Tales
Co-Authored with Keira Andrews
Flight
Levity
Rise

Leta Blake writing as Blake Moreno
The Difference Between

Audiobooks
Leta Blake at Audible

Free Read
Stalking Dreams

Discover more about the author online:
Leta Blake
letablake.com

Made in the USA
Las Vegas, NV
24 December 2020